ROSE THROUGH
TIME

ROSE THROUGH TIME

A Magical Bookshop Novel

HARMKE BUURSMA

ISBN 978-1-7374033-1-9 (hardcover laminated)
ISBN 978-1-7374033-3-3 (hardcover dustjacket)
ISBN 978-1-7374033-0-2 (ebook)
ISBN 978-1-7374033-4-0 (paperback)

Edited by Megan Sanders
Author photo by Patterson Photography
Cover design by Getcovers.com

Published by Illusive Press
info@illusivepress.com
www.illusivepress.com

For more information about Harmke Buursma and her books, visit
www.harmkebuursma.com

First Edition, 2021

To my husband Matthew, who is the most
supportive person I know

Contents

"I have a strange feeling with regard to you. As if I had a string somewhere under my left ribs, tightly knotted to a similar string in you. And if you were to leave I'm afraid that cord of communion would snap. And I have a notion that I'd take to bleeding inwardly. As for you, you'd forget me."
- *Charlotte Brontë, Jane Eyre*

I

A Forgotten Piano

Twelve pairs of bright young eyes stared up at me as I told them that a substitute English teacher would take over my classes next week. Well, maybe only ten pairs, as Tommy, a heavily freckled kid with glasses and a penchant for sticky fingers, was exchanging playing cards with his friend and classmate, Noah. A smart but easily distracted boy with piercing green eyes, who often wore Spider-Man t-shirts, and always had to show me his newest comic book.

I stopped talking and leaned against the desk which was cluttered with my students' homework, colored pencils and pens, and a "#1 Teacher" mug I had received as a gift. I scraped my throat until Tommy and Noah stopped their whispering and looked up at me with embarrassment. There were only a few minutes left, so I continued on with what I had to say.

"Now that we are all paying attention, I want you to promise me that you will be nice to Miss Singer who will be your substitute teacher next week. Your writing assignment will still be due on Friday and I will grade it when I return. I hope you all have a wonderful weekend, and I will see you all in a week."

"We'll miss you, Miss Hart," a tall girl with strawberry blonde braids and a small upturned nose chirped from the front row.

"We'll miss you," the other kids joined in as they stood, picked up their backpacks, and filed out of the classroom. I lingered for a moment, taking in the rows of students' desks and askew chairs, the motivational posters on the walls which were my idea to brighten up the room, and a large sheet of paper tacked up next to the white-board featuring impressions of the children's hands in multi-colored puff paint and their own hand scrawled names. My fingers traced the desks as I pushed in the chairs and tidied up the room before leaving.

My black purse started to buzz as I said goodbye to the receptionist. I reached around in its bowels until I pulled out my phone in its bejeweled case. The word "Mom" popped up on the screen in bright letters and I pressed the green button.

"There you are, honey, are you still coming over to help with the preparations? Maybe you can make a stop on the way and bring over more napkins; I'm worried we don't have enough. And since you are going anyways, can you also grab a bag of ice."

There was a local grocery chain near the school, so I swung by there to pick up the groceries. Snatching a shopping basket from the pile by the entrance, I wound my way through the aisles. My mother told me that we needed napkins and ice; so I grabbed those. Then I got myself a candy bar. I felt like I needed something sugary and chocolatey. Using self checkout, I paid for my items and dropped them in the trunk of my car. Once I settled back into the drivers seat, I took a moment for myself. I unwrapped the candy bar and bit into its chewy caramel center, savoring the sweet flavor. Then I stuffed the empty wrapper in my cup-holder, buckled my seat belt, and drove to meet my mom.

I parked my blue Nissan Sentra in the concrete driveway next to my mother's silver SUV and grabbed the napkins and bag of ice from the trunk. I walked up the ocher flag-stones lined with smaller decorative stones that formed a path around the cream-colored, stucco, two storied house that used to be my grandmother's home. My fingers trembled and I choked back tears as I remembered how, as a child, I spent many days running around in the backyard in my bathing suit, my grandmother laughing and following me with the water hose until I tired, or how I helped her whip-up extravagant sorbets which we promptly devoured. I would never again see her kind face surrounded by a halo of silver hair, bound back on top of her head as she strained over a crossword puzzle or taste the golden crusted cinnamon apple pie that she baked each fall with crisp apples from her own tree.

I used my shoulder to press open the side door leading into the garage and dropped the heavy bag of ice on top of the freezer box in the corner. I set the napkins on top of the stor-age shelf holding tins filled with a random array of screws and nails along with clear plastic bins that held a bunch of scarves and other cold weather gear. Then, I popped the top of the freezer which was still stacked with storage containers filled with my grandma's homemade stew and assorted casseroles. I moved some containers to the side and plopped in the bag of ice that had started to thaw, leaving the tips of my fingers moist.

"Is that you, honey?" my mom's voice shouted from inside the house.

"Yeah, I just put the ice in the freezer," I replied. My mom opened the door leading from the garage to the kitchen, her hair tied up in a messy ponytail, tendrils of copper hair framing her face like a halo of fire interlaced with shoots of silver. Seeing my mom with bags beneath her eyes spreading out like bruises and her clothing in disarray when she normally was groomed to perfection, brought home my reason for being there. "Mom," my voice hitched; she took one step towards me and enveloped me with her arms.

"I know," she whispered against my ear; her chest sunk as she exhaled deeply. Her hand gripped mine tightly, and she led me further into the house. The air was heavy with the sulfuric scent of eggs and the cloying perfume of the floral bouquets placed throughout the house, making my stomach turn. My mom had prepped her chunky potato salad along with deviled eggs, made special by the finely minced onion and pinch of curry powder she added as her secret ingredients. I moved them from the kitchen island to the fridge which was already stocked with drinks.

"I already cleaned the kitchen, but I could use your help with the other rooms. The nursing home isn't coming until tonight to pick up the equipment," my mom said. The foldable hospital bed my grandmother had spent her last days on stood stripped of its linen in the corner of the living room together with an empty IV pole, the only clinical distraction from the otherwise cozy but old-fashioned room. My grandmother had been fond of doilies, and she had them draped over every possible flat surface, including the big boxed TV that still worked. On the side table, next to the brown leather love seat, my mom had placed a poster-sized black and white portrait of my grandmother when she was younger. She stared straight at the camera with a smile that said she had a secret. Her hair was coiled up and fastened with a clip, wearing a white blouse and pearl earrings, the same earrings that now made their home in my jewelry box after she gave them to me for my eighteenth birthday.

"You look so much like her," my mom said. "She was about twenty-five in this picture, the same age you are now. I'm glad you got her chestnut curls and green almond shaped eyes instead of the reddish hair your late grandfather gave me."

"I miss her," I said.

"Me too, but I don't believe she's gone. She'll be here looking over us and I want to make sure she'll be proud of the reception tomorrow," she said patting my cheek. "I'll go outside to set up the tables."

My mom slid open the French doors and went into the backyard. I fetched the old Hoover vacuum and ran it over the carpet to make sure the floor was clean and fluffy. My grandmother was never satisfied until her beige carpet had straight streaks vacuumed into it. I glanced around the room again, taking in the wedding and family pictures framed on the wall behind the love seat, porcelain knickknacks on the heavy mahogany cupboard, and the Bavarian cuckoo clock hanging on the other wall above the stereo system that still played tapes, then I placed the vacuum back into the utility closet and joined my mom outside. She had started to set up the party tables; I helped her fold out the last one and set out the plastic chairs. It wasn't supposed to be windy today and tomorrow so we set up one of those pop-up shades but fastened it with ground-stakes just in case. Thankfully, May wasn't scorching hot yet, so we could host outside, otherwise my grandmother's house would have gotten cramped.

"Will you wait for the nursing home people to pick up the bed? I've got to go home and get your dad some dinner and lay my things out for tomorrow. Your dress is already ironed and hanging in your old room. You are staying with us tonight, right? That way we can drive together tomorrow morning," my mom asked.

"Yes, I'll be there as soon as the bed's picked up. Save me a plate," I said and walked her to the front door. She took her purse from the wooden coat rack on the left side of the door and fished out the car keys. I waved her goodbye as she reversed into the street and took off in the silver SUV. Once my mom left, the house turned extremely quiet and reverent, almost like a tomb. I shook that thought away. This was my grandmother's house, and besides her last days, it was filled with good memories. I took a seat on the bench in front of my grandmother's piano and opened the lid to reveal the black and white keys. I remembered her sitting at it with a straight back and her head held high while she played; it would be sad to see the instrument go but I didn't have the space and my mom never really learned to play, much to my grandmother's discontent. The piano beckoned me so I slid my fingers across the smooth keys, testing their sound, and then I couldn't help but play one of my grandmother's favorite songs. An hour later, around seven o'clock, the doorbell finally rang. I brushed my skirt as I stood, closed the lid to the piano, and went to answer the door.

"Hi, so sorry for your loss, ma'am. We're here to pick up the bed and IV pole," a young man, probably in his early twenties, with a Hillsbrook nursing home tag clipped to his blue polo said. I nodded and told him and his partner, a bigger middle-aged woman wearing a colorful scrub top, to follow me into the living room. There, the man started wheeling out the bed while the woman squeezed my arm sympathetically. She was holding a pen and some papers in her hand.

"I just need you to sign some paperwork while Ben loads up the van, okay?" she said with a warm tone. I nodded as she pointed at the sections I needed to put my signature on. Ben folded up the hospital bed then rolled it over the freshly vacuumed carpet and out the door. Now I'd have to vacuum the streaks back in, I thought, as I signed the paper-work. The woman was kind and didn't rush me, but her gentle concern didn't feel authentic. Instead, it felt performative. It wasn't her fault. She probably had to deal with bereaved fam-ily members all the time. It didn't take long for Ben to finish loading. The Hillsbrook employees and medical equipment being gone from the house made a huge difference. The living room looked like a living room again and not like a glorified hospital room. Without the clinical reminder, it looked al-most as if my grandmother could walk in again and sit down to watch her soap operas. I redid the vacuumed lines in the carpet and put away the old Hoover. Then, I straightened the decorative pillows scattered on the chair and sofa, walked out of the house with purpose, and locked the front door behind me.

2

A Family Gathering

I shimmied into the black cocktail dress my mom left hanging on my wardrobe door. She deftly coiled my hair up into a French twist while I applied waterproof mascara and dabbed on fuchsia lip stain.

"You look beautiful," she said as she brushed my cheek. "I'm going to finish up the last touches on myself, and I'll see you downstairs. Your dad is already waiting by the door, so we can leave in fifteen minutes."

My stomach filled with nerves as I stared at myself in the vanity mirror, the edges still covered in pictures from high school. Most of the pictures were of me and my friend Nicole; us in full glam at our prom, holding s'mores by a campfire during a camping trip with my parents, at fourteen dressed in matching bikinis at the pool. My favorite was the picture my mom took of us at the school talent show. We'd dressed up in matching sparkly leotards and performed a dance routine. I still cringed at the dance moves that were so corny. Nicole and I didn't realize this at the time, bless our teenage brains, but now every time we talked about it we were in hysterics. My mom still had a tape of the whole talent show in her media cabinet.

My eyes drifted to my jewelry box; my grandmother's pearl earrings prominently displayed. I picked them up and decided to wear them. My fingers shook a bit, but I stretched them a couple of times, stood, brushed invisible lint from my dress, and joined my parents downstairs.

"Oh, I forgot to tell you that the Realtor called about the house. I'm sorry I can't take any extra time off from work. Are you sure you still want to go through and pack up your grandmother's things this week to get the house ready for selling?" my mom asked. "I hate that I'm asking you to do this, but the idea of a stranger combing through the house to pack up all my mother's belongings just gives me the shivers. I want her things to be handled by someone she loved."

"Of course, Mom. I know it is important to you."

"If you find anything of your grandmother's that you like, please take it; I know she'd want you to have it."

"I'll sort through the sentimental items for anything you might like to go through at a later time together with Dad," I promised my mom.

"Thanks, sweetie."

My dad handed my mom her purse and held open the door for us. We shuffled into his white sedan, and he drove us towards the Sunny Acres Funeral Home and Cemetery. Parking in the large gravel parking lot, I could almost imagine we were going to a nice park, if not for the headstones lining the plots. Artificially watered, bright green grass covered the ground and palm trees lined the cemetery, belying an oasis in the middle of the desert climate.

It was a nice service, in how far a funeral can be nice. The priest covered my grandmother's life, reciting the highlights we had fed him. His deep voice comforted us as he relayed how my grandmother had worked as waitress at a local breakfast place before she became a piano teacher, where my grandfather, Gary Moore, had taken a shining to her. Every day, he returned to order two cups of coffee, then he would ask her to join him. After a month of declining his offer, she finally accepted and joined him for a cup after her shift ended. They were married forty-one years, and raised my mother, Holly Moore-Hart, together, when he died of a stroke in 2011. My grandmother was lost for a long time after his death, but thankfully she had found close friends in the ladies from her bingo group and gardening club. The three bingo club ladies— Patty, Wanda, and Shirley— stood together with us to pay their respects. Michael Jones, a gardening club member, had also joined the service. I was touched at seeing my grandmother's friends and our extended family all together to celebrate her life. My mom had picked out the wedding picture that stood displayed on a stand by the pastor's mike. Underneath the photo, it stated my grandmother's name along with her birth and death dates: Rosemary Scott-Moore, 1949-2020.

We all filed into each other's respective cars once the service was over, with my dad's car going first to lead the procession to my grandmother's house.

"That was beautiful, I think. Don't you agree? I'm glad her

friends showed up; I invited them to join us at the reception," my mom said as she fidgeted with her fingernails.

"It was very respectful, Holly," my dad said. "We made it through the service, and we will make it through the reception. Just remember we are all here to reminisce and celebrate your mother's life; you can take it easy. Everyone will understand if you don't serve them; the reception is potluck style anyway."

"Yeah, Mom, I think Grandma would have been proud of the service, to see her friends and family all gathered together. I'll take charge of accepting and setting out all the food so you can just grab a drink for yourself and talk to the rest of the family," I said as I squeezed her shoulder. My dad parked in the driveway and the other guests following us parked on the side of the road. I let my parents go inside first to give them a breather as I stood at attention by the front door to greet everyone and thank them for their food.

My cousin on my dad's side, Sofia Hart-Brooks, arrived first with her husband, Joshua. They handed me a potato casserole. Followed by her brother Ryan and his girlfriend Amber with green beans. Next, I greeted my Aunt Paula and Uncle Robert. They brought a container of salmon roll ups made with spinach tortillas and a fruit salad heavy with whipped topping and pistachio Jello mix. I told them to set out on the kitchen island next to the paper plates, napkins, and cutlery.

My second cousin on my mom's side, Eric Scott, hugged me and expressed his condolences. He and his boyfriend, Thomas, brought a vegetable platter with carrot, celery, and bell pepper with a ranch dip.

I let in a stream of other family members and close friends, which included Jason Scott and his girlfriend, Lauren. Most guests had already arrived when I welcomed my grandmother's brother, Lyle, and his wife, Terry. Finally, Nicole Moreno, my best friend since high school, showed up to give me emotional support. My grandmother's friends from the bingo group and gardening club arrived last. Patty Decarlo dropped a pan of lasagna in my hands. After closing the front door behind me, I took it to set out with the rest of the food. Everyone had come together and helped create a bountiful spread of food. Besides my mom's deviled eggs and potato salad, there were buttery dinner rolls, a cheesy and crispy potato casserole that made my mouth water, and a green bean casserole covered in fried onions. My aunt Donna baked a smooth and creamy cheesecake.

My mom thanked everyone for coming and loaded up her first paper plate with a scoop of Patty's lasagna, two of her own deviled eggs, and a dinner roll. Once she stepped away to sit down at the table in the backyard, the rest of the guests loaded up their plates and joined her. I waited until everyone else had served themselves before I took a moment for myself, slowly picking out the foods I wanted to try. Concern for my mother made me take care of all the greeting, but keeping up appearances was hard. The muscles around my lips were already strained from trying to keep a smile plastered on my face. With the back of my hand, I wiped away a tear sneaking down my cheek, careful to not mess up my make-up. I let out a sigh and started piling my plate with potato casserole and Patty's lasagna which scented the air with crusty Parmesan, savory beef, and tomatoes. For good measure, I also dropped a few carrots from Eric's vegetable platter on my plate. Just because it was funeral reception, didn't mean I shouldn't try to add something healthy.

My mom was listening to Lyle talk about his sister, my grandmother, when I dropped my plate on the table and sat down next to her. Terry, Lyle's wife, took a big bite of potato salad, wiped her mouth, and turned her attention to me. "Where is Michael? He's such a handsome young man. You are such a beautiful couple together; I can only imagine the cute babies you'll have," she said. I blanched and a hush fell around me. I mentally thanked my friend who came to my rescue, so I didn't have to answer.

"Michael ended up being someone who didn't deserve Rose, so they broke up. Serves him right in my opinion," Nicole said.

"You are right, Nicole, but Rose isn't getting younger," Terry continued. "You should really get back into the saddle and meet a new man," she said pointedly at me.

"I am content with being on my own for now," I said. "Please excuse me, I'm going to fetch another drink." I pushed out my chair and marched to the kitchen while my mom looked embarrassed; Nicole followed me on my heels.

"Don't listen to her. She still thinks it's 1940 and you need a man to provide for you so you can just pop out babies and medicate yourself with laudanum." She patted my arm and continued, "Let's just sit here for a moment so you can take a breather and eat some of this cheesecake." She pulled out a chair for me, which I took, then sat down opposite me. "So, how are you really?"

I sliced us both a share of the cheesecake and handed her

one of them on a paper plate. I poked at the creamy and tangy filling until it turned to crumbs before answering. "Honestly, I'm not sure. Between my grandmother dying and Michael breaking up with me, I don't know what to feel. Did you know he told me I was boring?"

"You aren't boring. He was just being rude."

"No, I am though. With everything, I play it safe. Why can't I just let go and live a little. He wanted to have someone to explore the world with, and he found that in someone that was not me. Can't even say I blame him. I'm hurt that he cheated, but I don't think I loved him. He was just a safe choice and it was better to stay with what was familiar than to dive back into the deep end. I don't want to end up filled with regrets; maybe something adventurous could still happen to me," I said, followed by a bite of dessert.

"I think you just need to turn your brain off and stop worrying sometime. We are young, and we'll get where we need to go. There's no need to be in a rush to get to some arbitrary finish line which we've been told we should wanna reach."

"Maybe you're right," I said with a sigh.

"Damn straight," Nicole said. "You know me, I'm always right."

"Unless you are wrong," I said with a wink.

"Ah, but that never happens." Nicole scooped some cheesecake into her mouth and licked her lips. "I think we should have a girls' night."

"We should. I'll be pretty busy packing up my grandmother's home, but we should hang out soon. We never get together as often as we used to."

One of the bingo ladies entered the kitchen. "Where is your bathroom," she said.

"Down the hall and on your right," I said pointing in the direction of the front door.

"Thanks," she said, then before leaving the kitchen she added, "I am so sorry for your loss. Your grandmother was a lovely woman."

"Thank you, I appreciate it," I said.

"It really was a lovely service, very dignified. I think Rosemary would have been proud." Nicole squeezed my hand when the woman left.

"Just a little longer and then you'll be able to rest. Promise me though, that if you need to talk for any reason at all, you will call me." I nodded. "I mean it. I am here, always."

"Thank you for coming, for being here for me," I said, returning the squeeze of her hand.

3

A Blind Date

I returned from Lowe's with new markers, packing tape, and a stack of moving boxes that had taken up all the space in my small car. My plan was to set up in my grandmother's living room and then systematically tackle every room in the house one by one, sorting items into: trash, donate, decide later, and keep. I brewed myself a cup of coffee from my grandmother's Keurig and decided to start upstairs. I figured I'd worked my way down, so I could do the kitchen last and still use the things in it. I drank the cup of coffee, rinsed the cup, and set it in the sink. Then I went upstairs to my grandmother's bedroom. I brought along a few trash bags to use while I emptied out the dresser drawers. Her underwear I would toss in the trash but most of her clothing was in really good condition and could go to Goodwill. The picture frames and jewelry I packed in a box for my mother to go through. I was sure she'd want her mother's necklaces, and pictures of herself as a child.

A couple of hours later, I was in one of my grandmother's

guest rooms, knee deep in old appliance boxes, keepsakes, shoe boxes filled with photographs, and musty smelling books. It was difficult to decide what I should throw away or what had value. But I figured that no one wanted random appliances that hadn't been used since at least the seventies, to judge by the faded labels. I stacked a box full of them and filled up the gaps with a bunch of old books. The box with photographs, I set aside for my mother. My phone rang just as I finished lifting the box of items to throw away downstairs.

"Hey, sweetie, how is the packing going?" my mom asked.

"I've made some good progress in Grandma's spare bedroom. There was a shoe box filled with photographs that I put aside for you to go through, and I just filled a big box with old appliances that I was thinking about bringing to the dump right now, so it doesn't fill up the downstairs. Is that alright?"

"She did love to keep everything, I bet they are more than a couple of decades old. They might be considered antiques," Mom laughed. "Don't worry, I asked you to help with packing up so do what you think is best. I trust you."

"Okay, I will. I'll probably head out to the dump soon then."

"Wait, before you go. I had something else to talk about. You know Susan?"

"Susan?" I said, wondering where the question was going.

"Yeah, Susan who's in my Wednesday yoga class."

"Sure, I think you've mentioned her before."

"Well, we were talking and I so happened to mention you, my smart teacher daughter. I was saying how you were single. And guess what?"

"What?" I said, worried that I knew where my mom was headed.

"She has a son who, I believe she said, is an accountant. Thirty-one years old, recently broken up as well, Nick's his name. She showed me a picture, and he looked like a nice man, so I gave Susan your number and—"

"Wait, you already gave out my number?"

"For Susan to give it to Nick, so he can call you to schedule a date."

"Mom, don't you think it's a bit too soon? Besides, I really don't want to go out with a stranger right now." I let out a sigh.

"Rose, it would do you some good to go out with someone else. Who knows, maybe Nick's the one. Susan spoke very highly of him."

"Of course, she did," I muttered under my breath. The woman was talking up her own son. "I doubt it would do me good, and I'm busy enough as it is. Unless you've forgotten." Perhaps I was being a bit unkind, but my mom could meddle a tad too much in my opinion.

"Just promise me you'll let him take you out."

"I need to continue packing," I said.

"Just one drink," my mom said, as she wore down my willpower.

"Fine, one drink."

"Good, tell me all about your date later."

I groaned when I hung up my phone, a date with a stranger was not something I was looking forward to. Hopefully, this Nick didn't like his mother meddling in his affairs either and would choose not to call me.

Turned out, my hope was in vain. My phone rang in the evening just as I was tackling the last of the books in the spare bedroom. I had made a lot of progress and managed to empty out almost everything else in the guest bedroom.

"Hi, my name is Nick Scranton. It seems our mothers arranged for us to meet," he said in a deep baritone. I had to give him points for his opening lines.

"Yes, I'm sorry about that. My mom likes to meddle."

"Well, I know a little about that," he said with a laugh. "But I figured that taking a chance wouldn't hurt. Would you like to go out to eat?"

"Sure, I'm free tomorrow evening."

"Great, I'll pick you up at six."

I gave him the address to my apartment and returned to the books. Dropping a few yellowed old paperbacks in the cardboard box, I reached my hand back into the unsorted stack and felt a zap. I pulled back my hand and looked at my fingers; it felt like an electric shock, but I didn't see any damage. A bit more careful, I continued to grab books, one at a time. Perhaps it was just a bit of friction, but it hurt. I picked up a pale blue covered book and immediately dropped it when I felt another zap, this time not as strong, merely mildly annoying. Gently, I lifted the book off the floor again; it felt so strange in my hands, almost as if it was vibrating. The title caught my attention— Rosemary, my grandmother's name. But I didn't see an author. I flipped the book open to see if it had the author's name on the title page, but it only had Rosemary printed on it. The only other identifier I could find was a stamp that said "Bookshop" and that didn't tell me much at all. It was strange but it had been a long day. I sorted the book with my grandmother's name into the stack for "decide later" and threw the last of the other books into a box that was headed for the dump, then I called it a night and went home.

My sleep wasn't peaceful. I dreamed about the book, Michael, my conversation with Nicole at the funeral reception, and my grandmother. They all got jumbled up, and over and over I kept being told that I needed to stop being so boring. In the morning, I told myself it was because I was sorting through my grandmother's belongings, that it made sense that I would feel a bit weird.

Later in the afternoon, after I shook off my disturbing dream, I actually managed to pack up the main bedroom and bathroom. My dad would have to come and help me lift the heavy furniture downstairs but everything else was gone, packed up, and sorted. The full boxes of things that were "to keep" I stacked in the garage. I could hardly believe I'd already finished the second floor. Now, I could continue on downstairs.

I checked the time on my phone. It was already four. If I didn't hurry, Nick would be picking me up dressed in sweats and covered in dust grime. My grandmother was a very neat woman, but somehow when digging through all her possessions, I still got dirty. Dust was everywhere.

At six o'clock, I was freshly showered, primped, and dressed in a cute maroon midi dress as I stepped into the passenger side of Nick's car. My mom was right; he was attractive. Although, he was wearing a pretty casual outfit. He wasn't as handsome as Michael, but then again, that hadn't worked out for me either. Besides, I just had to give him a chance.

"I hope you brought an appetite," Nick said, as he started the car.

"I can eat; where are we going?"

"Rolling Smoke BBQ, you like barbecue, right? Have you ever been? It's the best place in town."

"I haven't tried it," I said. I liked barbecue, but it wasn't really what I expected for a dinner date. My outfit felt somewhat overdressed now.

Turned out, my clothes were the least of my problems. Which became ever clearer the more Nick talked. He ate, barely chewed, and talked. Then talked some more. I barely got a word in.

"My mom said you were a teacher, that you work with young kids," he said in between bites. I was about to answer his statement, however, he continued again, "I considered going into teaching but then decided it wasn't for me. I think it would be tiresome to have to say things over and over. No, I'm glad I chose to go into finance."

"An accountant, right?"

"Yeah, I've been working for Hastings and Sons for a few years, but eventually, I would like to branch off and start my own company. I think Scranton's has a nice ring to it."

I just nodded and poked at my plate of pulled pork and Mac and cheese. Nick never once stopped talking about himself. I think I deduced why he was still single and regretted listening to my mom and agreeing to dinner. When he dropped me off in front of my apartment, he leaned in for a kiss. I backed up and told him politely that I thought he was a nice guy but that I didn't think we were compatible. He didn't look too happy with my dismissal but said goodbye and left. I was very glad to see him go and couldn't wait to lay down on the couch and not listen to someone talk about themselves.

"Thanks for that," I told my mom when she answered her phone.

"Why, what happened?" she asked.

"He invited me to dinner, so I dressed up in a nice dress and heels. Then he arrives in simple jeans, running shoes, and a sports shirt. And guess where we went."

"Where did you go?"

"A BBQ place."

"But, that's not that bad," my mom hedged.

"Well, then he spent the entire date talking about himself and telling me about what he heard from his mom about me while eating and chewing with his mouth open."

"Susan told me that he was a catch."

"I'm sure Susan thinks so," I said acerbically. "Can we agree that you can't arrange any more blind dates? My dating life is now off limits."

"Oh honey, that was just one bad apple."

"Yes, but I'd like to not make it a whole orchard."

"Okay, I won't pressure you into dating. But if you do find someone, let me know. I love you, Rose. I want you to be happy." My frustration with my mom melted away. She meant well, even if she sometimes went overboard.

"I know, Mom. I love you too."

My feet now snug in fluffy socks and dressed in pajama shorts and a comfy tee, I settled on the couch and put on a random show. While I checked my e-mails, my thoughts flitted back to the strange book in my grandmother's spare room. I searched the terms "Rosemary" and "bookshop" together but nothing popped up. What was I even thinking? No bookshop would name itself just that, and as for "Rosemary", all that showed up were recipes using the herb and random people I didn't know. I was being silly. It was just a static shock from the old pages combined with the dry desert air, nothing to be curious about. I would get them all the time from my clothes in the dryer, or my car door. I shoved my phone aside and watched a comedy show.

Later, on my way to the bedroom, I picked up the book from the "decide later" pile. I started reading the first few pages as soon as I settled down into the mattress.

Rosemary Scott stood gaping at her surroundings. The young woman had no clue what happened to her. Suddenly, she found herself in England during the Georgian era, standing in the middle of a gravel driveway flanked by a sumptuous garden. From behind her, she became aware of yelling and something loud inching closer. She turned around and froze as a horse and carriage was barreling towards her.

The driver shouted, "Get off the road." Rosemary lurched to the side and landed in a patch of grass. The driver swerved and halted the carriage. Someone traveling inside the carriage slid aside the curtain and peeked his head out of the window.

"Winston, what on earth is happening," he asked the driver.

"I apologize, Sir. There was a girl standing in the middle of your driveway."

"A girl? In the middle of my driveway?"

"Yes, Sir." The driver hopped off his seat and onto the ground. Then he opened the carriage door to let the traveler out.

Meanwhile, Rosemary brushed dirt off her petticoats. Though the damp grass had left a large stain on her pretty patterned sundress. She returned to standing only to see the traveler stomping towards her with a scowl on his face.

My eyes were getting heavy. I closed the pages and set the book aside. The story was so strange but the details about the main character made me certain it was supposed to be my grandmother. I rubbed my temples. It was important to relax, tomorrow I'd start packing up the living room, and since I was feeling a bit frazzled, I promised myself I would take an afternoon break to go for a run. There was nothing better to quiet the mind and get rid of frayed nerves than working your muscles and focusing on your breathing as your feet pound the ground.

4

The Bookshop

"How'd the date go," Nicole asked, her voice a bit shrill as it came through my phone speakers. I grunted. "That bad, huh?"

"You don't want to know," I said ominously while I packed up the knickknacks displayed on my grandmother's living room shelves. The statues and picture frames were headed for the box my mom would need to go through. "He took me for BBQ and didn't dress up at all. Then, he spent the entire date talking about himself and about what he heard about me from his mom, all without ever asking me a single question."

"Yikes."

"Yeah, definitely regretted the whole thing immediately," I said. "The next time my mom tries to set me up with another man I'm going to run for the hills. Dammit," I grunted as I cut my finger on a sharp edge of the cardboard box.

"What happened?"

"Nicked my finger," I said as I licked the wound. "Nothing serious. Packing hazard."

"Yeah, a very dangerous job that is," Nicole said. "Hold on a moment." She muttered something to someone then turned back to me. "Now, where were we. Ah, yes. You know, there's someone at my office I could set you up with. Josh Tiwari, he's a cool guy."

"Thanks, but I think I'm good. I don't want to go on any other blind dates right now."

"BBQ guy really scared you off, huh." Nicole laughed.

"Just a bit," I said. Mostly, I just thought back to the novel, the one that had shocked me. I wasn't in the mood to think about men. "I found a book," I said.

"What's it about?"

"That's the strange thing; the title is Rosemary, my grand-mother's name. I couldn't find the name of the author. I started reading the first few pages and it was very strange; the character really resembled my grandma or at least the way she was when she was young."

"Perhaps it was a special gift, and someone wrote her a story starring herself?" Nicole said.

"Maybe," I said, but it felt inadequate.

There were other voices talking to Nicole now and she said, "Hey, I have to run but we'll talk again soon."

I got up from the floor and stepped away from all the things that had yet to be sorted and packed. I found a band aid in the kitchen junk drawer, which was overflowing with random screwdrivers, old Christmas cards, dried up markers, and for some inexplicable reason, a single toothbrush. I figured, once I'd bandaged up my index finger, that it was as good a time as any to take a break.

I made a promise to myself to go for a run and I was intent

on keeping it. That morning, I made sure to bring yoga pants and a tank top so I would be ready to go. I brought another change of regular clothes for after. Packing up the rest of the living room in sweaty clothes wouldn't be necessary. I ran upstairs to the bedroom I was staying in while I cleared out my grandmother's home. I grabbed my yoga pants and a tank top from a duffel bag that I had dropped on the carpeted floors. It didn't take me long to take off what I was wearing and pull on my active wear. I made a quick stop in the bathroom to swipe on some sun screen; the desert sun was brutal on my fair skin. Then I retraced my steps to the kitchen where I downed a glass of water. With SPF on my face and fully hydrated, I was now ready to go. I swung my cross-body bag around my neck and headed out the door.

At first, I warmed up. I stretched my limbs which were sore from kneeling on the floor, bending in awkward positions, and lifting up boxes that were deceptively heavier than they appeared to be. Then I walked down my grandmother's street; when I reached the end, I picked up the pace. My plan had been to run down to the intersection and take a right which would lead me past the local park. There, I'd take another right, turning onto a residential road which winded its way around until it finally reached my grandmother's street again. Instead, something was telling me to go straight. I waited for the walking sign to turn white, then ran across the road and continued along the sidewalk. There was a 7-11 and Pizza Hut at the next intersection, and I still continued straight. What was I even doing? I'd gone a lot further than I planned to run. There was something in my mind that told me it was important to keep going, urging me on past the cars in the road, and the myriad of fast-food places. I took a few turns without knowing where I was going and passed by a few apartment blocks. My breathing had turned ragged and I was sweating through my clothes. The southwestern sun was beating down on me.

I wanted to stop; I should have stopped, but whenever I tried, I somehow didn't. My feet didn't listen and then my brain would tell me to take another turn, that is, until I reached the edge of a strip mall. The green and yellow Subway sign was the first thing I saw, then a dog grooming store, and a donut shop. I slowed down to an amble. Next up was a nail salon with a very bright pink logo, and a phone store advertising the newest iPhone. I continued on. Then, I had to look again, simply because the store I was staring at looked like it didn't belong in a strip mall. This building looked like it should be wedged in between other brick buildings somewhere in a city in Europe, instead of in the middle of a strip mall surrounded by pale cement and new storefronts with shiny facades. However, it was what I had been running towards; I felt it pull me towards its core, like it was gravity and I was the apple that had to fall and hit the ground.

Above the ornate wooden door, in the front, was a sign written in a beautiful cursive that simply said, "Bookshop". My hand reached for the doorknob but stopped just short, and instead, hovered above it. I had no idea what had drawn me to this shop that looked so out of place with its surroundings. How did I go from running around the city with my feet taking me wherever they wanted to go, to stopping in this place? Something about this bookshop was pulling me towards it; it felt eager, as if it was anticipating my arrival.

I hesitated. There wasn't time for this. I should return to my grandma's house, to continue packing. But even as I told myself that, I realized that I couldn't leave now. I shook off the strange sensation in my stomach. I loved books; I was already here, so I might as well go in and have a look. My hand grabbed the doorknob, swung open the door, and I stepped inside. A small little bell rang above my head to alert the staff of a new customer as the door fell closed behind me. I looked around in surprise as the inside of the bookstore looked a lot more spacious than the narrow storefront had indicated.

"Can I help you find something, dear? Are you looking for adventure or romance stories?" a middle-aged woman with pinned up, curly, graying hair and a kind face asked. She must be the owner, I thought. I walked over to where the woman sat behind a register.

"Hello, I do like adventures and romance books, but I'm just browsing for now."

"Alright, if you change your mind, just come up and ask. My name is Melinda, Mel for short. Take your time looking around and perhaps you'll find the right book for you."

I nodded in thanks and walked off to the right. It seemed as good a place as any to start in a shop full of rows of heavy oak bookcases, filled from top to bottom with books. My hand caressed the spines of the novels reverently as I trailed along the stacks. There were new and old books mixed together with no rhyme or reason. The owner must have never heard of the Dewey Decimal System because I found a Stephen King book tucked away next to a biology book written by an author whose last name started with F. How could anyone find what they wanted in this chaos?

I glanced at the different titles as I zigzagged my way through the shelves but didn't have a pull towards any of the books, that is, until I reached the back of the store.

There was a short staircase leading up to a small landing with more shelves lined with books. I wasn't sure if I was allowed up there, but something inside me pushed me up the steps. Surely, if there was no "Do Not Enter" sign, I would be okay to go up. I sneezed as I climbed the stairs. It looked like there hadn't been anyone to clean up there in ages.

My fingers skipped over the spines, disturbing the dust covering them. I didn't need or want to pull one out of the shelving until I reached a small book wedged in between two thick volumes. I brushed the dust off the spine so I could read its title. But the hardback held no clue to the author. I pulled it out. There was nothing written on its light green covered binding. I frowned at the book and sneezed once more, as the dust and fragile old pages tickled my nose.

I opened the book to figure out if anything about the author was written on the first page. But as I turned the page, everything around me turned black and a strong tugging sensation enveloped my body.

* * *

The shopkeeper, named Melinda, made her way up the stairs and picked up the book that lay open and abandoned on the landing. She closed it gently, swiping her hand along the spine, and placed it back into its spot on the shelf.

"May you have a great story," she muttered with a mischievous smile as she walked back down the steps towards the front of the shop.

The store that was simply named "Bookshop" was located at a strip mall in the Southwest of the U.S.A. in between a nail salon and a Dollar store, and then it wasn't. It existed someplace else. In another part of the world, another person was feeling the strange urge to head in a direction they hadn't planned on going, abandoning the things they were going to do that day. The spine of the light green book sitting firmly on the shelf now had one word written on it. *Rose.*

5

A Whole New World

What happened? I thought as I brought my hand to my temple and applied pressure. My head was swirling. Did I forget to eat? Is it low blood sugar? I blinked a couple of times while my equilibrium returned to normal before fully opening my eyes.

"Huh?" I gasped. I looked out at a lushly green meadow with a few clusters of trees scattered around and a low wooden fence with a stone border that ran through the land like a scar. It looked like something from a costume drama made by PBS. I must have been imagining things. Did I fall asleep? I closed my eyes again and pinched my hip. "Ow!" That hurt. Good, I thought. I was pretty sure I read somewhere that you couldn't feel pain in a dream. It sounded real or at least I hoped it was. I repeated the words, "I am at a bookshop; I am at a bookshop." As I slowly opened my eyes again, what I saw was green grass, trees, and a clear blue sky. Definitely no books and no store.

This must be what shock feels like. My breathing had increased rapidly. I pressed my hand against my chest to stop hyperventilating. Without meaning to, I took a step back. My foot slipped and I let out a shriek as my body teetered over the muddy edge of a pond. With a big splash, I tumbled backwards and hit the water behind me. I hardly knew what was going on around me. I had been too focused on the strange thing that happened to me and too shocked at finding myself in a different place. The fact that there was a pond immediately behind where I was standing had escaped my attention. Now, not only did I find myself inexplicably somewhere in the countryside with no idea how to return home, I also looked like a drowned rat covered in pond scum. I picked off some kind of weed from the crown of my head and let it drop back into the water with a splat, disgust etched on my face. There was someone running towards me while I splashed around in the pond. I was trying to catch my bearings and find a spot to stand. My purse was no longer on my shoulder. I was afraid it was now lost underneath a layer of sludge on the bottom of the pond. Goodbye phone. Goodbye wallet. I thought wryly. Using my feet, I tried to feel around the bottom of the pond, but I only sank deeper into the debris. The squelching feeling grossed me out so I kicked out my legs to swim up more. I couldn't see anything in the murky water.

A tall man, dressed in period clothing, pulled off his jacket, dropped it at the water's edge, and jumped in to help me.

"Miss, are you alright?" he asked in an attractive British accent. I couldn't help it; I loved how the Brits pronounced their words. It was probably one of the reasons why I watched so many costume dramas. "Pardon me." He put his hands around my waist and lifted me up and out of the water. His strong arms dropping me back on solid ground. Then he climbed out of the water himself and sat down next to me in the grass, his strange pants and billowy shirt clinging wetly to his body.

I vaguely noted that it was a shame that his clothes and boots were now also ruined. The outside of the polished black leather boots wasn't too dirty but the inside had to be filled with murky liquid.

After squeezing the excess water from his shirt, the handsome man started speaking to me.

"How did you end up here by yourself, in your undergarments no less?" His gaze raked over my soggy yoga pants and the tight tank top that had turned translucent. Something primal in his gaze made me feel self-conscious about my outfit. I crossed my arms in front of my chest. My skin was covered in goosebumps and the soaked clothes I was wearing added to my discomfort. I was cold, which was a strange realization. I was never cold in May. Wherever I was, it wasn't home. If the green fields hadn't clued me in, then the temperature would have. Summer, actually most of the year, could only be described as sweltering where I was from. Living in the Southwest meant living in a hot and dry desert climate.

"Umm, I don't know. Where are we?"

"You don't know where you are? Have you hit your head?"

"I don't think so."

The man seemed concerned as he leaned towards me. "May I take a look at your head?" he said.

"Sure," I said. He gently turned my head sideways, looking for blood or a wound.

"I don't see anything serious," he said. "Perhaps you are a bit shocked. Does anything else hurt?"

"I'm not sure." Maybe I was shocked. Nothing made sense to me at all. I hugged my knees to my chest and gazed up at the handsome man. "How did I get here?" I asked. I racked my brain for possible theories. "Is this a movie set?" It was the first thing that came to mind as an explanation for his weird clothes.

"Movie? I've never heard of that?" the man said with a puzzled face. Now, I was starting to freak out.

"You are joking, right? What is going on? Is this some kind of hidden camera prank type show?" I looked around for cameras. As far as I could see, there were no spots where they'd be able to hide the cameras or crew. But surely, they had to be here somewhere. I did wonder why they'd knock me out and bring me to a different country. That didn't seem like normal practices for a TV show, but I was grasping at straws.

"Hello, you can come out now; the jig is up!" I yelled, before turning back towards the man that helped me out of the water. "Very funny, taking me from the bookshop and having me wake up outside. What was used? Some kind of gas? I didn't ingest anything."

The man looked at me like I had three heads and ran his fingers through his wet blonde locks to sweep them away from his forehead. I scowled and scrambled to my feet. Dang it! I must have twisted my left ankle as I fell into the water. I tried balancing on one leg, wincing as I hopped. The man stood and put his arm around me. I gripped his arm so I could steady myself against him.

"Miss, I will take you to Hawthorne. You have to be seen

by a physician since you are clearly speaking nonsense. I am afraid you must have hit your head or be in shock."

His presence rattled me, so instead of taking a moment to breathe and think rationally, I lashed out. "You can stop the act. Return me home. Get me back to my own city." I pursed my lips and glared. "Contact whoever you need to." But the man just kept staring back at me in puzzlement. My stomach started to sink. This couldn't be real, could it? Was I in a different time?

"Can you stand on your own for a moment?" I nodded. He hesitated, as if assuring that I spoke the truth, but then he let go of my waist. He retrieved his coat from the ground and placed it around my shoulders; I had started shivering from being drenched in the pond. Thankfully, the heavy coat helped a bit. The man didn't look too warm either. His shirt clung to his chest and his hair was plastered to the sides of his face. I imagined I didn't look much better.

"I am going to lift you up and carry you to my horse. I apologize but you will have to ride with me. Fortunately, we are only a mile away from my estate." The man frowned. "You are wearing the most peculiar outfit," he said as he scooped his other arm behind my knees and lifted me up against his chest.

I felt incredibly awkward as he strode towards his horse while carrying me, both waterlogged, and my arms clinging to his neck for dear life. Like I was some kind of damsel in distress. He plopped me on the horse's back and then took his place behind me.

"Hold on to him," he said, as he took the reins and urged the horse to move. As we rode, an expansive mansion came into view, framed by tall hedges. Two stone columns stood guard beside the wooden front door. This must be the Hawthorne Estate he mentioned. Was I transplanted into Pride and Prejudice? Lush British country side? Check. Pond? Check. Large estate? Check. Handsome man in period clothing? Check. I shook my head at the strangeness of it all.

"We are almost there, then we can get you warmed up." He must've taken the shake of my head for shivering. I really was cold though and hoped I could change out of these wet clothes soon. A woman ran out as we reached the mansion.

"John, John. What happened? Who's this? Oh, my, you are both drenched. We've got to warm you up before you catch pneumonia." Her eyes lingered on the state of my clothes, worry lines crossed her face.

"Beth, we are fine. Don't fret, but could you please notify Mrs. Avery and have her send for a physician? And perhaps prepare some warm water? For Miss..." He turned towards me.

"Umm Rose."

"For Miss Rose. And could you retrieve one of your spare dresses, sister?"

"Yes, I know exactly which one of my dresses would suit Miss Rose's complexion." Beth was almost jumping up and down in excitement before running back into the house, her high-pitched voice shouting for Mrs. Avery.

From that point on, everything happened so rapidly. A short and busty middle-aged woman, wearing a grease-stained apron, rushed out and scolded the man that had brought me here.

"John, what are you still doing outside? Bring the girl to

the guest room," she ordered. "I've already got water heating. And once you have her settled, you need to dry off too." She pointed towards a different man that stood gawking outside near the side of the looming building while holding a rake. "Hugh, can you take John's steed to the stables?" The woman was a whirlwind of action and orders.

The man named John lifted me back into his arms and carried me through the wide wooden double doors. We passed through the spacious foyer lined with portraits and climbed up a flight of heavily carpeted stairs. Once we reached the landing, he set me back down in front of the first door on the left. He opened the door and let me in to the most beautiful room I had ever seen. It was everything you could dream of thinking about antique homes.

"Mrs. Avery will be here to assist you soon, as I'm sure my sister will also be, with dry clothes," John said. He helped me towards the edge of a stand that held a washing basin; it was perched against the wall near the fireplace. "Thank you," I muttered, as he left the room and closed the door behind him.

I stripped out of my yoga pants and tank top, the wet fabric clingy against my skin, and left them, together with my bra, in a wet pile at the edge of the stand. The pond water had left a gritty texture mingled with dark smears behind on my body. It didn't feel right to leave my dirty clothes on top of the hardwood floor, but I wasn't sure where else to put them. By now, my teeth had started chattering. I felt uncomfortably nude and exposed. Having the soggy itchy fabric removed from my skin felt nice but I kind of regretted taking my clothes off. Now, I would have to face the unknown women dressed in my birthday suit.

My limbs shivered as I tried to warm up by the flames that burned low in the fireplace. I stood awkwardly in the strange bedroom, my eyes roaming every inch of my surroundings. A huge mahogany bed stood front and center, its pointed head-board placed against the back wall, a sheer cream-colored canopy draping over and down the sides. A pretty floral rug was strewn on front of it, and satin embroidered pillows were stacked on top of plush sheets that looked extremely inviting. On the other wall, there was a small secretary and a wardrobe with beautiful feminine woodwork in the corner. Was feminine even the right word? It was the only descriptor that came to mind when I wanted to describe the soft rounded etchings and loopy details. I could imagine Jane Austen sitting there, in front of the secretary, writing her books. How did I end up in a place like this?

There was a small knock on the door and Mrs. Avery entered the room. I hurriedly crossed my arms in front of my chest. She was hoisting a large bucket of water towards the washing basin. Steam wafted up from the surface as she emptied the water into the porcelain bowl.

"Mr. Easton said you fell into the pond and might have hit your head. The physician has been summoned. However, he might not be able to visit until the morning. How about we first get you cleaned up, dressed, and into bed?"

I had no response to that, so instead I nodded.

"Don't be shy," she said, nudging my arms. "It's nothing I haven't seen a thousand times before." Hesitantly, I dropped my arms. Mrs. Avery held out a washcloth, which I accepted.

"That's a good girl," the woman said, as she helped me wash the pond scum off my face. I made sure to scrub away the grit gathered beneath my breasts and in my armpits. Not even the back of my knees were free from sediment. Bending over, Mrs. Avery picked up my wet clothes and dumped them into the empty bucket. She looked scandalized as she picked up my black lacy bra and examined it. Poking at the wire, she gave me an odd look. Footsteps could be heard running up the stairs. Mrs. Avery quickly dropped my clothes and bra in the bucket when John's sister, Beth, entered the room. Together, they helped dress me in a nightgown, a long billowy cotton that covered me from my collar bone to my ankles. I was feeling lightheaded. Beth and Mrs. Avery supported me by my arms as they walked me towards the bed. Mrs. Avery covered me with the plush sheets. They were even softer than I could have imagined, the texture like butter against my skin. I yawned deeply. Exhaustion reared its head when I finally felt warm and comfortable. I could hardly keep my eyes open. There was another knock on the door as I snuggled deeper into the sheets. Mrs. Avery grabbed the bucket holding my dirty clothes and slipped out through the door together with Beth. I could hear John's voice, only slightly muffled through the heavy wood.

"Did she say anything? Tell you where she's from?"

"The poor thing was too exhausted to talk," Mrs. Avery replied.

"I need to ask her some questions."

"John! She needs to sleep; any questions you have, you can ask in the morning," his sister chided.

The last thing I heard before I drifted off to sleep was, "Fine, I'll get to the bottom of it in the morning."

6

A Spoonful of Medicine

Ugh! My head weighed a million pounds, my scalp was tender, and I could swear that every single strand of my hair hurt. I tried to sit up but the muscles in my arms trembled and dropped me back into the mattress. The jarring movement sent me into a deep rumbling coughing fit that traveled straight from my head all the way down to my toes.

"Good morning, Miss Rose. Careful, you don't look so well. How do you feel?"

Dang! It wasn't a dream; I was still here, and I was sick. I groaned out loud which sent the woman, named Beth, into action.

"Oh dear, I will fetch the doctor; he just arrived," she said, fidgeting. "You haven't eaten yet," she continued more to herself than to me. "Oh, yes, I will order some broth, so you can have something to eat. That might help you feel better. Don't worry, Dr. Marlowe is a good doctor; he's treated us whenever we were sick." Beth's skirts rustled as she hurried out the room. I re-examined the bedroom I was in; my yoga pants and tee were folded neatly on top of the wooden desk chair with my bra resting on top. The short and stout Mrs. Avery must have already washed them. I couldn't believe I was still in this strange place. Maybe it was too much to ask that falling in a pond was just a dream. What was I supposed to do now. My body felt weak and exhausted. My stomach cramped from the lack of food. Not much time passed before Beth's light footsteps returned with two heavier ones following her up the staircase. I also caught a whiff of something hearty that made my mouth water; that must be the broth she was talking about.

"Hello, Miss Rose, my name is Doctor Marlowe. I'm here to make sure you are well. Mr. Easton told me you made quite a tumble into the pond and that you twisted your ankle?"

"Yes, sir," I croaked. I gingerly touched my throat and winced. The elderly man, with a sharp nose and bright eyes behind a set of spectacles, bent forward towards me.

"Miss, if you could stick out your tongue for me?" He took a small stick out of his doctors' bag and used it to press down on my tongue as I stuck it out at him, then he made me say "Aah".

"Good, good, you can close your mouth again. I'm just going to check your throat and listen to your lungs." Mr. Easton looked a bit embarrassed that he was standing at the doctor's side, observing me while I was being treated. He turned around, looking intently at the floral wallpaper when the doctor pressed at the sides of my neck, checking for my lymph nodes, I assumed. Finished with that, he took out his stethoscope and placed the cold metal on the bare skin of my chest. I jumped a little at the sensation and started off into another coughing fit. "There now, Miss Rose, when you are ready, if you could take a deep breath for me?"

I did my best to inhale and exhale, but it went a bit shaky. "Good, can you breathe in once more? Perfect. Now, let's go and take a look at that ankle of yours." My ankle was a bit bruised and the doctor dressed it in some linens. Then he rested his hand on Mr. Easton's shoulder and pulled him to the side.

"I'm afraid Miss Rose has a slight fever and a cold. She must stay warm in bed and drink plenty of fluids. Her ankle is sprained and will be tender for a couple of days at least, but should heal with no difficulties. Just keep the lady off her feet while she heals and keep the leg elevated whenever possible. I'll leave some medicine with you for her cold."

"Thank you for your help, doctor. However, Miss Rose is a stranger. We don't know who she is; if I find out where she's from, is it safe for her to be moved?"

Beth's face revealed shock. "John, how could you say such an unfeeling thing? This poor girl is sick because of something that happened on our estate. We have to take responsibility and nurse her back to health. We can talk about returning her to her family when she's better. Besides, I'd quite like to have some companionship other than you for once," Beth said, aghast. My body chose that moment to let out another lung scraping cough. Beth quirked her brow and stared at John as if to say; see? John grimaced.

"Beth, we don't know who she is or where she's from. We can't just let a stranger into our house."

"John Easton," Beth said, thrusting her hands at her sides and raising her voice. "This is my home too. We can't send her away in the state that she's in. She could get worse." Beth shot me a worried glance. The young woman was right though. I felt awful and I had nowhere to go. What if John did kick me out; where would I go? Doctor Marlowe shuffled awkwardly side-to-side while the siblings argued. He seemed too mortified to cut in.

John rested his palm against Beth's arm. "You know I am only thinking about your safety."

Beth's face softened and she dropped her arms. "Of course, brother. However, we can't turn away someone in need." She pointed at me. "She can stay here until she gets better or until relatives claim her. She looks to sick to be moved currently." John looked to doctor Marlowe for confirmation.

"I am afraid I must agree with Miss Easton," the doctor said. "Miss Rose is much too ill to be moved at the moment. Keep an eye on her, and if anything changes for the worse, send word for me immediately. For now, I have more patients waiting, so I must bid my farewells."

Beth smirked. The young woman was obviously very proud of standing up to her brother. My motives were selfish but I couldn't help but cheer for her victory. I much preferred the pillowy bed I was in right now over the outside. There I'd probably have to rough it on some patch of grass; or be thrown in jail; or committed to an insane asylum. My brain was sifting through any and all historical movies and tv-shows I'd seen. None of them particularly positive about my outcome as a woman alone during these times.

"Thank you for your help," Beth told the doctor. He nodded and picked up his bag of instruments.

"I'll be off then. Send word to me if anything changes."

"Of course, let me walk you out, doctor." John led the way out the door and the elderly doctor followed him down the stairs.

"You must be positively starving," Beth said.

"The soup smells delicious, " I said softly, to spare my throat. Beth pulled up a chair next to the bed and fluffed up a pillow behind my back so I could sit upright. "Thank you."

She smiled at me as she brought a spoon filled with broth to my lips.

"You heard the doctor's order, plenty of fluids." She lowered her voice a little. "Don't worry about my brother. He really isn't as unfeeling as he pretends to be. He's just careful. But, I'll make sure that you'll be nursed back to health." Then she straightened and her voice returned to normal. Now, Rose, do you have a last name?"

"My name is Rose Hart." I slurped some of the broth off the spoon she was holding but found it a bit awkward. "Thank you so much for the broth but would you mind if I try eating it myself?"

"No, of course not," she said. Beth looked a bit dubiously between me and the bowl. "Are you sure you are strong enough?"

I nodded. "I don't feel great, but I think I can manage." Beth handed me the bowl of broth and I ladled some more into my mouth. I didn't remember what the last thing I ate was, all I knew was that I hadn't had food in too long.

"Rose is a pretty name. I don't think I am acquainted with anyone named Hart around here; perhaps there isn't anyone left or they've all emigrated. Do you know when your family moved to the Americas? Where is your family from?"

My mind raced as I tried to remember early American history and what cities were already established during what, to my limited knowledge, appeared to be Jane Austen's time period, the Regency era. I had seen plenty of period dramas to recognize the empire gown Beth was wearing and I knew my city sure didn't exist yet. It was probably safest to stick with the most well-known and historically densely populated city.

"My family lived in New York," I said.

"Lived? Where are they now?" Beth asked. It was difficult thinking up a story on the fly and the guilt at spinning an elaborate lie to tell Beth when she was so caring and kind didn't help. She had taken me into her house without any reservations, unlike her brother. To give myself some more time to think, I raised the bowl of broth to my lips and finished the now almost cool liquid. I thought of my grandmother's funeral and grief flooded my brain, it felt wrong to use that experience, but it made for the most plausible explanation.

"My parents passed away."

"Oh no, my deepest sympathy. John and my parents passed away when I was still very young; I know how difficult it must be for you, adrift without the kind words and support of a parent. Were you here to be taken in by relatives?"

"Umm," I started before John Easton cut in and I turned toward him. He was leaning against the doorway with a dark look on his face.

"Yes, please Miss Rose, do tell us of your relatives."

"Well," I stammered. "My dear parents didn't tell me much before they passed away. My grandfather had a falling out with his family and moved to America. All I know is that they live on a large estate somewhere around here." I made sure to mention an estate so they hopefully would assume I wasn't working class.

"So, your plan was to knock on the door of every building in and around Westbridge until you met someone who said, 'Hart? Yes, I know a Hart family.'" I blushed at his inquisition.

"Well, yes, my father had debts and didn't leave me with much. I used everything I had to travel here in hopes of finding my extended family."

I kept surprising myself. That was a pretty convincing lie, I thought. Now, I hoped Mr. Easton believed me.

"Oh, John. We have to help Rose find her relatives. I do so love a family reunion. I wonder who they are and if they live nearby. Oh, can you imagine! Rose, maybe we would be neighbors, and we could stay the best of friends!"

Beth looked excited. However, Mr. Easton wasn't convinced. His eyes pierced mine for a moment as if he was trying to read my soul. I tried my best to act sincere and stared back without flinching.

He scratched his head and said, "I can send out some inquiries; perhaps we will resolve this mystery sooner rather than later."

"Thank you, brother," Beth said, as she jumped up and down, holding his hands.

"You are welcome, sister, Miss Hart." He nodded his head and left the room.

I was glad I had thought up a cover story but worried what might happen when Mr. Easton couldn't find any relatives. I hoped I wouldn't be here anymore when that happened. How did I get here? The last thing I remembered was opening the book in that bookstore. Was the owner a witch? That thought was so ridiculous that I laughed which turned into another coughing fit.

"Oh my, you have to be careful. I hope you will feel better soon. And don't mind John; he is very protective of me, so I hardly get to have any guests. I would love to get to know you and find out about your family while you are here," Beth said, clasping her hands.

"You are very sweet," I told Beth. "I'd love to know more about you as well. Although, I'm not really the best company at the moment," I said, grimacing at the throbbing at my temples. I wondered how long I'd be sick and stuck in this bed. I was never ill. My mom would joke that I had the immune system of an ox. My co-workers would have to take sick days multiple times a year; any germ the kids in their class had, they would get. But not me, and here I was, God knows where, sick as a dog from falling in a pond. Wonderful. I was stuck here with more questions than answers. And a lot of those questions I couldn't even ask because the person that I needed to ask them had passed away. Why did you have a book with your name on it, I thought. Why did it shock me, and why did it lead me to that strange bookstore? Because there was no other explanation, all of this had to do with my grandmother's book.

My head was pounding, and I laid back against the pillow. Beth gave me a spoonful of medicine from the bottle the doctor had left. The mixture left a bitter, unpleasant coating in my mouth but soon I started drifting off again. Every once in a while, I would wake and find Beth watching over me, touching my forehead, and sitting on the chair beside me reading.

7

Bread and Butter Pudding

The days passed swiftly. I was on the mend thanks to Mrs. Avery's attentions, who I found out was the housekeeper in charge of everything that happened in the house and also served as the main cook. The Eastons, despite their large home and obvious wealth apparently preferred keeping the staff to a minimum. Beth herself also barely left my side and helped me eat and dress though that usually was a maid's job. I'd briefly been introduced to Estelle, a French woman, who insisted she should be dressing me while Beth was waving her concerns away. When they were away, even John peeked in through the door a couple of times.

"I do think the worst has passed; your fever is gone and your cheeks have color in them again. How do you feel? Do you think you might be getting better," Beth asked.

"I think you are right. I do feel a lot better." And I did, the tenderness and pounding in my scalp and temples had stopped and my coughing had receded. My chest was still a bit sore from over exertion but that would go away soon. I flexed my ankle and moved my foot up and down. Beth followed the movement.

"Is your ankle still sore?" she said. "I know the doctor said to keep it elevated and that it might take a couple of days."

My ankle felt fine as I moved it and I told Beth as much.

"Splendid, it is a beautiful day outside, so we should go for a walk, catch some fresh air. I will fetch one of my walking gowns for you to wear."

Beth hurried out and returned with a shift dress, petticoat, and stockings hanging across her arms. She helped me pull on the shift dress and petticoat. I rolled the stockings up my legs as Beth fastened my hair. It was odd to wear these old-fashioned clothes.

"There isn't any underwear?" I asked Beth. She looked confused and then scandalized.

"Underwear? Do you mean drawers? Do ladies wear those in America?"

"Umm, you don't?"

"No, I've only heard women of ill repute wear those." She let out a gasp and slapped her hands across her mouth. "Oh, I'm sorry. I didn't mean to imply that you, that you... well, you know."

"It's okay, Beth, I'm not offended. It's normal to wear, you said drawers? In America."

"Oh, thank you, I didn't mean to sound so callous. Here, you are ready. Let's go and have a stroll through the gardens." We stopped at the front door where she helped me put on a bonnet, a kind of weird hat. She linked her arm with mine and led me along the paths winding through the garden.

The few days of bed rest left me feeling weak. However, I was sure that would pass soon. The watery English sun warmed my skin. I was in desperate need of some vitamin D. I turned my face toward the sky to soak up the sunshine. The faint heat made me miss the southwest sun. I loved going to the river to lay out in the sunshine or go canoeing. Though, every summer Nicole and I would drive to Los Angeles or San Diego so we could sunbathe at the actual ocean. Those road trips brought up fond memories of eating sliced mango topped with chili powder from fruit stands at the side of the road, and digging in to cold creamy custards with the sound of waves in the background.

"Do you like our garden?" Beth said. I turned my head towards the young woman.

"It is very pretty," I said. And it was. The garden was set up with small pathways and nicely manicured topiaries. Some marble statues and stone benches were scattered throughout. Beth and and John had to be fond of roses since those bushes were planted everywhere. Their buds barely started to bloom.

"Hugh, our gardener and driver, works magic with the hedges and grass," Beth said. "But the roses are originally planted by my mother. They were her favorite flower."

"Roses are my mother's favorite as well. I prefer peonies."

Beth grinned. "I guess I should have known that. Roses for Rose."

"My family likes naming their children after plants. It's a bit of a tradition."

"That is nice," Beth said. "I've always liked the name Daisy."

"Or Juniper," I added.

"Marigold."

"Lily."

Beth tried to think of more flower names. "There are so many," she said.

"Definitely a lot of choices," I said, as we continued walking.

We turned a corner and walked straight into Mr. Easton.

"Ah, Miss Hart, how nice to see you up and about."

"Thank you," I said as I dropped into an awkward curtsy and stumbled. Mr. Easton had to steady me while Beth let out a giggle.

"Does your ankle still bother you?"

"No, my ankle is fine; I think I'm just still a bit faint from being confined to a bed for so long."

"Ah, if that's the case, I hope I will get to see you and my sister at dinner tonight."

"I would love to," I said, while pushing down the urge of doing another awkward curtsy. All this formal behavior really awakened my inner 19th century maid. Next, I'd be saying "my lord" and "my lady" and sweeping out the ashes or milking the cows are whatever it was that a maid did all day. Beth nudged me in the ribs after John strode away.

"Was that supposed to be a curtsy?" Beth asked still giggling. Her laugh was infectious and soon I joined in with her.

"I tried," I managed to blurt out.

"Isn't there any polite society in New York?"

"There is, but my father was protective of me and didn't let me mingle with anyone my own age."

"No tea? No social calls, or balls?"

"No, none of those."

"Well, you have to experience a ball! It is great fun, and I haven't been to one in ages. John never wants to host a party, but I will persuade him! Oh, I shall introduce you to the ladies in town. I will send Hugh out with a note to ask if Mrs. Blakeley is free for tea tomorrow morning. With you here, John can't possibly refuse."

"What does tea entail?"

"Oh, we catch up on all the gossip. Mrs. Blakeley generally knows about everything that happens in Westbridge. We drink tea and eat some small bites of food. She'll be able to help spread the word about you and your predicament and start your venture into society. Who knows, maybe she even knows something about your family."

"That sounds amazing," I said, though I worried what would happen if they all saw through my fabricated story. Whatever I thought up on the fly couldn't possibly hold up under scrutiny. Beth spent most of the day showing me around Hawthorne, leading me through the various down-stairs and upstairs rooms. I personally loved the hothouse that was built against the backside of the huge stone building. Back home, I used to love lounging in a sun room with a tall glass of iced tea, except during the summer months when the temperatures would be sweltering. The hothouse made me think of one, except it was filled to the brim with all kinds of plants and flowers— petunias with their funnel-shaped flowers with green hearts, vibrant yellow tulips, and pink to white ruched petaled carnations.

"These are beautiful," I told Beth.

"Thank you," John Easton said, as he sneaked up behind

us. "This one is my favorite." He pointed towards the violet flowering wisteria whose vines were threading up a trellis in the corner of the hothouse. "But if left unchecked, it smothers all the other more delicate flowers." He moved to the plant and snipped one of the vines snaking towards another potted plant with his shears, then he turned back towards us and raised his brow at me.

"My brother is fond of horticulture. All these plants are his work," Beth said.

"Oh, how wonderful. You must be gifted to grow so many beautiful flowers," I said, trying to sound pleasant more for Beth's benefit than Johns. His veiled warning shook me, but Beth didn't notice. I wondered how long I would have to stay here. What would I have to do to return home? It was honestly exhausting being a woman in a period drama. The bodice pinched everywhere; I couldn't bend over properly, or draw in a deep breath. I got a hard-won new appreciation for anyone walking around wearing corsets or stays or whatever else kind of torture device.

John held out his arm and said, "Please, let me escort you ladies to the dining room. I was merely coming to fetch you on Mrs. Avery's behalf. Her cooking waits for no one." I nodded and grabbed his right arm a bit awkwardly.

Beth on the other hand chirped out, "Lets," and deftly linked her arm with his left.

The dining room was bathed in a warm glow coming from the candles on the two candelabras arranged in the middle of the long wooden table. A white cloth had been draped across and on it were the place-sets for the three of us, although with many more plates and silverware than I thought we'd need.

The best word I could use to describe the room would be opulent. Still-life paintings in gilded frames depicting a variety
of foods were hanging in between the wainscoting on top of
dramatic burgundy wallpaper, glass oil lamps fixed symmetri-
cally between them.

John Easton strode towards the table and pulled out two
ornate dining chairs; Beth sat down at one and I took the
other on her right. John ambled around and settled himself
down across from us. Two servers sat dishes out on the table
in an impressive pattern.

Beth leaned towards me and said, " Since it's just the three
of us, we are only having one course; although, Mrs. Avery has
made today a little special with her bread-and-butter pudding. You should see the variety of dishes when we are having
a dinner party!" I couldn't imagine the amount of food there
would be with a dinner party because I already thought there
was way too much food for the three of us to eat already. The
centerpiece was a golden-brown roasted duck, and around
it, the two waiters had placed a silver terrine with a brown
aromatic liquid that had to be some kind of onion soup,
pickled carrots, the bread-and-butter pudding Beth had mentioned topped with plump currants, asparagus topped with
melted butter, and a bowl with what I assumed were pieces of
chicken.

One of the waiters served me some onion soup; I grabbed
a spoon from the many cutlery options next to my plate. Beth
gave me a little nudge and pointed at the other spoon. I never
had to learn which plate went where and what piece of silverware to use with each dish, so I felt a bit embarrassed. John
studied me like a hawk as I switched spoons.

"Curious," he said. "You say your family is connected to a wealthy family here, but you haven't been brought up with proper table manners. Surely, polite society in America can't differ that much from England's." His doubts were loud and clear from his tone of voice. I took a sip of savory onion broth with a hint of tart white wine to save time for an answer.

"As I said before, my late father unfortunately fell on hard times, so I wasn't raised learning dinner etiquette or polite conversation. I do hope you can forgive my lack of knowledge; perhaps Beth will be able to teach me. On that note," I said, as I turned towards Beth, "could you tell me what the dish with pieces of chicken is?"

"Oh, of course. That is chicken fricassee; you must try it." The waiter added some to my plate and I took a bite of chicken breast smothered in a fragrant sauce with hints of sage and rosemary and acidity from a splash of wine.

"This is delicious," I said.

John rolled the stem of his wine glass between his fingers, sniffed the red liquid, and took a sip. "Mrs. Avery is a good cook. I'm sure you aren't used to these luxuries." I rolled my eyes at his remark. He probably thinks I'm poor, but there's no reason to sound like such a snob. John was getting on my nerves. Beth sensed our animosity and changed the subject.

"Oh, John, you must let me invite the other ladies over for tea, so they can meet Rose."

"That isn't a good idea, Beth. I have to leave for some business in London tomorrow morning and I might be gone the whole day or possibly overnight."

"Please, brother. I'll send out Hugh with invitations. Besides, it's only tea, and Mrs. Avery is here to keep an eye on us." John glanced at me, bit his lip, then with a big sigh spread his hands.

"Fine, but only invite a couple of ladies." With a big smile covering her face, Beth started on the bread-and-butter pudding.

8

New Visitors

John had left for London before dawn, the noise his carriage made on the decorative gravel in front of estate had woken me up. Thankfully, I'd managed a few more hours of sleep before Beth burst through the doors. I really did not want to leave the warm and cozy bed, but Beth was full of excitement and dragged me out of it.

"Come, Rose, I've got the perfect dress for you in my room, and Estelle is waiting to do our hair." Estelle, a petite and pretty French maid with honey-blonde hair and a button nose, who picked up all kinds of odd-jobs like dressing Beth, cleaning, and helping in the kitchen, stood by the vanity in Beth's room.

"Bonjour, madame, 'ow would you like your hair styled today?" the maid said.

"I think both of us will wear it in a chignon with ringlets framing our face," Beth interjected, "Rose already has beautiful curly hair and I picked out one of my dresses to compliment her eyes." Behind her, hanging over the wardrobe, was a soft green empire gown with pearl beading on the cap sleeves.

"That's a gorgeous dress. Are you sure you don't want to wear it?" I said, but she brushed the thought away.

"No, green suits you and I have chosen a pink dress."

Estelle's fingers turned deftly as she gathered my hair in bunches and wrangled them into a chignon. I'd never been able to tame my mane into shape like that. The maid's features were delicate and laser focused as she worked on both of our hair. The end result wasn't something I would normally ever wear but I had to admit that it looked sophisticated. The shape accentuated the length of my neck and my heart shaped face.

"Thank you," I told Estelle. The maid smiled and curtsied. Once I pulled on Beth's green dress, I looked like a whole different person. I had to do a double take in the vanity mirror. I wished my grandmother was here to see me. She would be so impressed with the way I looked. I could imagine her voice telling me how beautiful I was. She always said so. I was her beautiful Rose. "Don't let anyone tell you otherwise," she would tell me as a little girl. Beth had sent Hugh out with invitations early this morning and around one in the afternoon, the guests started to arrive. Beth introduced me to Mrs. Blakeley and her two daughters; Anne who was a younger version of her tall mother, with black hair and a face resembling a Roman statue, and Mary whose bubbly attitude lessened her severe features. I liked Mary as she oohed and aahed about my dress. She was a bit younger, maybe fourteen or fifteen and her demeanor reminded me of a little girl in my class; Noelle Mary and her had the same zest for life. Thinking of Noelle made me miss my classroom. How much time had passed? Was everyone back home worrying about me, wondering where I had gone? I hoped not. Even though my mom had set me up with a horrible blind date, she still didn't deserve to have her only daughter go missing. Someone was talking to me and I shook of the memories.

"I'm sorry, I didn't hear you. I'm still recuperating from a cold and a sudden drowsiness overtook me," I said, as an excuse to Mrs. Blakeley.

"Ah, we'll have to sit you down so we can all get acquainted. It is ever so lovely to meet a new person, especially one so mysterious." The last person had arrived and stepped through the door with her manservant. Beth had told me she'd invited Mrs. Ashbrook, an elderly widow with a huge fortune and no heirs to Granhope Manor, a vast estate bordering Hawthorne. The low stone wall and fence I had seen the day I fell into the pond marked the border between the two estates. Apparently, the future of her inheritance was the talk of the town, according to Beth. The stately woman with gray coiffed hair commanded the foyer as she pulled off her gloves and handed them, together with her coat, to the servant standing beside her.

"How lovely of you to invite me," she said to Beth. "Mrs. Blakeley, Anne, Mary," she acknowledged the other three guests.

"Wonderful, let's retreat into the drawing room," Beth said, as she led Mrs. Ashbrook through the doorway on the left to a chair by the round table, set-up in the middle of the room, laden with petite-fours and a teapot with strong herb scented steam still wafting up through its spout. Mrs. Blakeley and her two daughters followed behind; I trailed after them. Beth sat down on Mrs. Ashbrook's right; Mrs. Blakeley nudged Anne, and she hurried as casually as she could to sit down on the left. I wasn't sure what was going on with them; I would have to ask Beth afterwards. This was the room Beth would go to so she could embroider. There was a nice royal blue settee in the corner of the room with a small side table and two lounge chairs. On the other end, there was a piano; the room was set up so guests could sit down to observe the person playing.

Estelle, the maid, curtsied and poured our tea as I sat down next to Beth. I thanked her as she poured mine.

"So, Miss Hart, how did you end up in Westbridge?" Mrs. Ashbrook asked, while she picked up a cucumber sandwich shaped as a triangle. The Blakeley's all stared at me with interest.

"Well, my father passed away, leaving me with no family, but he told me his father originally came from here from a wealthy family before they had a falling out. So, I used the last of my money to travel here to find them."

"How exciting, our very own mystery in Westbridge. I wonder who your family could be," Mary said. I smiled at the girl, but her older sister wasn't as pleasant.

"Such a quaint accent. American doesn't sound as refined as ours, does it?" Anne said as a general statement. "So nice of Beth and Mr. Easton to let you stay with them. Perhaps they will hire you and let you stay on as a maid if you can't find your family." Disdain was apparent on her marble face. Even her mother looked a bit perturbed at Anne's thinly veiled slights and nudged her side, but the girl kept going. "Speaking of Mr. Easton, is he around?" She craned her head as if she could spy him if only she cranked her neck out far enough.

"No, he had to go to London on business. He should be back either tonight or tomorrow. Also, I am glad for Rose's company; she teaches me about things in America and has already become a great friend. No matter what happens to her search for family, she is welcome here." Mrs. Ashbrook seemed to study us all with her lips pursed and her eyes flicking between Anne, Beth, and I. Anne's rudeness irked me on Beth's behalf; the sweet girl had been so excited to host afternoon tea.

I wanted it to live up to her expectations, so I made sure to praise Beth in front of her visitors. Peering at Anne I said, "Beth and Mr. Easton have been incredibly kind to me. I never wanted to impose on them, but Beth made me feel right at home. When I was felled with pneumonia, she stayed with me and nursed me back to health. In my opinion, I couldn't have asked for a better friend to introduce me to Westbridge and all you kind ladies." I emphasized the kind.

"Well said, dear," Mrs. Ashbrook said as she patted the side of her mouth with a napkin. I took the lull in conversation as an opportunity to eat an apple tart doused with crunchy sugar and drink a sip of tea.

"Have you heard," Mary said, clearly pleased she had something to share. "There is a new gentleman in town, a Mr. Danby. Mama and I saw him introduce himself in town; he was ever so handsome. I wish I was already out in society so I could go to a ball and only dance with him."

"Mary!" her mom squeaked while Anne looked calculating.

"Beth, you should ask Mr. Easton to host a dance here

to introduce Rose to society. There hasn't been a dance at Hawthorne in years and surely it's time for you to be introduced to society as well?"

Beth looked at me and twiddled her fingers. "A dance would be nice," she hedged.

"Wonderful, that will be a great start of the season. I shall have to go into town to have a new dress fashioned at Norah's dress shop," Anne said.

"Oh Mama, can I go dancing as well?" Mary said, bobbing her head in excitement.

"You are still too young, and we haven't secured a good match for Anne yet. Perhaps you can join your sister in society next season," Mrs. Blakeley said.

"We can discuss my matches later, mother. Perhaps after the dance here, Mary will be able to join society as well," Anne whispered slyly. Beth looked a bit worried. Her brother was strict and had only let her host this afternoon tea after she pleaded with him. I didn't think he'd be happy to find out he'd be hosting a dance. Maybe we could still salvage this and say the dance wouldn't happen, but with the way Anne was prodding Beth, I didn't think that would be the case. As soon as she left Hawthorne, word would spread— of that, I was sure.

After all four guests left, Beth went to fill me in on the gossip while Mrs. Avery and Estelle took away the dirtied plates and the tray of food. I wondered if they'd finished off the leftover cucumber sandwiches and apple tarts in the kitchen, such a strange world with such clear divides depending on your supposed station. Anne's words still rang in my ears and I guess I should be glad Beth took me in. With no idea how to get home, I could've ended up as a beggar on the streets or in the loony bin. Beth sat down on the blue settee and I joined her.

"Randolph Blakeley, Mrs. Blakeley's son, has a gambling problem," Beth blurted out. "He owed a lot of money to debtors which his father managed to pay off, but now there isn't much left of their fortune. Anne and Mary will have to make a good match to ensure their families place in society. Mrs. Blakeley has her eyes set on Mrs. Ashbrook's fortune and hopes to ingratiate one of her daughters with the widow in hopes of inheriting, the same as any other down on their luck family in town. It's why we were fortunate to have Mrs. Ashbrook visit us for afternoon tea; she hardly leaves her manor with so many society ladies vying for her favor. She must have been intrigued by you."

"I'm not interesting; maybe she wanted to see you. I do wonder why people are trying to inherit from her; doesn't an estate usually go to a family member?"

"Yes, usually the firstborn male and then it keeps going down the line, skipping to first cousins and second cousins, but Mrs. Ashbrook has no children and no distant relatives left. This means she gets to choose who inherits her estate unless a distant relative happens to appear."

"I think Anne has her sights set on your brother and not on Mrs. Ashbrook's money."

"I dare hope not; Anne is positively ghastly the way she spoke today. I'd much rather have you join me as a sister-in-law," Beth said, as she gripped my hand.

"I don't think your brother is fond of me," I said. "And I can't help but feel the same."

9

Accusations

"Can you explain to me why there was talk of a dance being hosted in my home when I stopped in town on my way
back from London?" John Easton thundered as he strode into
the drawing room late the next morning. The color drained
from Beth's cheeks; she looked lost for words and dropped her
embroidery piece into her lap. "I let you host an afternoon
tea, not enter society. How come, after being gone for only a
day, do I find you to be the talk of the town." Beth was on the
verge of tears and John paced around in angry struts. I didn't
agree with his admonishments; none of it was her fault.

"Beth doesn't deserve to be yelled at," I shouted at John.
The irony wasn't lost on me. However, I couldn't help myself;
I felt protective of Beth. John didn't deserve to be yelled at either but he didn't need to stride into the drawing room hot-
headed making unfounded accusations.

He turned towards me with a scowl and said, "Is this your
doing? Is a dance part of some kind of plot of yours to find

suitors and you just happened to drag Beth into it? If so, I think you might have stayed out your welcome."

"John, please. Rose has only been kind to me," Beth said. "It wasn't her fault; it was mine."

"No, I will not have anyone take advantage of you and your kindness," John said firmly. "I'm the head of this family and it is my responsibility to keep you safe. Maybe, if we can't locate her family, Rose needs to find somewhere else to stay."

"John, will you let me explain?" Beth pleaded.

"I will not," he said. "She's clearly a bad influence. This would never have happened if Rose wasn't staying here."

"Fine, John Easton," I shouted as anger seethed beneath my skin. "I'd rather sleep in the streets than spend my nights under the same roof as the likes of you. I'll have you know that I am not interested in finding a suitor; I'm just dandy on my own. Thank you very much!" I stood up and walked towards John. "Beth didn't come up with the plan to host the dance; it was Anne Berkeley."

"Rose is right. It was Anne, although I didn't know how to decline the idea when she brought it up," Beth said, with her eyes downcast.

"I was only trying to protect Beth from your accusations," I told John. "Anyway, I don't understand what the big deal is. What is wrong with having a dance if Beth wants to host one?"

John took one perplexed glance at me, steeled himself from his emotions, and grabbed my wrist. "Beth, you wait here, and you," he said to me. "You come with me." Mrs. Avery peeked around the corner of the kitchen as John gripped my wrist and led me outside through the front door, then around to the back of the mansion and into the hothouse.

"What are you doing," I said, while John closed the glass doors behind us. I scowled up at him, my arms folded in front of me. Who did he think he was, dragging me away like I was a misbehaving child? I stood alone with him hidden from view between pots of flowering plants, the scent of them perfuming the air. John started pacing again, moving between the violet Wisteria in the corner to the crimson Azalea's in the middle.

"You don't understand anything, and I refuse to be talked to like that in my own home where the staff and my sister can hear," John said, a vein pulsating at his temple.

"What is there to understand? I don't get why you have to be so uptight that you can't even host a party so your sister can have fun. Besides, she didn't even suggest it. Like I said, Anne Blakeley was the one who brought it up."

"I don't know what uptight is, but I think I understand the meaning. And yes, you are severely mistaken!" John said sternly, before his demeanor changed and his voice became gentler. "I'm supposed to protect Beth; I've been her only guardian since our parents passed away six years ago. My sister has a large dowry and without our mother to advise her, it would be easy for her to be taken in by someone wanting her for her money. I'd like to spare her that and keep her happy and safe. Is that so wrong?" John's handsome features pleaded for understanding as his bright hazel eyes gazed into mine. His words rang true, so I reached out my hand and rested it on his left shoulder. The definition of his muscles was clear, I noted, even beneath the gentlemanly outfit he was wearing.

I briefly wondered where he would have the time to work-out since they definitely did not have gyms in this time, but I shrugged off the thought and continued with our conversation.

"I'm sorry, I shouldn't have interfered and yelled at you. It is none of my business; I was only trying to defend Beth since it truly wasn't her idea. She does seem a bit lonely though. You should have seen the way her face lit up when the ladies were visiting for tea. Beth likes to be in the center of things.

John placed his left hand on his shoulder brushing his fingers and palm across mine and said, "Maybe a dance would be a nice occasion, and I am sorry too; I shouldn't have threatened to throw you out. I might not know you, but so far, you've been a diverting companion for my sister. You do need to promise that you won't raise your voice against me in my own home again. I am the master of the house and I don't appreciate being spoken to thusly in front of my sister and staff, especially by someone who's barely been here, knows hardly anything about our lives, and who apparently doesn't understand anything about social conventions either." Heat from his palm seared the skin on the back of my hand and his eyes pierced mine. A bit flustered, I swallowed nonexistent saliva and pulled my hand back to my side with a quick jolt.

"I won't yell at you again unless it's warranted," I said. "That's all I can promise. I do apologize for being angry with you today even if you were unnecessarily taking your frustrations out on Beth."

"I don't think an apology counts if it comes with a clause," John said, with a quirked brow. He stood close enough that I could feel his breath against my skin. My heart hammered in my chest, partly because John managed to really get under my skin, and the other part because despite the rude and dismissive behavior he had shown me, I couldn't help but want to reach out to him. To cross that final distance between us until he would stand flush against me. I wondered what it would feel like to run my hands through his wheat blonde hair. Why did John have to be both so attractive and so difficult. I didn't have time for this. John was staring at me, waiting for a response, but I didn't have one. Any and all thought had flown out of my brain and into the wind.

"Yes, um, I'll go back to Beth," I stammered and turned on my heel, leaving John Easton to stand alone, between his flowers, looking entirely too tempting in his handsome period clothing. You are imagining things, I told myself as I hurried back to the drawing room.

Beth scrambled to her feet as soon as she saw me enter the room, her face worried. "What did John say? You shouldn't have defended me. He didn't tell you to pack your things, did he? You can't leave, I won't have it. Not until we've found your family."

John's sophisticated accent sounded from the doorway before I had a chance to answer.

"Don't fret sister, lest you get worry lines," he said, as he once again sneaked up behind me. This man managed to pop-up everywhere too quick for his own good; he must have followed me immediately after I stormed off. "Rose and I have had an enlightening conversation, and she's promised to bite her tongue every once in a while, for as long as she's staying with us," he said, with a pointed look at me. Beth caught my gaze, question marks evident in her eyes. Then John continued, "I've also decided that a dance might be fun. However, you will have to be chaperoned at all times. It has been a long time since there has been a dance at Hawthorne; I think our parents would enjoy knowing the ballroom is once again being used. However, I can't let you host a dance without a new dress. So, sister, please purchase a new dress from Norah's, and one for Rose as well and perhaps a few extra pieces for her to wear around town. Hugh can take you both into town. I'll give him a list of things we need to prepare for the party, so he can run errands while you pick out fabrics."

Beth's face lit up at John's words and I couldn't help but smile; her happiness was infectious. Her bubbly personality made her appear younger than her actual age; nineteen years. John gave me a quick wink as Beth was throwing out thank-yous, and I blushed. He walked off as Beth started talking about the latest fashions from Paris, heat pooled in my stomach as I saw his tall lean figure turn around the corner. Maybe my initial view of him was wrong and there was more to him than the rude man I met the first day I arrived. The jury was still out.

Hugh had the carriage prepared and ready for us out front, the horses bristling as they waited. The decorative gravel in front of the mansion crunched beneath the heeled leather boots that were a gift from Beth as I stepped up to the colorfully painted wagon. Hugh held out his hand so I could use it for support while I clambered up the steps, ducked my head, and took my place on a velvet upholstered bench. He closed the door behind Beth once she sat down across from me.

"I can't wait to see and touch all the fabrics; we'll have to get you a day dress, a walking dress, a riding dress, and a dress for the dance. Oh, how fun," Beth said.

"Beth, I can't possibly need that many dresses, not to mention that I really don't want you and John paying for everything for me."

"Nonsense, you are living with us until we find your family so you will have to dress the part. What would the town think if we let you wander around in those strange pants you have," she said. "You must tell me what you and my brother talked about; I am ever so curious. He was much calmer when you both returned; I don't think I could have calmed him that fast. Not that he gets angry often," Beth rushed to say. "No, John is the best brother I could wish for."

"I really didn't do much," I said. "John wanted me to apologize and promise I wouldn't yell at him again, so I did. I don't think he fully accepted it though."

"He must have," Beth said joyously. "Since the dance is still on and we are headed out to go shopping. Why else would he change his mind?"

"I guess so."

The carriage shook as Hugh moved to his seat upfront and cracked the whip at the horses, but after the initial start, movement slowed to a slight jostle. I hadn't left Hawthorne since I appeared; therefore, I couldn't help but stare out the window as we passed through the British countryside, the carriage riding across dirt roads. We left Hawthorne behind and passed Granhope Manor, Mrs. Ashbrook's estate. As we started nearing the center of the town of Westbridge, Beth pointed out the Blakeley's home, a picturesque cottage like house with rose bushes lining the front. Looks were a bit deceiving though, because it was still a pretty sizable building, though, not as big as Mrs. Ashbrook's or John's. I guess it made sense why Anne Blakeley and her mother thought John was a good catch. If I were from these times, I might think the same thing.

10

Eligible Bachelors

Hugh stopped the carriage when we reached the center of Westbridge. I had been staring out of the window the entire trip, taking in the scenery. For some reason, the fact that I was in a different time hadn't fully sunken into my mind until we got further away from Hawthorne, as if this whole time we all had been pretending to be old-fashioned in this kind of drawn-out play.

Beth chattered animatedly about dresses, ribbons, and other frippery. It confused her that I was staring out of the window instead of talking to her about the different lace trimmings and color combinations, and what accessories might be nice for her bonnets; she decided on feathers. As she droned on, my mind kept going back to John and his conflicting behavior. How could he be so rude to everyone, but when we were alone in the hothouse, show his vulnerable side. I didn't understand him. However, he wasn't the only thing I didn't understand. I also wanted to figure out why I ended up in this time and place. John's behavior was unpredictable, but my own emotions kept getting the better of me as well. I could blame it on stress. Lord knows, I was thrown into a situation that would be challenging for the most patient and unbothered person. But, I'd never been that type of person, even in the best of times. I could be hot tempered myself and I could certainly be quick to judge. Thinking back to how I yelled at John, I had to be grateful he didn't just kick me out. If our positions had been reversed I probably would have. The change in his behavior once we were alone definitely left me with something to mull over. When he wasn't angry, I could clearly see the brother that Beth was so fond of. A gentle, caring man who loved his family. Beth was lucky to have him, even if he was a bit too strict. I wasn't sure if that was his personality or just a sign of the times.

The creaking of the carriage door pulled me back from my thoughts. Hugh opened the door, and Beth and I clambered out to the paved road.

Westbridge wasn't a huge town, especially compared to towns in America. Hugh had dropped us off in the heart of it, and I did have to say that it was charming and quaint. The paved road Beth and I stood on had sidewalks and was lined by impressive storefronts with lots and lots of windows, some of them had awnings inviting you into their shaded depths. Most of the buildings were made from a reddish brick and the wooden trim was painted a dark green. Along the trim or on signs hung from the buildings were the names of stores elegantly written in gold, black, or white depending on the owner's choice.

Beth grabbed my hand and said, "Let's take some air first; we can stroll up and down the promenade before we go to

Norah's." There were other people out and about as well, a few couples walking stiffly beside one another, a family with a young boy and girl dressed in frilly matching outfits, two men in military dress gawking at a stand with wares from a barber shop on the right.

Beth talked to me about the town, the different stores, and the delicious buns you could buy from the confectioner's shop. She pointed out the delicacies on display in the window when a small copper bell attached to the door post rang and the shop door opened. Mrs. Blakeley stepped out of the store, accompanied by Anne and Mary and a waft of rich buttery pastry.

"How wonderful to see you, Beth, and you too, Rose. Are you both also shopping for new dresses?" Mrs. Blakeley said as she smiled at Beth.

"Indeed, we are. John said I could purchase a new dress for the dance, and he wanted to make sure Rose would also receive a new wardrobe since her luggage has been lost on the way here," Beth said. Anne glared at me while Beth was focused on Mrs. Blakeley.

"That is so kind of Mr. Easton to take in a stray and clothe her too," Anne interjected. Beth shrugged off the comment, and I bit my lip to stop from speaking. That girl was a high school bully's dream come true. Her sister, Mary, on the other hand was sweet and oblivious.

"Mama, we still have to go shopping for Anne's dress. We could all go together!" Mary said.

"That would be wonderful," Beth said while I suppressed a groan. I wasn't looking forward to spending more time around Anne.

Mrs. Blakeley led our way across the street and back down to Norah's dress shop. The name was written in large white letters on the dark green facade. The windows let me take a glimpse inside the store filled with colors and fabrics. One of the shop girls opened the door for us, and we stepped over the threshold into a seamstresses' paradise.

The shop girl that opened the door joined Mrs. Blakeley, Anne, and Mary in their search for fabrics. Another one joined Beth and I at the display showing fabric swatches.

"How may I assist you today?" the short brown haired shop girl asked.

"Rose and I need new gowns for a dance and Rose also needs some everyday clothes, a walking and riding gown, some accessories," Beth said, ticking her demands off on her fingers. The shop girl shuffled through the drawers and pulled out an apple green satin she called Pomona green; I let the smooth material glide through my fingers. "That color suits you, but I think it needs a white robe as an accent piece," Beth said. "I would like an evening primrose satin gown," Beth said, as she turned towards the shop girl.

"Good choice Miss, evening primrose is a most fashionable color," the shop girl said. She pulled out a deep yellow fabric for Beth and then added white cotton that was supposed to turn into robes to go over the evening gowns. Beth selected some more fabrics and picked out a heavier slate fabric for a riding gown for me. I told her firmly I wanted as little as possible, but she waved the notion away. Fashion was her forte; it definitely turned her from easy going into a strong-willed director. With her mind made up, I had to give up and let her decide which things were right for me.

The shop girl took all the different fabrics and laid them out behind the heavy wooden register. Mrs. Blakeley, Anne, and Mary walked over to us when they finished choosing their colors. Anne studied our choice of fabrics.

"I would never have chosen Pomona green which is so last season. My gown will be salmon, the new color of choice of Paris ladies," she said, with a flutter of her eyes. "Evening primrose will suit you though, Beth; you have the same complexion as your brother, Mr. Easton. I think he would look handsome with a yellow cravat."

"How is Mr. Easton? I regret missing him when we were at Hawthorne," Mrs. Blakely said, with eager eyes. If I wasn't wrong, I thought she was fishing for another invitation, this time one where John was also around. I rolled my eyes and Anne glared at me before turning back towards Beth.

"My mother does enjoy Mr. Easton's insights and I enjoy the tarts your cook makes," Anne said, her voice dripping with honey.

"Unfortunately, Mrs. Avery and Mr. Easton will be too busy planning the dance to be able to host another social call in between," I said, causing Mrs. Blakeley's face to droop and Anne's lips to purse. They looked back to Beth hoping she'd say something different, but Beth nodded gravely.

"I'm afraid Rose is right; however, we shall be delighted to see you at the dance. We have a few more errands to run, so we will be off," Beth said. She linked her arm with me and left the Blakeley's behind in the dress shop. She took me to the stall in front of the store with random ribbons and accessories, "haberdasheries" it said. Beth turned to me and whispered, "I really didn't want another social call with the

Blakeley's; Anne acts ghastly when her social standing doesn't allow for it. However, you can't be so frank with them; it isn't polite."

"I'm sorry, you are right. I just didn't like the way she was sneering and fishing for an invitation," I said. Part of that was true, although the idea of Anne and her statuesque features flirting with John caused a twinge in my stomach. I was being ridiculous. My plan was to find a way back home, not date an old-fashioned man whom by all accounts distrusted and maybe even loathed me. He deserved Anne and the sneer permanently plastered on her face.

"Anne and Mary are under a lot of pressure. Since their father passed away, their mother has been trying to find an advantageous match for Anne. She needs to marry well to ensure a home and allowance for them since their house is now owned by their brother, with no guarantees for their continued occupancy. Anne likely sees you as a real threat to her future when she doesn't have many opportunities to meet wealthy bachelors and now you are living in the same home as my brother, one of the few bachelors in Westbridge."

I hadn't thought of it that way. If my livelihood depended on marrying a man, then I would probably also be angry at whomever just showed up out of the blue and moved in with said man. Even if that woman didn't have any intention of staying and marrying.

I picked up something called a reticule, which was a small purse, in a pretty purple velvet from the stand outside the haberdashery shop and swirled around to show Beth. My head knocked against someone's firm chest. The man dropped his walking stick and I scrambled back and picked it up with flaming cheeks. "I apologize, here is your cane," I said as I handed him the smooth carved walking stick. He smiled warmly and accepted it. The man was dressed sharp for the times in his navy tailcoat accented with baby blue lapels, his elaborately knotted cravat, black woolen top hat, and his polished brown knee-high riding boots.

"Allow me to introduce myself," he said, with a flourish as he took his top hat into his left hand. "My name is Percy Ambrose Danby, and who might you lovely ladies be?"

Beth giggled shyly and said, "Pleased to meet you, Mr. Danby. My name is Beth Easton and this is my friend and house guest, Rose Hart." I nodded my head at him.

"Perhaps you will accompany me to the confectioners? I am new in town and would love to make some new acquaintances."

"We would love to, wouldn't we Rose? Where are you staying in town if I might ask?" Beth said, fluttering her eyelashes. I kept my face neutral, but I enjoyed seeing Beth happy and flirting.

"I am currently staying at Pemberton's lodge, but I am looking for a permanent place to live in Westbridge."

"How wonderful, you must come to the dance my brother is hosting at Hawthorne in two weeks on Saturday. It would be the perfect occasion to meet all the influential people of Westbridge."

"I shall indeed if you'll grant me a dance, Miss Easton," he said with a charming smile and a small bow. Beth added the purple reticule to John's tab for me, or puce as the shopkeeper called the purplish color, then the three of us followed the scent of pastries. Mr. Danby appeared to be a nice man, and we had a fun afternoon taking bites of flaky buttery pastry and talking about his travels. John should let Beth out of the house more often to have fun.

11

Dancing The Waltz

Mrs. Avery had outdone herself. Hawthorne looked like something out of a fairy tale. Bright sconces led the way from the front door, through the foyer, past the drawing room, and into the ballroom which was bathed in the soft glow of candlelight. The flames accented the gilded frames on the walls revealing classical paintings and the large glass chandelier hanging from the ceiling. A setup for a small group of musicians was placed in the corner, ready for them to sit down and play their instruments. Servants had decked out a table placed on the side of the room covered in white linen with small plates of food and drinks; different little seating areas were created along the outer rim of the room. Someone, I assumed Hugh, had set up a trail of lanterns in the garden for anyone who wanted some fresh air. The warm flickering lights visible through the windows that covered that side of the house nearly from floor to ceiling, lined with cream-colored valences.

I smoothed my hands against the silky material of my new

dress, which made me feel like a princess, and twirled around in the empty ballroom. My skirts billowed out, and I laughed. A slow clap sounded from the doorway and I turned my head towards it. There John stood leaning against the frame with the side of his mouth turned up into a small smile, his hands lifted to clap.

"Brava, Miss Hart. I didn't know you were a professional dancer," he quipped.

"I thought I was alone," I said, blushing. John was handsome tonight, the warm candlelight added a depth to his features that made him more approachable, even dressed as he was in the black waistcoat that peeked out from beneath his burgundy tailcoat with a cream silk cravat tied at his neck. He didn't have the dark-haired look of Mr. Darcy but I could imagine him playing a fine Mr. Bingley, just with a bit more personality.

"Perhaps you will honor me with a dance later tonight," he said with a nod. "Come, our guests will arrive soon; let's join Beth so the servants and musicians can take their places. I joined John and Beth in the foyer; servants were hustling around us, putting everything in order. We joined the musicians in the ballroom once they had taken their places.

The servants let in the first arrivals and John nodded at or greeted every guest that entered and introduced Beth and I. Mrs. Ashbrook complimented my dress and commented on the lovely decor of the room. Beth pointed out an older gentleman named Mr. Abernathy who took his seat near the musicians.

"I wonder why he never married," Beth said.

Mrs. Ashbrook's brows lifted, and she turned towards us

conspiratorially. "This was long before both of you were born; Mr. Abernathy fell in love with a woman. Come to think of it," she said, as she studied me. "Rosemary looked a lot like you, the same wavy hair and green eyes. We all thought they were going to marry, but she disappeared just as suddenly as she arrived. Mr. Abernathy never recovered."

My heart thumped loudly in my chest. It couldn't be, could it? "What was her full name?" I asked Mrs. Ashbrook.

"Rosemary Scott," she said. "What's the matter? You look like you've seen a ghost." I definitely felt like I did. This couldn't be a mere coincidence. My grandmother had been here when she was younger and now, I was also here. What was the meaning of this and how did she get back home? My mind raced back to the strange book I found in her home which led me to the bookshop that appeared out of nowhere. I would need to find a way to speak to Mr. Abernathy.

"I apologize, I presume the heat is getting to me. I might need to sit down for a moment."

"Of course, I will join you," Beth said. I thanked Mrs. Ashbrook and linked arms with Beth. We walked over to the two chairs arranged next to the table laden with food. Beth handed me a glass filled with watered down wine. I glanced over at the elderly Mr. Abernathy again while I sipped the drink. Age and probably loneliness had made him portly, but judging by his strong jawline, he probably would've been quite handsome in his youth. It was a strange idea to imagine him with my grandmother. I never thought she could've been with anyone except for my grandfather. Even if I made it back home, she wouldn't be there anymore to ask.

I got pulled out of my rumination when Mrs. Blakeley

stepped towards us with Anne, Mr. Danby, and another gentleman which I assumed had to be her son. He had the same strong features as Anne, his cheekbones smooth as if they were carved from stone. Beth and I moved from our chairs.

"Let me introduce my son, Randolph Blakeley, and Mr. Danby who is new to town," Mrs. Blakeley said. The two men bowed, and Beth and I curtsied.

"We've met, but I am pleased to renew our acquaintance," Mr. Danby said with a mischievous smile. He held out his hand for Beth. "Miss Easton, could I ask you for this dance?" Beth blushed and grasped his hand. Mr. Blakeley repeated the gesture towards me.

"Miss Hart, would you do me the honor?" I took his hand and joined Beth and Mr. Danby in the middle of the dance floor together with two other couples. The musicians played a slow-paced cheerful piece of music. I kept my eyes firmly on Beth, so I could mirror her movements. I think she noticed my worried face, and she mouthed the word quadrille at me. Now I knew the name of the dance, but I still didn't know the steps. Every couple turned towards each other and curtsied. Beth and Mr. Danby started towards Mr. Blakeley and I in little skips. Mr. Blakeley gave me a little nudge and I tried to repeat the same movements he was doing. He knew all the steps and throughout the dance, steadied me when I lost my footing on the polished wood floor. Dancing had made me a bit winded, and I was glad once it was over. Mr. Blakeley had been graceful about my missteps and I thanked him for his patience.

"It is my pleasure, Miss Hart; practice makes perfect," he said. The way Beth had talked about the Blakeley's financial situation, I thought he must be an awful person. I was surprised he acted so gentle and kind. He behaved more like his sister Mary than Anne. Mr. Blakeley led me back to the chair near the table and I watched Beth start another dance with Mr. Danby. Her face was glowing from a mixture of exertion and happiness; Beth's yellow dress and fair hair made her stand out in the crowd like a ray of sunshine. I smiled at the joy I saw on her face as she and Mr. Danby leaped around each other in their dance. He whispered something to her, and it must have been something sweet because her eyes lit up and her cheeks reddened some more.

I lifted the glass of watered-down wine from the edge of the table where I had left it when I went dancing with Mr. Blakeley, but before I could take a sip, someone tapped on my shoulder. I turned around in my seat to see a gaunt man with greasy unkempt hair bowed down in front of me. His eyes grazed down the front of my dress as he lowered his upper body. His stare sent a shiver down my spine. I wasn't sure what to do with so many people around; this was Beth's moment to shine and I didn't want to embarrass her by causing a scene.

"You must be Miss Hart, the house guest of Mr. Easton and his sister. My name is Mr. Willoughby, the vicar at St. George's church. If you'll allow me this dance," he said pompous, while stretching out his long thin fingers towards me. I nodded and took his hand so he could lead me to the dance floor. Thankfully, another quadrille was playing which meant we didn't have to touch each other during the dance. We skip-hopped around each other while he kept up conversation.

"I heard you were hoping to find your long-lost relatives.

It is such a difficult position to be without circumstance and family," he said. Then with a slick tone he added. "I happen to be in the market for a wife. Now, I am highly eligible, but I could be persuaded to marry beneath me to someone with the right connections like, let's say the Easton's." He must have taken my shock as agreement because he inched closer to me when the song ended and placed his bony hand on my hip, giving it a little squeeze. Disgusted by his touch, I tried to think of a way to excuse myself. The scrape of a throat sounded behind me and Mr. Willoughby reluctantly took his eyes off me and turned them towards the intruder.

"Excuse me, may I cut in. Miss Hart has promised me this next song and I intend to honor her wishes," John's warm voice said.

Mr. Willoughby appeared to get ready to object, so I smiled and curtsied and said, "Yes indeed, thank you for the dance." I took John's hand, relief flooding through me when the music turned into a waltz. If John hadn't cut in, Mr. Willoughby would have had an excuse to lay his hands on me for an entire song. Mr. Willoughby looked miffed at his dismissal as it was. I made a mental note to avoid him for the rest of the evening. The thought of more dances with him wasn't something I wanted to contemplate.

"I'm afraid I am not a good dancer. I don't even know the steps," I told John.

"A waltz is easy to master. I will lead and you just try to follow my steps." He grasped my right hand with his left and placed his right hand on my left shoulder blade. I rested my left hand on top of his right shoulder. He whispered the instructions as he stepped his left foot forward. "Right foot back, step left foot out and connect. Good! Then left foot forward, right foot out and connect." My eyes were focused on our feet. John was right, it wasn't too difficult. I grinned up at him. "See, now you can waltz," he said.

"Thank you for saving me from Mr. Willoughby," I said, while we kept twirling. His hand on my shoulder blade warmed my skin. Up close, his hazel eyes had small flecks of gold in them and his blonde hair a bit darker than Beth's framed his face beautifully. Even his proudly set mouth seemed inviting, especially with the hint of smile upon them.

"I thought you weren't looking for a suitor," he said with mirth.

"I surely am not! And especially not that man," I said, offended.

"Our vicar certainly is an acquired taste," John said. "However, I can't blame him for trying just like Randolph Blakeley did and I'm sure others will when you are dressed so enticing. Look, I see multiple men staring at us this moment from the side of the ballroom wishing they were dancing with you in my stead."

"You are such a scoundrel!" I said.

"The scoundrel that bought you that dress," John whispered with a wink. I stumbled and stepped on his foot. Perfect timing to cut the dance short and make a run for it.

"I am going to get some air," I said, and walked off, leaving him behind in the middle of the dance floor. He was so infuriatingly hot and cold. I never knew what to expect.

12

An Old Lover

My shoes click-clacked along the polished wood floor as I strode past the other dancing couples. John's eyes burned a hole between my shoulder blades as he stared at me while I walked away. I looked around the room for Beth and spotted her near the refreshment table chatting with Mr. Danby. He was handing her something to drink, and she batted her lashes at him. Smoothing my dress down, I gathered my thoughts.

Maybe I could take this moment of reprieve to talk to the old man, Mr. Abernathy. What if I could learn something about my grandmother and how she got back home. The man hadn't left his seat near the musicians, so I walked around the room and stopped near his chair. I pretended to stumble and gripped the back of his chair. Confused at the sudden jostle, he looked around and sprang up, faster than his advanced age would have suggested, to steady my arm.

"Are you alright, my dear?" Mr. Abernathy said. "Here, please sit down," he continued while supporting me, so I could take a seat. The gallant young man he might have once been hidden behind his aging skin, gray hair and larger frame.

"I apologize, sir. I got a bit lightheaded." He stared at me with a hint of shock then squinted his eyes for a few seconds and opened them again.

"Are you related to a Rosemary Scott?" he asked. So he did recognize my features. I couldn't tell him she was my grandmother; it wouldn't fit my cover story and if word got out, it would raise even more questions. However, I did want to keep him talking to find out if he had any information.

"No, I don't know a Rosemary. Who is she?" I asked.

"I just thought. You look so much like her. For a moment, I thought you were her. That she'd returned to me. Never mind. You must be Mr. Easton's guest. I heard he was hosting an American. My Rosemary was also an American. How are you finding Westbridge?" Mr. Abernathy's expression saddened.

"Maybe it's my accent that reminded you of Rosemary; what happened to her?" The elderly man's hands trembled, and his voice grew shaky. "I asked her to marry me, but she said she couldn't. That she had obligations somewhere else. She ran off, and I curse myself every day that I didn't follow her immediately. When I did go after her, she was nowhere to be found. I never found out what happened to her." He straightened his hands and steeled his face. "I apologize, this isn't a good topic during a dance. I would like to continue to listen to the music if you don't mind."

I nodded at the man and stood so he could reclaim his chair. "Of course, thank you for your concern. I shall go and find my friend." I had a lot to mull over. Unfortunately, Mr. Abernathy didn't know anything, so I was no closer to finding a way back home. It was a strange idea that my grand-mother could have been married to that man. How different her life could have been? I for one was grateful she hadn't stayed though; that would have meant my mother wouldn't exist and in turn I wouldn't have either.

I crossed the room, observing the couples that were danc-ing a polka. Mr. Willoughby caught my attention and I hur-ried around a few couples to the corner of the room near the exit before he could come over. I hoped he lost sight of me in the crowd. My nerves were frayed enough as it was; I didn't want to have to navigate his creepy behavior as well. The room was heavy with the mingled smell of sweat barely masked by floral perfumes and sweets from the refreshments table. The combined heat from so many guests dancing in one room was getting to me; if I had pretended to feel faint ear-lier, I really did feel faint now.

Anne's snobby grating voice came from the doorway as I stood, hidden from sight, with my back pressed firm against the wall paneling. "-taking advantage of poor Mr. Easton and Beth," Anne said.

"Where did she come from?" another woman's voice spoke.

"By boat from America apparently. She says she has family here, but I think she is trying to swindle Mr. Easton out of his fortune. Did you notice the dress she was wearing? Beth took her shopping and bought her a whole new wardrobe," Anne said, with a sneer.

"How uncouth," the earlier woman said, with apparent shock.

"She was shamelessly flirting with our vicar and with your

brother. I even saw her dance with Mr. Easton," a third woman with a high-pitched voice piped up.

"I will make sure she will not sink her claws into Mr. Easton or my brother," Anne bit out. I had enough of her belligerence, so I stepped away from my hiding spot and stormed through the doorway glaring at Anne and the other two women as I passed them by. The other two at least had the decency to look ashamed at being caught gossiping, but Anne just smirked at me and crossed her arms in front of her chest. I shook my head in anger and continued my stride through the hallway and foyer until I reached the front door.

The crisp night air hit my face, gently blowing the small curls Estelle had put so much effort into creating away from my forehead. The breeze divine against my skin, I stepped out to lean against the brick facade. Lanterns lit up an ethereal path in front of me. Hugh had outdone himself on the garden. It had looked beautiful when I saw the lights flickering through the ballroom windows earlier, but standing outside with the sky lit up with stars and surrounded by candlelight, it felt like I was the sole inhabitant of a fairy garden.

A tear snaked its way down my cheek, and I wiped it away with a deep sigh. My feet slowly followed the lit path. I didn't even fully understand why I was crying; everything going on felt so overwhelming. Anne's comments were the last drop; I hit my max and now my emotions were overflowing. Losing my grandmother, navigating this place and the people in it. Perhaps I was the butt of a joke and everyone was in on it and snickering at how gullible I was. My chest rose and a let out another hitched breath.

"Miss Hart, are you hurt?" Mrs. Ashbrook said, concern

tinting her warm and weathered voice. She sat with her hands folded in her lap on a small bench near the hothouse.

"I'm not hurt; I just had to get some air," I said as I wiped my cheeks some more.

"Come." She patted the spot next to her on the bench. "Sit down next to me and tell me what is wrong." I did as she said but her concern reminded me of my grandmother and only brought on more tears. Mrs. Ashbrook pulled a handkerchief out of her pocket and handed it to me. "Was someone unkind to you?"

"Living here so far away from my home has been difficult," I started while I dabbed at my eyes with the handkerchief. Someone, maybe even Mrs. Ashbrook herself, had embroidered her last name on it with pretty silver thread. "I tried to get away from the vicar who was trying to make unwanted advances, and Anne has been gossiping and telling lies about me to the other guests. Now they all think I'm some kind of gold digger because Mr. Easton and Beth purchased some new clothes for me. I didn't even want new clothes; I tried to persuade Beth, but she insisted." I sighed and held out the handkerchief to Mrs. Ashbrook. She grasped my hand and closed my fingers around it.

"You keep it," she said. I nodded and tucked it away in my dress. "Hold your head high and pay the others no mind. Anne and her mother are social climbers; they've been after my wealth for a while by pretending to care for me." My eyes widened at her remark. "Oh yes, I know what the people of Westbridge are talking about. That I am too old to know any better, that I will choose one of them as my heir. The families are like hens fighting for scraps. I can't go a day without some conniving society mother finding a ploy to stop by my house. Come," she said, as she linked her arm with mine. "Join me on my way back to the ballroom."

I slowed my pace to match the steady reverent steps of Mrs. Ashbrook. We moved away from the crisp night and candlelit garden to join the other guests back inside the estate. The soft sweeping tones of a waltz was being played by the musicians. Mrs. Ashbrook stopped to the right of the ballroom and I joined her side. My eyes followed the dancers in the middle of the polished floor, gracefully turning and stepping in time with the music.

Anne was smiling up at John. He had his hand braced against her shoulder blade while her hand caressed his upper arm. John was leading her with his other arm, their fingers interlaced. Something gnawed at my stomach. Why did he have to look so at ease with Anne. There he was, laughing at something she'd said, while they continued to glide across the room, the corners of his eyes crinkled. What could have been so funny? She fluttered her eyelashes at him, and I scowled. I was being silly. I tried to relax my facial muscles so no one else would notice my furrowed brow. In no way did I have the right to be jealous of Anne. This wasn't my time, and John and I weren't even close, but still. I couldn't stop the pangs of jealousy from clouding my judgment, from wishing it was me dancing with him again, being so close together that I could feel his breath against my skin.

"Rose, isn't the ball splendid!" Beth said, as she came to my side and grasped my hand, distracting me from my jealous train-of-thought. "Mr. Danby has danced with me three times and has kept me company and brought me refreshments most of the night. Isn't he wonderful?"

I took another quick glance at John Easton and Anne Blakeley. Mrs. Blakeley was watching them intently from the sidelines, looking as pleased as a cat with cream. John had to be put out of my mind.

I plastered a smile on my face and responded to Beth, "He does seem to like you. I am glad you enjoyed your dance."

"Perhaps we can find someone else for you to dance with?" Beth said, with a quick turn of her neck, so she could glance across the room.

"Dancing has worn me out. I'm a bit tired and might retire for the evening," I said, with an apologetic face.

"Are you sure?" Beth said.

"Yes, I am. Thank you for the wonderful evening, Beth. And thank you, Mrs. Ashbrook, for your advice. I hope we'll meet again." I nodded at both women and strode out of the room. Anne and John were still dancing in the middle of the dance floor. She's perfect for him, I told myself as I trudged through the foyer and up the wooden staircase. My fingers slid across the banister and the heavy silk skirt tangled around my legs. However pretty the dress I wore was, I still wanted out of it. It was stifling, the tight fabric trying to conform me into something I wasn't. I couldn't stay here in the past and learn more about John. He clearly liked Anne and her manipulative behavior. They deserved each other.

I struggled out of the heavy silk dress and hung it gently over the back of the chair in my guest bedroom. A good night's sleep would erase the marks the fabric had left in my skin. I wished for a good dream, one where John wouldn't show up to torment me. Something as simple as a tropical vacation or a memory of showering.

13

A Piano Forte

"Good morning, Rose," John said, as he looked up from the newspaper he was holding. A cup of freshly brewed tea was letting off steam on his right.

"Good morning," I mumbled back at him as I crossed the room and sat down at the table facing him. John focused his attention back on the newspaper, a soft rustling every time he flipped a page. I grabbed a yeast bun from the platter in the middle of the table and set it on a small white plate. Slowly, I tore some pieces of dough away from the bun and stuffed them in my mouth. Then I took the tea pot and poured myself some tea. John lowered the paper and stared at me as if he wanted to discover my secrets.

"Are you upset about something?" he said. "You are usually more talkative. Why, I can't recall a time where there was an opportunity for you to speak where you chose not to. I've reminisced a few times here and there the days of quiet solitude I had before you ended up in our pond." John gave me a little smirk.

"Very funny. I'm fine," I said brusquely, and quickly stuffed more of the rich buttery yeast buns decorated with caraway seeds drenched in sugar syrup into my mouth. John scoffed and looked a bit perturbed. He took a swig of his tea and set it back down as Beth entered the dining room.

"I am famished!" she said, and dramatically dropped herself into a chair next to me. Beth snatched one of the yeast buns, took a big bite, and let out a moan. I grinned and shook my head at her. "All the dancing last evening had me work up an appetite. Maybe you would be as hungry if you stayed longer," she said to me.

"You danced multiple times with that newcomer, Mr. Danby. He appeared quite taken with you, sister," John said. "He stayed by your side the entire evening,"

"Yes, and you were quite close to Anne Blakeley if I remember correctly," Beth retorted. I tried to keep a scowl off my face as I remembered how handsome Anne and John looked together on the dance floor.

"Speaking of Anne, she and Mrs. Blakeley are invited over tonight for a social call. I also received a letter from William; he will join us tonight and be our guest for a couple of days," John said, ignoring Beth's remark.

At this news, Beth perked up. "William is back in town? How long will he stay?" she said.

"His orders changed; he is now permanently posted in London. In the letter he sent me, he said he had already found an apartment in London, somewhere in Albany. He's on furlough for a few weeks and wanted to come visit us."

"It will be wonderful seeing him again," Beth said.

"Who is William?" I asked.

"William Chambers was my brother's closest friend growing up," Beth said. "They did everything together, including teasing me," she said, with a pointed look at John. He grinned back at his sister.

"You did make it easy with your flower crowns and pretend tea parties," he jibed. Beth glared back at him and winked.

"Nevertheless, William was like a second brother to me. He joined the army as an officer to follow his father's legacy a couple of years ago. His service has taken him to Belgium and more recently to south England near the coast. I'm sure John has missed his company," Beth said to me.

"I'm sure it must be wonderful to see him again; I bet you will have lots to talk about," I said to John. While he nodded, I picked up the teapot, poured Beth a cup of tea, and topped my glass off as well. "Would you like some more?" I asked John.

"Yes, please," he said as his eyes tracked me while I poured the fragrant hot liquid into his cup. John took a sip of tea and lifted the newspaper back up to his face. We continued our breakfast in comfortable silence then, once John left the room, I spent the rest of the day with Beth chatting and picking out our dresses for the evening.

We had a light supper around five P.M. and once the sun began to set, the three of us retreated to the drawing room. I barely had time to sit down in the blue velvet settee in the corner of the room before the doors to the drawing room burst open again and a tall man with light brown eyes dressed in a red colored uniform strode in with his arms spread wide.

"Old friend," the man exclaimed as he headed towards

John and gave him a bear hug. John smiled and patted the man's back.

"It's good to have you here, William," John said. As John's friend got nearer, I noticed the scar that ran through his eyebrow and curved around the left side of his face. It looked like whatever had happened must have hurt but it somehow didn't detract from his gentlemanly charm. Instead, it just lent him another layer of ruggedness that caused intrigue.

"Beth, lovely as always," William said, as he bowed with a flourish, grasped Beth's hand and kissed the top of it. "And who is this lovely lady," he continued and gave me a wink.

John stepped in and said, "This is Miss Rose Hart; she's staying with us until we find her distant relatives."

"Nice to make your acquaintance Miss Rose. My name is William Raphe Chambers," William said to me. I smiled and curtsied, this time without stumbling.

"Much improved," John said, with a grin that made me blush.

There was a knock on the door and Mrs. Avery walked in and announced the arrival of Anne and Mrs. Blakeley. They joined us near the blue settee and Anne immediately gravitated towards John's side. Her dark hair was pulled back and small curls framed her high forehead. She had once again picked a red dress to wear. To make sure she'd be the center of attention, I thought. The Blakeley's already knew Mr. Chambers and Mrs. Blakeley went to ask him questions about his service.

"I heard from a friend that your battalion was sent to fight in Belgium," she said. "How ghastly." Her eyes glanced at the scar framing the left side of his face. "How was your experience? Were the French very uncivilized. You must be glad to be home."

A painful expression crossed Mr. Chambers' eyes at Mrs. Blakeley's barrage of words, then he smiled a bit watery before answering. "Yes, I'm fortunate to be back home amongst friends."

"Mama, let's not talk about war and the French. Mr. Easton, will you join me in a duet at the piano forte?" Anne said, while fluttering her eyelashes at John.

"It would be my pleasure," he said as he held out his hand. Anne took it and together they sat down on the bench in front of the piano forte, facing towards us. Mrs. Blakeley and Beth sat down on the chairs to the right of the couch while Mr. Chambers and I sat down into the plush velvet cushions of the blue settee. Anne's mother looked shrewdly at her daughter and John, the gears in her head turning as she paid close attention to the couple.

I saw Anne whisper something to John while she moved some pages of sheet music. John agreed with whatever she said and joined her on the piano bench. She stretched her fingers and started to play an upbeat tune I didn't recognize. John started in with the first verse, his singing voice rich and deep. Anne's voice was light but not unpleasant and a stab of jealousy hit my heart as their sounds combined. She had a smug smile while she played and sang. Her mother looked pleased and proud at her daughter's ability to woo John; although, he was a bit too willing in my opinion. I was glad when their duet was over and clapped halfheartedly together with Mr. Chambers, Beth, and Mrs. Blakeley.

"Thank you, thank you," Anne said, while curtsying. She pinched the sides of her dress to flare it out as she sank down.

"You played wonderfully," John said, while resting his hand in the small of her back as he led her back towards us. Anne turned towards him with a big dazzling grin.

"It wouldn't have been as enchanting without a beautiful voice as yours to mingle with and bring the song to life," she said.

"My daughter is particularly talented and so is our Mr. Easton, of course. Now, who shall play next?" Mrs. Blakeley said.

Anne's eyes raked over me, and she quickly piped up so no one else could volunteer. "Why not hear from our newcomer, Miss Hart," Anne said, with a conniving look that meant to pass as sincere. "We would all love to listen to your musical prowess, wouldn't we? Unless, you don't know how to play? Maybe they don't teach music in the Americas?" Anne looked so pleased with her little ploy to make me fail. She probably thought that if I made a fool of myself in front of everyone, John might notice how much of an accomplished lady she is. Well, today the joke was on her. I had years of piano lessons throughout middle school and high school. My grandmother had been a piano teacher. I thought of her favorite piece—"Claire de lune" by Debussy. The notes rang through my mind as I remembered how she used to smile at me while I played it for her. Fitting, I thought, to play it today. I met Anne's gaze and said with a confident face.

"I would love to."

"How wonderful," Beth squeaked with delight. Anne looked a bit perturbed by my confidence. It must have rocked her off kilter when instead she thought she had me at a disadvantage. I sat down at the piano forte and lightly brushed my fingers across the ivory and black keys. John fanned out his coat and sat down on the blue velvet next to Mr. Chambers; Anne looked petulant as she sat down in a chair next to her mother.

Muscle memory took over as I played the first few notes. My eyes shut, I swayed with the sounds as the music poured out of me. My grandmother would have been proud of the way I played, I thought. The keys, cold beneath my fingertips, were the only things I focused on. Once I hit the final note, I inhaled deeply, then, finally, opened my eyes. John and Mr. Chambers stood clapping loudly.

"Brava, we have a virtuoso in our midst," John said. I stood and moved away from the large wooden instrument.

"Where did you learn to play like that?" Beth said.

"My grandmother taught me." My eyes caught John's again. He looked pleasantly surprised, but there was also a glimmer of something more. Perhaps admiration? I had to withdraw my gaze when Mr. Chambers grabbed my hand.

"You must play something else. You would do us the greatest honor listening to such beautiful music from such an accomplished woman," Mr. Chambers said.

"I think Miss Hart could use a break. We all should play a game of cards instead," Anne quickly said. Her eyes were glaring daggers at me and her already small mouth had turned to a thin stripe, but as soon as the men's attention turned back towards her, she plastered on a fake smile.

"Miss Blakeley is right. Let us play a game," John said as he waved at the table and chairs previously used for afternoon tea. I paid attention to the rules and had an otherwise fun time the rest of the evening. Mr. Chambers stayed by my side to help me with my cards until it was time to say goodbye to the Blakeley's.

14

Nightmares

Someone was yelling. At first, I thought I was still dreaming when I realized I was awake I bolted upright, confused and groggy with sleep.

"No, James, stay with me. Please God, let him stay with me," a deep voice shouted from another room. I stumbled out of the heavy sheets and planted my feet firmly on the plush rug. Did anyone else hear his voice, or was everyone else too fast asleep? I stretched my hand out in front of me to make sure I wouldn't walk face-first into furniture or a wall while my eyes acclimated to the dark. The man was still desperately shouting "no".

My fingers reached for the silky robe draped across the chair and pulled it around me. On my tiptoes, I made my way over to the door and opened and closed it gently behind me. The sound of my feet was dampened by the heavy decorative rug in the hallway. I didn't hear anyone else stirring, so I crossed the hallway. The yelling was coming from the guest room across from me. I entered the room as quietly as I could;

amidst the heavy draperies and blankets on the queen-sized bed, I spied the figure of Mr. Chambers. The moonlight coming through the windows just bright enough to lighten the darkest shadows. He was thrashing around in his sleep, muttering now instead of shouting. It seemed to me he was having a bad nightmare. I wasn't sure what would be the best approach to help him, but I also didn't want to leave him in distress.

I sat down next to him on the edge of the bed, sinking down into the plush mattress, and placed my hand on his forehead. The room was heavy with the smell of sweat and his forehead and temples were slick and shiny with moisture; his hair was plastered to his face.

"Mr. Chambers, wake up," I said, as I gently touched his shoulder. "Are you alright?" I continued, but he didn't react to my voice. Pained expressions crossed his face and I decided to shake his shoulder a little harder. "Wake up, Mr. Chambers."

His back stiffened, and his arm shot out and grabbed me, then he looked at me confused. "What is going on?" he said.

"You were having a nightmare. I heard your screams across the hall," I said in a soft voice.

"Oh," he uttered, he noticed his tight grip on my wrist and let go. "I apologize, I didn't mean to frighten you."

"You didn't, I promise."

"Did anyone else hear? Did I wake anyone else?"

"Just me, probably because the room I'm staying in is across from yours."

His face relaxed as I said that, but he still looked thoughtful and weighed down, as if his thoughts were too heavy and important to keep inside at all times, and he might burst from the burden of carrying them. "I apologize for waking you," he said.

"Don't worry about that." I scanned the room for his washing basin. "I think you might like to wash your face," I said as I moved from his side on the bed to the washing basin on a stand in the corner of the room. William nodded. I grabbed the cloth hanging from the edge of the bowl and dipped it in the cool water, then wrung it until it was moist but not dripping wet. "What did you dream about," I asked innocently while I handed him the wetted fabric.

"Military service has left me with some demons which prefer to prey on me during the nighttime. I'm afraid that any particulars aren't suitable for the ears of a gentle woman such as yourself. Would you perhaps do me the kindness of not mentioning this to John or Beth?" He sponged his temples with the cloth.

"If you prefer to keep it quiet, then I won't say a thing," I promised. "I was wondering though; you were calling out a name, James. Is he someone you know?" I wasn't sure if I should even mention it, but the name had made me curious. Pain flashed across his features, and he absentmindedly touched the scar cutting along his temple.

"Many great men die in war and I mourn their loss but there is no pain that cuts deeper than the loss of someone important, the loss of a friend or family member fighting by your side," he said with a hitch in his voice. He swallowed deeply and turned his head away from me to wipe away a tear, presumably, so I wouldn't notice. William scratched his throat and tried to perk up his countenance. "I'm afraid all this talking has left me a bit thirsty. Would you care to join me in the kitchen for a late-night snack?"

"Of course, Mr. Chambers. I'd be delighted," I said and stood. His deflection was clear; I had hit a nerve, and he wanted to forget it for the moment. If every time I slept, I had to deal with nightmares about some of the worst moments in my life, I wouldn't want to talk about them either.

"I think we should do away with the formalities," William said, on his way out of the bedroom. "You may call me William. After all, you have seen me asleep in my private chamber," he said with a hint of flirtation. He was trying to be the same charming man as last night, albeit a bit shakily.

"Okay, you may call me Rose," I said with an encouraging smile. William led the way down the stairs and through the corridors until we reached the kitchen.

It looked a lot larger without Mrs. Avery's presence filling the room. I'd watch her sometimes prepping dishes and kneading dough for breads and pastries, her aging arms much stronger than mine because of the way she had to exercise her muscles every single day to bring food to John and Beth's table. I was spoiled with modern inventions like hand-mixers and microwaves. Seeing how everything has to be done by hand here made me realize how privileged I was growing up with so many machines and tools to do the hard work for me. I missed modern technology, especially a warm hot shower and a perfect steaming cup of coffee at the press of a button. If I closed my eyes, I could almost smell the freshly ground beans; tea didn't hit me the same way that a cup of coffee did. Tea went to your stomach, but caffeine went straight to your soul.

"Would you like some water?" William asked, as he pulled out a seat by the butcher's block.

"Please, sit down. I will round us up something to eat," I said. "You were the one having a nightmare."

"Well, alright. Since you insist," William said, the corner of his mouth raised into a tentative smile. He sat down on the stool and rested his arms on the wooden top. I opened the kitchen cupboards and grabbed two glasses. There was a filled pitcher of water next to the sink which I used to fill them. I deposited both glasses on the butcher's block in front of William and continued on my scavenger hunt. I found what looked like a block of cheese, some stale bread, and some kind of dried sausage in the pantry. I sniffed it to be sure it wasn't spoiled but it smelled hearty with a hint of peppercorn and maybe something like nutmeg or cloves.

"Look what I rustled up," I said when I sat down on a stool next to William with a plate of snacks. I used a knife to cube the cheese, slice the sausage, and added the stale bread for some added visual flair.

"Looks delicious," William said as he grabbed a piece of sausage. "I do believe the night terror has left me famished. I wonder if every step you take in a dream counts in real life; it certainly feels so after the dream I just had."

I nibbled on a cube of cheese with a firm but creamy texture. "I've had dreams before where, when I woke up, it felt like I was falling, or I'd dream I was drowning, and I would wake up out of breath. You know," I said, keeping my tone even. "If you want to talk about your dream, I am here to listen." I took a quick glance at him and saw his lips purse before he let out a deep sigh.

"I've been having nightmares ever since I returned from Belgium." He paused and the silence in the room enveloped us with its weight.

"What happened," I hedged.

"My squadron was camped together with Prussian troops near this abandoned windmill on the outskirts of Ligny, one of many cavalry outposts to stop the French advance. By mid-afternoon, we heard cannon fire and saw the French cavalry approach much sooner than expected." William paused. "Are you certain you want me to continue my story? I'm half of a mind to not continue myself."

"I'm certain," I said. "But only if you want to."

William nodded and continued his story. "Field Marshal Büchel of the Prussian army ordered his men to the battle-field, a vast expanse of grain fields with high stalks boxed in by rivers. We hadn't received word from Duke Wellington, so without his orders, our general decided to join the Prussians in the field. We were low on ammunition and the Prussian army was in shambles with many men deserting before the start of the battle."

"Is this where you got your scar?" I said, looking at the jagged line of flesh marring the side of his face from the corner of his eye to the side of his lip.

"Yes." William had his hand clenched into a fist, his knuckles turning white. I laid my hand on his arm to soothe him. "I apologize, war isn't a proper subject for a lady."

"I don't care," I said.

"I'm not sure if anyone has told you this, but," he said, as he looked up from his hands, "you really are quite different."

"I shall take that as a compliment."

"You should, I meant it as such," he said, with a glimmer in his eye. "I predict it shall be entertaining to get acquainted with you Miss Hart."

"Rose," I corrected him.

"Rose," he replied with a smile. "For now, though, I for one think I should try to close my eyes again. I've had enough talk of war for tonight. I do thank you for your kind concern and friendship this evening."

"Good night," I said as his stool scraped over the flagstone floor and he stepped away from the butcher's block. The last piece of cheese found its way into my mouth and I cleaned off the plate I had used to hold the snacks. There had been more William had wanted to say, at least his pregnant pauses had made me think so. I wondered about the horrors he must have faced. I didn't understand much about old-fashioned warfare except for what was depicted in movies. However, I was sure they could be just as brutal as the things the military were capable of in my time. After all, death was death, and the people who loved the soldiers that became casualties of war would mourn them just the same.

Except for his scar, William seemed too gentle of a man for fighting. I couldn't picture him, or John for that matter, with a weapon. If I was stuck in this place and had to befriend them, I was glad John wasn't a military man and that William was now permanently posted in London. It would be nice for John to have his friend back. From what I had seen, there weren't many people in town that John was close to. Most were simple acquaintances at best. William brought an air of lightness and fun to Hawthorne, brightening everything around. I just hoped the man himself would also succumb to those same effects and heal from his mental wounds as he had done his physical.

15

Family Connections

"Rose, a letter has arrived for you. You must let me know what it says," Beth said, as she stormed into the kitchen. I was helping Mrs. Avery with cooking, so I was covered in flour. The cook took over from me rolling out the dough and I brushed my hands off on the slightly soiled apron.

"Here," Beth said, as she thrust the cream-colored envelope into my hands. I looked back at Mrs. Avery, but she continued on with the chore in front of her.

"Go on, child, you can help me bake another time; Beth loves her pastries so there will be plenty more to be made," she said.

"Thank you, Mrs. Avery," I said, and the woman smiled kindly. "Okay, let's go to the drawing room," I told Beth. I untied the apron and hung it on the nail by the larder then followed her to the settee in the other room.

"Go on, open the letter; let's see who it's from," she said as she sat down next to me and watched me like a hawk while

I tore open the envelope and took out the heavy textured paper.

"It's from Mrs. Ashbrook," I said as I noted the name and signature at the bottom of the paper.

"Mrs. Ashbrook?" Beth said, snatching the empty envelope and turning it over for possible clues. "Why would she send a letter to you?" I was just as confused as I read Mrs. Ashbrook's words.

"It says here she wants to invite me over for tea this afternoon."

"How odd," Beth said, looking thoughtful. "Is the invitation for you alone or for the both of us?"

"I'm not sure," I said, handing her the letter. "It's addressed to me and it invites me directly." Beth scanned the words.

"It seems to be an invitation solely for you," she said, a bit deflated. "You must have made an impression on her when she came round at Hawthorne. I wonder what she wants to talk to you about."

"Perhaps I can ask for an invitation for the both of us when I meet with her," I suggested. This appeared to brighten Beth's mood.

"That would be lovely," she said. "If you are to visit Mrs. Ashbrook, then you must wear one of your new dresses. Estelle will arrange your hair, and Hugh can drive you to Granhope Manor." Beth seemed to think. "Would you like to borrow one of my bonnets?"

"I'd love to," I said, grateful she was no longer feeling excluded from the visit.

"Oh, you must tell me everything when you return, and

put in a good word for me. I would love to have tea somewhere that isn't Hawthorne for once," Beth added.

"I will make sure to sing praises of your every accomplishment, but first I'll have to make sure I won't make a fool of myself," I said, with a smile. The invitation was curious, and I wondered why it was directed at me and not Beth. There wasn't anything I could think of that Mrs. Ashbrook might need me for and if she wanted to socialize with a lady, then my friend would surely have been the better choice instead of me.

"You will be perfect," Beth said, unaware of my thoughts. "Everyone that has met you has taken a liking to you. Just look at William, he has been trying to attract your attention ever since he arrived last evening."

"Except Anne," I shot back at her, thinking of the dark-haired beauty that kept a close watch on everything that John was doing. "And I think William is just trying to get to know me because I am staying with you and John; he's probably curious."

"Perhaps, but Anne is interested in John, and you are new and exciting and you are an unmarried woman living at Hawthorne; therefore, she has decided that you are her competition. I don't necessarily want her for my sister-in-law but you both might have more in common than you think, and she isn't all bad. Or at least she hasn't always been," Beth amended.

"It is suspicious how nice you are," I said, poking Beth in her arm. "How can you point out the good in everyone and everything."

"It is a gift," Beth laughed. "Now, let's get you ready for your visit with Mrs. Ashbrook."

Two hours later, I found myself squeezed into a cream-colored dress, with an aching scalp from all the pins and tightly coiled curls in my hair, standing in front of the steps leading up to Mrs. Ashbrook's estate. Now that I stood there, surrounded by the opulent home and intrinsically manicured garden filled with Roman or Grecian busts and statues, I was glad Beth made sure I looked my best. As it was, I still felt out of place, even if not a single strand of my hair dared to jump out of its securely fastened spot. The architect of this place must have loved Ancient Rome because even flanking the entranceway were Roman columns.

I knocked on the door and a footman let me into the hallway. "I'm Rose Hart; Mrs. Ashbrook invited me," I said.

The man with dark, gelled back hair nodded. "Please follow me this way, Miss Hart," he said, holding out his hand to take my hat. I trailed his heavy steps from the foyer through the main hallway, then he turned right into another corridor leading to the left wing of the house. I gawked at the round half tables lining the walls, decorated with porcelain vases that were beautifully designed with gold. Family portraits had lined the entrance way but here they were paintings of women and men wearing toga's, dancing or eating fruits from large platters. The footman stopped at a closed door and rapped his knuckles against the wood three times.

"You may enter," Mrs. Ashbrook's voice said. He opened the door and waved me in.

"Miss Hart ma'am," he said as he bowed.

"Thank you, you may go," she ordered the man. He simply

nodded and closed the door behind me. "Now come sit by me, dear," she said as she patted her hand on a tufted chair next to the velvet couch she was sitting on. "You'll have some tea?" A servant girl stepped away from the corner of the room and headed towards the teapot on the small table. I hadn't noticed the thin young girl when I first entered the room; she had almost blended in with the wallpaper. "You may go as well, Demelza," Mrs. Ashbrook said as the girl finished pouring the tea. I made myself comfortable on the chair, although, I was a bit nervous being there, especially when I had no idea what the stately woman might want with me. I did remember her kind words on the day of the dance when Anne was trying to make me feel excluded. Perhaps it was best to start with a praise.

"Thank you again for being so kind to me at the dance. I really appreciated it," I said.

"Of course, dear," she said, with a kind smile. "Women should support each other during difficult times. We already have to navigate a restrictive society, so we shouldn't add to another woman's misery."

"I didn't think you would have many restrictions."

"Ah, but I've got the privilege of wisdom and being the lady of a wealthy estate." Mrs. Ashbrook's face turned serious. "While the banter is enjoyable, I do have a reason for inviting you today."

"I was wondering that," I said matter-of-factly.

"We'll have a lot to discuss. Do you perhaps have an idea as to why I invited you?" I couldn't think of any reason, so I just said the only thing that came to mind.

"Since it isn't to socialize, is it to tell you about Mr. Easton or Beth? I'm afraid there isn't much to tell and even if there was, I wouldn't."

"Oh heavens, no dear. Although you have shown yourself to be a kind and interesting person, and your loyalty to your hosts is commendable, I have something more important in mind. I wanted to discuss something without prying ears which is why I've sent Demelza and Bert away." She drank the last dregs of tea from her cup and placed it on the table. "Would you be so kind as to take over for my servant girl and pour me another cup," she said, leaning back into the velvet fabric. "Now, I have been mulling this over for the last few days and I have decided to declare you, my heir." My mouth sagged open at her words and I spilled some tea on the table-cloth. "Now, think about your composure," she chided. "As I have told you at the dance, I have no relatives to bequeath my home and fortune to, so every dilettante in the area is vying to be in my good graces. I am simply exhausted dealing with them, and I would like to live out the rest of my years in peace. This is where you come in," Mrs. Ashbrook said.

"How could it help you to make me your heir?" I asked.

"Your story of arriving here and looking for your long-lost family doesn't add up." I tried to explain or make excuses, but she cut me off. "Now don't try to deny something we both understand to be true. You must have your reasons, but knowing that you aren't who you say you are is something I can use."

"Will you tell Mr. Easton," I said, worried.

"I don't plan on telling anyone. You caught my attention during tea at Hawthorne, especially the way you handled Miss Blakeley and the affection you showed for Miss Easton. Regardless of how you ended up here, I feel your kindness and affection for the Easton's is sincere. I hope by making you my heir, I will get your loyalty, and in turn, it will get those vultures of my back. I swear they are counting down the days till I drop dead."

"But, wouldn't everybody know we aren't related? It might anger people."

"I thought about this and I have come up with a plausible story. One of my brothers took passage to the Americas and never returned. Who's to say he didn't change his name and had a son who married and had you? I shall claim you as my long-lost grandniece, reunited with me once more through good fortune and luck. You will leave here today with a letter for Mr. Easton informing him of your family connections to me and your status as heir. I assume you'd prefer staying at Hawthorne," Mrs. Ashbrook said, with a sly wink.

I thought of Beth's friendship so far and even John with his hot and cold behavior. "Yes, I would prefer that," I said. The idea of staying with Mrs. Ashbrook was definitely not preferable, not that I had many choices.

"I thought so. However, if you do change your mind, you are welcome to move to Granhope and take up residence in one of my guest rooms. Regardless, we will announce your entrance into society with a ball in your honor." Mrs. Ashbrook got up off the couch and pulled on a cord hanging from the ceiling. I could hear a faint ringing noise coming from somewhere far away.

"How may I assist you" the footman said just a few seconds later, as he entered the room. "Please fetch me a pen and paper," Mrs. Ashbrook said. I stood by her side as she wrote the letter meant for John, sealed it, and then handed it to me. "I shall contact you about the date and time. And remember, you cannot speak about this to Mr. Easton or Beth, or anyone else for that matter. This is to stay between us. If you are in need of any financial support, for example, for the procurement of a dress for the ball, please send me a note and I'll arrange for Bert to handle it."

16

Fortuitous News

"How was your visit at Granhope Manor?" John Easton asked as he looked up from the book he was reading. I had taken off my bonnet and gloves and sat down near him in the drawing room.

"It was interesting," I said, hesitation clear in my voice. John cocked his head and closed his book.

"Did something happen?"

"No, well, yes, actually," I blurted. "Perhaps it's better if you just read it for yourself first."

I handed John the letter Mrs. Ashbrook had written. The doors to the drawing room opened and William and Beth walked in.

"You are back," she said, excited. "How was your visit? Did you manage to see the art gallery in the right wing? Mrs. Ashbrook has one of the largest collections in Westbridge. Next time, you should see if you could invite me along." John hadn't looked up from the letter yet, his brows furrowed.

"I did ask for an invitation," I told Beth. "We only need to send her a note to give her advance warning of our intent to visit."

"What's going on," William said to John, who still looked a bit concerned. John stood and handed the letter to William, then looked at me. "It seems we have found Miss Hart's family."

"Really, who?" Beth said.

"Mrs. Ashbrook," William said with shock, clutching the letter.

"Can I see the letter?" Beth said to John. "I wasn't expecting that at all. Rose did say it was a wealthy family," Beth said. "However," she said, turning towards me. "You must be so excited to have found her. You should have told me immediately. How did she know you were related?" John answered before I could.

"A letter from her brother before he left where he said he'd changed his name, so he wouldn't be associated with the Ashbrook name anymore, and apparently Rose's countenance. Mrs. Ashbrook writes that Rose's features resemble those of her great grandmother."

"How fortuitous," William added.

"I wish I could have been there when you found out. That must've been so exhilarating," Beth said.

"It seems you had an exciting day as well," I said, trying to direct the conversation away from me.

"William and I went riding. You should join us next time," Beth said, then she frowned. "Wait, does this mean you will move in to Granhope Manor?" Beth looked sad, and both John and William were curiously awaiting my answer.

"Well, if it would be alright with Mr. Easton," I said, looking up at John. "I would very much like to stay at Hawthorne. I'm still new to Westbridge and I have come to enjoy Beth's companionship. Of course, if you would like that as well, Beth," I said, clasping her hand. "I wouldn't want to impose on you any longer if you didn't want me to."

"I think this can be arranged," John said. "You know I can't deny my sister anything that might make her happy."

"Oh, Rose, I am so happy for you," Beth said, hugging me. "I do admit, I worried you would leave Hawthorne, but I am so glad you will stay here with me. We've only known each other for a short while but I have come to regard you as my sister, if not by blood, then by heart."

"I agree," I said, squeezing her tighter. "I do have one request for all three of you," I said, once I let go of Beth. "Will you please keep it a secret that I am Mrs. Ashbrook's grand-niece, at least until after she has sent out the invitations for the ball that she is planning on hosting."

"Why would you want to keep that a secret?" William asked. "Soon enough, the entire town will find out anyway."

"I'm just not used to being the center of attention; it makes me a bit uncomfortable. I just need some time to process all the new information of finding out that I'm related to Mrs. Ashbrook, without people gossiping about me." John actually smiled at my remark. I wondered why. Maybe he didn't believe me or maybe he thought I was weird for wanting to keep this a secret when instead I should have been jumping for joy and shouting the news off the rooftops. I'm sure that's what Anne would have done, I thought, with a bit more vitriol than I should have.

"We can do that," he said. William and Beth both nodded.

"I can't imagine why you'd want to keep it a secret for now, but you have to tell me everything," Beth said. "Come, let's leave my brother and William to pontificate by themselves and go for a walk."

I happily recounted the fictional version of my visit with Mrs. Ashbrook to Beth all afternoon while fielding her questions on the more strenuous details. Thankfully, she was easily distracted with descriptions of the paintings and vases and other decor so abundant at Granhope Manor. Eventually, I did tell her that I needed some time to think everything over. Beth understood and left me to my own devices the rest of the evening and most of the next day.

John and William had gone into town for the day, taking care of business or for pleasure, I wasn't sure. Beth was also absent. I went to her room, but it was empty, and I didn't find her in any of the other usual spots either. She didn't leave with William and her brother because I had waved them off early in the morning. More than likely, she went out riding and I would see her whenever she returned.

I took it upon myself to take stock of Hawthorne and go over my options. So far, I had done my best to fit in and it worked. Even without Beth calling me her sister yesterday, I had gotten close to her. She had quickly become one of my favorite people, sweet and funny with just enough fire in her to make it interesting. If we were both back in my own time and I met her somewhere random, like at a park, I could see us becoming fast friends. It scared me how rapidly Hawthorne and its inhabitants grew on me. My grandmother's funeral seemed ages ago. Did I really complain to Nicole about my ex and my lack of adventure? I guess I got what I wished for. Landing in the 19th century with no way out definitely constituted an adventure. Maybe that's what the bookstore did; it sniffed out my lack of a life and decided to change it.

There were no rules that I knew of and being in the middle of things made it easy to forget that I had a life that didn't involve mansions and men in period clothing. I pictured my mother's face. Did she miss me? Had my disappearance turned into a missing persons case, and was my father consoling my mother at this moment? Or did time not continue in the present so that if I found a way home, I'd return to the same time I left? I should have watched more time-travel shows with Nicole, maybe then I could come up with some better hypothesis.

"Are you alright?" Mrs. Avery asked as I slunk into the kitchen. I chose to answer with a version of the truth.

"I miss my family," I said, feeling the truth of it down to my soul. Though Mrs. Avery couldn't be more different than my mom, something about her reminded me of her— a nurturing and caring quality that said that a hug would make everything better. My throat hitched and while I tried to fight the tears building up in my eyes, the feelings of loss— losing my grandmother, losing the world I knew, missing my parents, and the feelings of worry about how to navigate the new place I was in, how to get back home, why I ended up here— finally bubbled over and I cried. The housekeeper and cook held me in her arms and let my cry against her apron. Her hands, sticky from the food she'd been prepping, holding me tight.

"There now, love. Let it all out." Then, as my crying petered out, she said, "Come help me with dinner. Nothing better than cooking to soothe the soul." She put me to work chopping vegetables and browning meat. Together with her help, I also prepared the dough and filling for a fruit pie. Tart and sweet strawberries a scullery maid had brought in from town, reduced over heat with some sugar.

Beth returned to Hawthorne in the early afternoon but retired to her room for some personal space. She wasn't dismissive exactly, but she did seem preoccupied. I made a mental note to talk to her later; I hoped she wasn't upset with me about anything, not that I could think of anything I might have done.

Only Mrs. Avery and I were working in the kitchen, besides Estelle occasionally wandering in for supplies. Quiet busywork drowned out my worries and by the time William and John arrived back at Hawthorne in time for dinner, I felt a lot better. Mrs. Avery was right, creating meals by focusing on one task at a time did help.

John announced that he had some news once we all sat around the dining room table, topped with dishes I'd helped make. "William and I ran into Mrs. Blakeley and her two daughters." A pang of jealousy hit me when I thought of Anne spending time with John, but immediately chided myself. There was nothing going on between John and I, and even if he was interested in me, I sure wasn't, so there was no reason to envy Anne. "Mrs. Blakeley remarked upon the weather and how lovely it has been and how soon it would be too cold to enjoy the outdoors for long. Then she suggested a picnic would be wonderful and that Anne and Mary should greatly enjoy a day of fun. So, I hope you and Rose will join us tomorrow," he said to Beth.

Beth looked thoughtful. "Will Mr. Danby be joining us? If not, we should invite him. He is new in town and might like a social engagement."

"How thoughtful of you, dear sister. As it is, Mrs. Blakeley was planning to send out an invitation to Mr. Danby, so we shall find out tomorrow if he'll be joining us."

"A picnic sounds like fun; don't you agree, Rose?" William said. "Maybe I can feed you grapes, and we all can play some games to pass the time."

"I'm afraid I will need your assistance with entertaining Mrs. Blakeley and her two daughters; otherwise, I'm afraid they'll get even more invitations out of me," John said, with a shrug. "Besides, you can't monopolize Miss Rose's attention."

"And why is that?" William asked.

"Well," John hurried to say. "Rose will be a great distraction with the Blakeley's."

"I think I like William's idea better," I retorted.

"See," William joked. "It is settled. The lady has spoken, and she shall be fed grapes."

"A picnic might be fun, and I think it will be especially interesting to see John juggling Anne and her mother."

"Good luck," Beth told her brother in faux horror. William guffawed.

"I wouldn't laugh if I were you," John said to William, with a pointed glare. "Might I draw attention to the fact that you are now an eligible bachelor with apartments in London? I merely need to suggest as much to Mrs. Blakeley and not only will she be trying to snare you for one of her daughters, so might all the other society mothers. You know how fast gossip spreads in Westbridge when Mrs. Blakeley is concerned."

"You wouldn't dare," William said, in mock outrage.

"Would you take that chance," John said, smirking. "If I'm to be sacrificed, and brought as a lamb to the slaughter, then so shall you."

"No one would compare you to a sacrificial lamb," Beth cut in. "Prized pig sounds more like it." Earning a snigger from both William and me, and another glare from John.

17

A Game of Croquet

Mrs. Avery and Estelle had packed us a feast inside a pretty rattan box. Hugh lifted it off the back of the carriage and set it down on the grass. John picked the place to have a picnic, a pretty spot in a meadow that overlooked the river which ran through the center of Westbridge, and the stone bridge that functioned as the main entrance into town. He and William were struggling with the over-sized picnic blanket; the wind kept picking it up and twisting it before they could lay it out. There was a bit of a breeze but with my hair tied back and pinned down by the bonnet I was wearing, it didn't bother me. Eventually the two of them managed to stretch it out with the help of Beth who plopped down on a corner.

Mrs. Blakeley and her daughters arrived with Mr. Danby in tow as we were setting out some appetizers in the center of the blanket. "How wonderful to be out and enjoy nature on a day such as this," she said to John, waving her arms at the sky.

Mary hurried out from under her sister's shadow and joined Beth on the blanket.

"Indeed," John said, holding out his elbow for Mrs. Blakeley. "Here, let me assist you with finding a place to sit." He supported the woman's arm and let her sink down on one of the small pillows we had strewn in a circle on top of the blanket.

"I hope it is alright that I joined," Mr. Danby said to John. "Mrs. Blakeley informed me of the invitation and I was pleased to accept. Perhaps you remember me from the dance, my name is Percy Ambrose Danby."

"Yes, I do remember," John said, as he scrutinized the man. "Are you perhaps related to the Danby's from Hertfordshire? I believe my late uncle used to hunt with a Fitzwilliam Danby."

"I can't say that I am," Mr. Danby said. "My family hails from the north."

"I've always wanted to travel up north," Anne added.

"What brings you down to Westbridge?" William asked.

"I joined the militia when they traveled through my hometown. As we traveled down, I fell in love with the area and have decided to make it my home."

"How brave of you to join the militia to protect us," Beth said with rounded eyes. "We are lucky to welcome you to Westbridge society."

"Very brave indeed," Mrs. Blakeley and her daughters echoed.

"Did you know Mr. Chambers is also a military man," Anne continued, fanning out her dress and making a show out of sitting down. William frowned at Anne's mentioning of his career. Mr. Danby appeared a bit uncertain on how to continue the conversation.

"Never thought of joining the army and fighting with the men overseas?" William said sharply to Mr. Danby.

"I'm afraid that by the time I joined, the war with France was already over, and I felt my skills would be more useful to serving the people at home," Mr. Danby said. William exchanged a quick glance with John before straightening his face.

"You are right," Beth gushed, not paying attention to anyone but Mr. Danby. "Serving our own people is very commendable indeed." She patted a seat next to her. "Come, let's sit down. Would you like a small cake? Mrs. Avery, our cook, makes the best tarts."

Mr. Danby smiled pleasantly and sprawled out next to Beth. John didn't look pleased when his little sister was handing Mr. Danby bites of food and laughing.

"Oh, John, will you sit by me?" Anne called out. "You must tell me which foods I should try." She fluttered her eyelashes fast enough to launch a plane.

"Go ahead," William said, smirking while nudging John's ribs. John joined Anne, and I had to watch her hand feed him a grape while her mother looked at the scene with a smug expression. I bet Mrs. Blakeley was already imagining her daughter as the lady of Hawthorne.

"Jealous?" William whispered with a quirked brow.

"Who, me?" I said, glancing between William and John, who was now laughing at something Anne said. "No, I'm definitely not jealous. I have no clue what you are talking about; I don't even like John."

"And I'm supposed to believe that when you are clearly regarding our dear Anne over there with the same disdain you'd show dirt stuck underneath your shoe." He smirked.

"Not at all, she seems lovely," I said, turning up my chin. "John clearly enjoys her company as well."

"So, we've established that you have no interest in John in the slightest." William emphasized. "Which means I get your companionship all to myself today then," William said, with a wink.

"I guess so," I said flatly.

The leading topic of conversation during the picnic was mostly about what Mrs. Blakeley had seen in town, intermingled with the constant boasting of Anne and Mary's accomplishment, that is, until Mr. Danby took his focus off of Beth and the cucumber sandwich he held in his hand, and turned towards me.

"Miss Rose, Mrs. Blakeley was mentioning during the ride here that you were still looking for your family. It must be challenging for you to find your place in this town without any familial connections."

"You haven't found your family yet?" Anne said, a sneer plastered on her face that didn't instill any kind feelings in me towards her. "What are your plans if you don't; will you go back to America?"

"I'm not sure," I said. No one except for John, William, and Beth knew about Mrs. Ashbrook claiming me as her grandniece. I really wanted to keep it that way, at least a little while longer. However, it was incredibly tempting to blurt out. I knew if Anne found out, it would've wiped the sneer off her face.

"If you are looking for a reason to stay, I hear Mr. Willoughby is looking for a housekeeper." I bit my lip and thought about the slimy man and the way he danced with me at the ball, a shudder passed through my spine. Beth tried to speak, but I knew what she wanted to say, so I gave her a stern look and shake of my head.

"My, these tarts are exceptional; you must thank Mrs. Avery for me," William said, coming to the rescue and defusing the situation. "You know what would be fun?" he said to us, before turning towards John. "You did bring the set, right?"

"Ah, yes," John said, hopping up.

"What would be fun?" Anne asked, a bit upset that her interrogation of me was being put to a halt. Not to mention that she wouldn't be able to feed John more bites of food anymore now that he was walking towards our carriage. The thought of Hugh sprawled out on the bench inside taking a nap while we were outside having a picnic was brightening my day. The man deserved a break from all the hard labor around the estate.

"Anyone up for a game of croquet?" William asked.

"Ooh, will we play in teams?" Beth said. "If so, would you be my partner?" she asked, canting her head and looking shyly at Mr. Danby.

"Naturally, with you by my side, I venture we'll be the winning team," he boasted.

"Will you show me how to play, Mr. Easton?" Anne asked, like a true seductress. I had to bite my lip so I wouldn't say something rude or roll my eyes.

"Do you need me to show you how to play as well?" William whispered in my ear.

I swatted at him and said, "I think I know how the game works but explain it to me if I do something wrong."

The three men set up a course with the metal hoops that the croquet ball would have to be shot through. I had a rough idea of how to play the game but no idea of actual sports terms or scoring. The wind had picked up a bit more and seeing Anne try to keep her hair out of her face was giving me some evil delight. Even though Beth had told me some good reasons as to why the brunette behaved the way she did, it still didn't change my feelings as soon as I saw her actions in person, most of them negative and directed at me.

The first round of croquet, I taught William how to high-five with lots of amusement from everyone else. I actually managed to use the mallet and shoot my ball through the first hoop or wicket, as William explained to me. However, I celebrated too soon. The second round, I tried to reprise my success and almost missed the entire ball; it rolled only a couple of inches before stopping.

"I guess it was just beginner's luck," Anne sneered; she grabbed on to Johns arm and looked up at his face. "Can you teach me the proper stance?" John awkwardly stood behind her, adjusting her grip on the mallet while she kept leaning more and more into him. She was pulling out all the stops. Her mother must have thought the same thing because she called out to her eldest daughter. Anne flashed me a quick cocky smile as brushed John's shoulder with her hand and joined Mrs. Blakeley. Her mother whispered something in her ear and the grin on her face thankfully disappeared. The pit in my stomach, however, didn't as John turn around and focused his eyes on Anne.

I stepped away a bit angrily as Mr. Danby was taking his shot, but William handed me a pastry and said, "You'll do better the next round." It turned out that he was right; the next few rounds, we both managed to get our balls through the wickets. We were now tied with John and Anne. Beth and Mr. Danby were two wickets behind us, mostly because Beth couldn't stop giggling every time it was her turn to shoot, and Mrs. Blakeley and Mary both kept shooting off to the sides despite Mary trying her best. Now, Anne was posturing in front of her ball swinging her hips as she tried for the best shooting position. John was giving her more pointers on how to hold her hands for the best swing. William and I had both missed, so I was hoping Anne would miss the ball so we'd get another shot. A gust of wind came out of nowhere and behind me came the tinkling sound of porcelain being smacked against each other. William and John ran to hold down the blanket so there wouldn't be more damage to the plates. Just as I turned back towards the croquet set, I caught Anne using her foot to guide her ball through the wicket. She stepped back and acted as if she had shot the ball and won.

Everyone else congratulated her while she looked pleased as punch.

"This is a perfect time to call an end to our picnic," John said. "The wind is picking up."

"We should have another outing again soon," Anne said. "I could use some more advise on how to play."

"I think you play well enough, even with using your foot to score," I said, a bit salty.

"I would never," Anne said, feigning innocence. "How dare you speak to me like that."

"Now, ladies. This is just a friendly game. Besides, has anyone else seen Anne use her foot?" John said. Mrs. Blakeley and Mary shook their heads no; Beth and Mr. Danby had been too preoccupied with each other to see anything, and William and John had been out saving the picnic blanket and its contents. "I think Anne was this game's rightful winner." Anne shot me a smug smile which made me seethe.

"Thank you, John, I couldn't have done it without your help," she said, her voice sugary. I was glad the picnic was over; I wanted a break from John and the rest. A quiet night in my bedroom with a book from Hawthorne's library sounded like just what the doctor ordered.

18

Puddles of Water

A good night's sleep put most of yesterday's ordeal out of my mind; I decided I wanted to do something outdoors. It had rained during the night, leaving puddles of water behind on the dirt pathways snaking their way around the estate. I liked it that way though; it rained so seldom in my home-town that anytime it did, it was like a special treat. My favorite scent was the smell that clung in the air after a good downpour, clean and earthy, as if all the world's sins had been washed away. My grandmother would chide me when I'd run outside, letting the drops fall around me, soaking my clothes and plastering my hair to my face. I knew she was never really upset with me though; she would hand me a towel, and as I dried my hair, I would smell cocoa heating up on the stove. She would use real pieces of chocolate which made the hot drink taste much richer than a single hot chocolate packet. Then I'd top the mug with a mountain of mini-marshmallows. It was funny how a simple thing like a puddle of water could trigger a memory of her. I'd been busy dealing with being dropped back in time, but still, even in an unfamiliar place like this, there would be something that pulled at me and triggered a memory, then the sadness over losing her would hit me like a gut punch. I never lost anyone before, not like my grandma. My grandfather passed away when I was much younger; not understanding the finality of death meant that much of the loss and grief passed me by.

In that moment, with the memory of my grandmother on my mind, I didn't care that, to anyone who paid attention, I would look like an idiot. I wore shoes that were way too flimsy for what I was doing but it felt liberating as I twirled and jumped and danced through the puddles. The rainwater soaked through my slippers and the fabric at bottom of my dress. Just for a few seconds, I wanted to recapture that feeling of freedom I had when I was a child, when my grandmother was alive, and any difficulty I might encounter would be resolved by ice cream and a hug from my parents.

"What are you doing?" William asked, a bemused look on his face. He was leading a horse from the stables.

"Enjoying the rain," I said, both giving him the full answer and no real answer at all.

"Indeed," he said, at a loss for words. "And this is a regular activity?"

"Not very often." I stopped twirling. "Where are you going?" I asked, pointing at the horse.

"I'm just going into town for a bit. There's some mail that needs sending and I've got to run some other errands. John can tell you more as I am in a hurry," he said. "Look, there he is now." William pointed at the figure of a man walking towards us. "I have to go; I will catch you later." William led his horse further down the path, then once he was clear of any puddles, he mounted the mare.

John caught up with me as William rode off. "What are you doing outside? The weather is unsuitable for the light clothes you are wearing," he said, scowling at the sight of my ruined slippers and dress. "Why were you near the stables?"

"I felt a bit stifled staying in the same room, and I like the rain, so I wanted to enjoy the outdoors," I said.

"I prefer taking some air when the weather is dreary. Would you perhaps like to join me for a ride," John said.

"I've never ridden before, I'm afraid, unless you count the day we met when you carried me home on your horse."

"Yes, I don't think that counts," he said with mirth. "Come on, there's nothing to be afraid of," he said, leading me into the stables. My eyes had to adjust to the low lighting. "This here is Brutus, but of course, you've met," he said, pointing at his horse.

"Hi, Brutus," I said, holding out my hand. Brutus pressed his nose against my fingers and with my other hand, I patted his mane.

"See, he remembers you too. Now," John said, moving to the next stall. "This here is Molly; she's Beth's horse, and she is very gentle. I'm sure Beth wouldn't mind if you took her out for a ride today."

"Are you sure?" I questioned. Looking at the spotted mare, she did seem calm with big gentle eyes, but the idea of riding her made me hesitate.

"Trust me," John said. "You will be fine."

"You promise?" I hesitated.

"I promise that you will be fine, but you'll have to learn how to ride."

"Okay then, I'll give it a try." I nodded. "Can you give me a moment while I find something different to wear?" I said, lifting the dirty hem of my dress.

"I'll get started with saddling Brutus and Molly. By the time you return, we should be ready to head out."

"Yay," I exclaimed, and darted off towards the house. The anticipation of horse-back riding with John was weirdly exhilarating. While John saddled the horse in the stable, I found Estelle, the French maid, dusting the furniture in the drawing room. She would be able to help me with a very specific request. John's eyes grew a couple sizes when I returned.

"Why are you wearing a pair of my trousers and one of my shirts," he exclaimed.

"You can't expect me to ride a horse while wearing a dress, can you?" I asked. Estelle had had a similar reaction to my request.

"Non, madame. We women don't wear men's clothing. It iz not done. I don't know 'ow the fashion in America is but this iz England." I however insisted, and finally, after some grumbling, she had found me a pair of John's castaways. John shrugged and gave me a boost into the seat. I did catch him staring at my legs a few times as he jumped in the saddle himself. He led Brutus towards my horse and grabbed my reigns as well. He explained to me how to move with Molly and what commands to give, so she would stop and go. Mostly, he did all the work leading my horse around the property.

"William said as he left, that you would tell me what he was up to," I said, trying to make small talk.

"I thought he might want to announce it himself over dinner, but I might as well tell you," John said. "William invited us to stay with him in London for a couple of days. He is sending out letters to inform his staff, so they can ready our rooms. I'd assume you'd like to join us and act as a companion to Beth."

"Oh, that sounds like a lot of fun. I would love to come," I said.

"Splendid," John said, then he pondered something. "I saw you earlier, when you first went outside to stare at the puddles of water. Your gaze was so far away and such sorrow clung to you. I hope I am not overstepping, but I would like to know what you were thinking about."

I patted Molly on the back and gave John a watery smile. "I was thinking about my grandmother."

"Was it a happy memory," he asked.

"Yes, but also sad. She died not too long ago."

"My condolences, it's apparent you have had to deal with a lot of loss for someone so young."

"Thinking of her hurts, but the pain is lined with love. I feel sadness about losing her but also joy when I remember her smile and the way she smelled. A large part of who I am is because of her. She was my friend, my teacher, my greatest fan. It was her dedication as a piano teacher that got me to learn to play at all even though at times, I wanted nothing more than to stop."

"Your grandmother sounds wonderful; I wish I could have met her," John said, his voice deep and gentle. "What was her name?"

"Rosemary," I said, a small hitch in my voice.

"That's a beautiful name. Your family must be fond of plants."

"It's a bit of a tradition on my mother's side," I said.

"My mother loved plants and flowers; it's because of her that I have a love of horticulture. She taught me how to plant and seed and take comfort in every growing thing in our garden." John's smile faltered a bit. "Once my mother and father died, I couldn't bear the idea of the hothouse being empty or overgrown with weeds. The place feels like a refuge. Whenever I am there with my hands in the dirt pulling out weeds, or watering plants, or pruning back leaves, I sense her with me. I know they are gone. However, I can't help but feel like she's watching over me and nowhere is that feeling stronger than in the place she loved the most."

"Can I ask what happened to your parents?" I asked hesitantly.

"Father had to go to London on business and my mother joined him. Beth and I stayed behind which ended up being for the best; although, Beth, young as she was, had really wanted to come with. From the moment mother and father left, she was crying and angrily striding through the house. My mother had asked father if it wasn't possible for us to join the trip, but he'd said he would be too busy to entertain his kids. I was glad for his dismissal afterwards." John looked at me now. "There was an outbreak of cholera that summer, many people died including my parents. Manfred, my father's valet had said it was quick, which I suppose is some kind of comfort. They went from perfectly healthy to dead within a couple of days and I became the head of the household and had to be a parent to Beth."

"I'm so sorry," I said, I reached out and squeezed his hand.

"I've had some time to deal with the loss, but the ache never really goes away. Sometimes, I walk through the hallway and this floral scent of rose and lily of the valley hits my nose and it's my mother's perfume, the one I'd smell when I hugged her, the one she'd dab on her wrists in front of her vanity when she would go out with father. I can almost imagine her standing behind me. But then I turn around and she's gone and so is the scent of her perfume. Anyway," he said, cutting off his story. "This is a nice and even trail. Perhaps you can try to ride Molly without my assistance," he said, leading me to a grass path lined by knotted willow trees.

The ground underneath us made squelching noises as both Brutus and Molly continued their trot. I took a hold of the reigns and was expecting the mare to veer off in another direction. Instead, I found I didn't have to do much. Beth's horse gladly followed along Brutus.

"Let's try a canter," John said. I gave Molly a slight squeeze with my heels, and she sped up. John followed suit next to me. Once I fell into a rhythm of riding together with Molly, I had fun. The wind in my hair, feeling Molly move beneath me, and for the first time in a long while being free from the constricting clothing of this time period. Granhope Manor loomed in the distance. John was leading us close to the border between their estates before we veered around to head back to Hawthorne. It was an enjoyable loop to ride and showed the magnitude of John's home. He grew up in such an enormous house with so much land to roam.

19

Midnight Confessions

"Did you miss me?" William said with a grin, as he swaggered into the library.

"Like a toothache," I said with a wink. I had curled up on a soft seat near the large bay window, with a book from John's library; Moll Flanders by Daniel Defoe.

John had made himself scarce as soon as he returned the horses to their stalls, both Brutus and Molly were wiped down and relieved of their saddles, bridles, and stirrups. Even if John had servants to take care of every little thing he could want and need, he still insisted on getting his own hands dirty.

"My father taught me that to own and form a bond with a horse, you must be willing to care for it; you can't enjoy the pleasures of riding without also mucking stalls, filling the feed buckets, and wiping down their sweaty flanks. However, I must confess that I rarely muck the stalls nowadays," he said conspiratorially.

"I promise I won't spill your secret," I had said, then he

showed me how to take the gear off Molly and get her ready to be put in her stall, his muscles working hard while he patted her down. Just the two of us in the barn, besides the horses. He must've had the same thought, and practically ran away from me as soon as he was able. I turned my thoughts back to the present and closed the book I was holding.

"John told me the reason you were sending out mail; it will be a lot of fun to visit London, and to see where you live. I believe you've mentioned that you haven't lived in London for long?"

"Yes, I've hardly been to my new apartments, so I figured it could use some good company to liven it up. And, I really had no choice but to invite you all, because Beth has been dropping hints about things in London she's missing out on while I've been visiting Hawthorne," William said, with a laugh.

"How can anyone deny her the latest fashions? It would be a crime," I retorted. "I'm fond of Beth and I can't imagine how excited she'll be to visit London; she might never want to leave. I hope you are ready for a permanent guest," I laughed. "Seriously though, thank you for inviting me as well. I know you didn't have to, especially since I'm just a guest here."

"It seems that for the time being you are a part of the family," William said. "Who knows, perhaps you will enjoy London so much you will never want to leave my apartments," he laughed.

"Oh, you flatter yourself," I said, sticking out my tongue. "Besides, I'm here as Beth's friend."

"And it is only Beth you are staying here for," William said with a raised brow. My cheeks heated as I thought of John and the vulnerability he had shown today. "That's what I thought," he said, pleased with his deduction.

"I am just grateful to be a guest here," I said, testing the words.

"How strange that both you and John have such similar reactions to my innocent remarks," William said.

I turned up my nose. "Strange indeed. Perhaps, since you are the common denominator, it is you in particular that warrants such a similar reaction."

"Let's go with that if you prefer," William said with a shake of his head. I wasn't about to confess to William that I had mixed feelings about John Easton; they had been friends since childhood. John was both exasperating and interesting. He pulled me in with his vulnerability, and not the least bit important, he was very attractive. The memory of him up on his horse was doing things to my insides. The way his muscles stretched taut as he turned Brutus around would take up permanent real estate in my brain. But then, he'd run away from me like I had leprosy. It was too bad that John never seemed to make up his mind. He was either kind and honest, moody and rude, or he ignored and evaded me completely. I didn't need to read too much into his actions. His avoidance of me, and his willingness to help and stand by Anne yesterday, spoke volumes. Why did I care about what John did? I wasn't even meant to be here. If I wasn't looking for a man in my own time, then I for sure wasn't in need of one now.

Beth, John, William, and I all reconnected during dinner where John announced we would leave for London the next day over the munching of bread. Beth, as I'd expected, was brimming with joy; although, with her excitement, she was still worried about how long we'd be gone.

"Why do you ask? Are you planning to stay longer than a couple of days?" John asked. "Perhaps William is in need of a younger sister full-time. We can ask him."

"Oh no, a couple of days is more than enough," she hurried to say.

"Are you sure? I could use someone to chat my ears off and beg me to go shopping," William said, laughing, shooting a knowing indulgent glance at John. "Well, if you are sure. Perhaps I can still persuade Miss Hart to stay behind."

At that, Beth looked aghast. "Rose? Stay with you?" She looked at me and narrowed her eyes. "That's not what you want, is it?"

I threw my hands up in the air. "I have no idea what's going on," I said. "I think Mr. Chambers is speaking nonsense."

"Good, because you are my friend and I would miss you too much," Rose said, appeased by my comment. "Besides, you are the heir to Granhope Manor; it wouldn't do to move to London without a chaperone." William and John snickered, and Beth scowled at them.

"Okay, let's stop teasing Beth," I said, giving both William and John the same stare I would give the kids in my class if they would misbehave. "I for one am looking forward to London. Beth, you should show me what you are going to bring and maybe you can help me pack as well."

"I'd love to," she squeaked.

"I will see you both tomorrow," I said, nodding at John and William as I left them behind, seated at the table, with Beth by my side.

"Can I say that I'm grateful my sister hasn't been introduced to London society yet?" John muttered to William while we left the room.

Upstairs, Beth was opening every drawer and taking out every piece of clothing she owned, while I sat on top of the plush blanket covering her bed. There were a bunch of dresses hanging over her armoire doors, the chair in front of her vanity, and even her nightstand. Every other available spot was reserved for laying out matching accessories.

"I overheard William and John talking this afternoon," she said, as she was comparing two different silver necklaces, one dainty with a geometric design and the other with a stone inlay of what looked like jade. "John said he told you about what happened to our parents."

"He did," I said. "When we were horseback riding."

She paused, added the jade and silver necklace to her "take to London" pile, and put the other necklace back into her jewelry box. "He hardly ever speaks of them," she continued. "He thinks I don't notice, but ever since they passed away, he has carried such a weight on his shoulders. He considers himself responsible for me and, I think, he thinks he is protecting me by not mentioning them. As if feeling sad or grieving is somehow wrong. But I know that he is still. So, I try to lighten the load and not add to his burden by being happy all the time, if I can make him believe that I am perfectly fine, then maybe he will start to heal. Sometimes I just want my brother back, the jokes and spontaneity and carefree attitude that left when Manfred returned with the bad news."

"You both have been through a difficult time," I said.

"I don't need to pretend all the time though, so don't feel

sorry for John and I," Beth said. "I do love shopping, so that excitement is all real, and I enjoy your company."

"Me too," I said, embracing her.

Today had been a bit of a strange day for me. There was this strange feeling running through my veins almost like an electrical current, a slight buzzing sensation that set my teeth on edge. With the plans to leave for London in the morning, I had tried to go to sleep early but now it was already past midnight and I still lay awake staring at a small rip in the canopy above my bed. The suitcases Estelle had brought for me were packed and ready next to the door.

I finally gave up trying to sleep and crept out of my room at the top of the stairs. Mrs. Avery had left a kettle filled with water next to the stove in the kitchen. I used some matches to light a fire and waited for the water to boil. In the pantry, I found some dried chamomile which would be perfect for tea. Hopefully, the steeped flower buds would help me relax and get back to sleep; otherwise, I'd be like a zombie in the morning. I blew on the hot tea and took slow sips as I wandered around downstairs, weaving in and out of the empty rooms like a specter that was haunting Hawthorne. I was staring out the window in the library when a hand rested on my shoulder.

"You couldn't sleep either?" William asked, his face looking tired.

"No, I think I'm feeling a bit anxious. So, I came down for some chamomile tea. Here," I said, holding out the still steaming cup. "Maybe it will help you."

"Thank you," William said. I followed him to the cozy

chairs near the window and sat down. "You know I meant what I said earlier," he said.

"What do you mean?"

"My offer for you to stay in London, it would be nice to have a friendly face near me. I don't have anyone left that I get along with and trust besides John and Beth, and they are too far away to visit regularly. Perhaps," he trailed off, a pained look on his face.

"Perhaps what," I hedged.

"No, never mind," he said, shaking his head. "Just understand that my offer stands even though I believe you won't take me up on it, and a part of me hopes you wouldn't to begin with."

"Did you have a nightmare again?"

"Not tonight; I just couldn't fall sleep."

"You can talk to me about it if you need to," I said, with concern.

"Perhaps," he said in a curt tone. "My plan is to look forward to tomorrow, and hopefully, settling in London with a visit from my friends will help me find my place."

"I hope you find what you are looking for."

"I do too." With a last nod to me, he stood, taking my cup of tea with him. I lingered behind, taking a deep breath as I leaned back into the chair, drawing my knees to my chest. William was an enigma. He acted so carefree and fun when we were away and around other people, but at night, his personality changed and a sense of sadness clung to his every pore. He was right; I wouldn't take him up on his offer. But not because of the reasons he probably had running through his mind. He didn't know my secret. No one did. Not even Mrs.

Ashbrook knew; although, she had more of an idea than anyone else. For reasons I didn't know yet, I had appeared here at
Hawthorne, and my guess was that it was also where I would
need to be if I wanted to go home. I just wish I knew what to
do. So far, I had no clue.

20

A Fur Hat

The version of London we rode through by carriage didn't remotely look like the London I had visited with my classmates during senior year of high school. Back then—or in the future, I thought with a wry smile— our class walked along streets full of cars, with skyscrapers, and large video screens on Trafalgar Square. We even took a ride on the giant Ferris wheel called the London Eye. None of that existed, yet. I stared out of the carriage window, making sure to take in every detail of the city.

"Is this your first-time visiting London?" Beth asked, as she handed me a small flaky pastry, a traveling snack provided for us by the cook at Hawthorne.

"Yes, I haven't had the chance. I traveled straight to Westbridge from the port." I broke off a piece of sweet flaky crust and nibbled on it.

"My sister loves the shopping in London," John Easton said, with a wink. "We usually go a couple of times a year, and she has been begging me to start her first season here."

"Her first season?"

"Oh, I simply adore seeing all the latest fashions. You and Mr. Chambers must escort us to Bond Street," Beth said, ignoring John's comment.

William turned to me. "It's when an eligible lady of the British upper class gets introduced to the London marriage mart. Usually, families will stay in London during the summer months to attend all the varying social engagements in hopes of snaring a husband."

"And Beth is not yet ready to enter," John cut in.

"Brother, might I remind you that I'm almost twenty years old. Anne is the same age as me and will be entering her third year."

"So, Anne's been trying to find a husband since she was seventeen?" I said, incredulous.

"I suspect the reason that she hasn't yet is because her mother has set her sights on our dear John over here," William said. "But he avoids London, and society as a whole, like the plague during summer. It could be that Mrs. Blakeley thinks Anne has a shot simply because John doesn't go anywhere."

"I have no need of the hustle and bustle and myriad of social engagements in London," John sniffed. "Nor do I need to attract the attention of society mothers. And neither does Beth."

"Beth can speak for herself," Beth said. "I, for one, want to go to dinners and parties. Or, if I can't do that, I want to at least go shopping." Her face lit up as she talked about all the things she wanted to do. John Easton and William were indulging her excitement and nodded along to all her exclamations, even though, I assumed they didn't really care for fripperies and frocks as much as Beth did. The support and encouragement they were showing her made my heart warm.

John caught my gaze as I glanced at him; I blushed, and he asked me a question. "So, Miss Hart. Is there anything you'd like to find on Bond Street? My sister can't be the only lady leaving London with new purchases. What would our friends back home say if you returned without so much as a new handkerchief?"

"Perhaps a pair of boots or something else sturdy," I offered.

"Wouldn't you rather show of your feet in a pair of fancy slippers? Or just splash about in them when it rains?" Mr. Chambers said jokingly.

"No, I'm not much of a dancer. I'd rather get something to wear outdoors, so I can go for a hike."

"A hike?" Beth said, as she tested the word. "Do you mean walking. I like going for a stroll. I'm sure it would be lovely to go on one together when we return."

"Yes, it would," I said. I smiled at Beth and sneaked another quick glance at John.

"Perhaps, we will make it an outing we can all go on," she added. The trip to London excited me. It was a reprieve from the constant worries plaguing my brain. The situation I found myself in was still very disconcerting. I was living at Hawthorne by the good graces of John and Beth, but I didn't have a clue how I had ended up there or how I could leave. My only clue into my grandmother's book and the secret of the bookshop was the old man, which had already been proven a dead end. My life here was an elaborate lie facilitated by Mrs. Ashbrook's scheming plan. Despite all of that, I found life with Beth and John disturbingly comfortable. I had gotten accustomed to the routines of the estate, helping out Mrs. Avery in the kitchen, the grand dinners. And I felt close to Beth, and John, I had to admit grudgingly. A change of scenery might be for the best. Maybe it would shake things up and get my head back in the game. This London was completely new to me and evoked a sense of wonder and possibility when we arrived at Mr. Chambers' apartments.

William showed us around his place, and I was pleasantly surprised by how many rooms it had. For a bachelor, the size of the place was downright decadent. My guest room was smaller than the room I occupied at Hawthorne, but it had all the necessities and then some.

"I sent word of our imminent arrival so housekeeping could prepare the rooms," Mr. Chambers said as he led us past the guest rooms and back into the seating area. I enjoyed the company of William, John, and Beth, but after traveling by carriage, I was glad to retire to my room.

John and William wished me a quick goodnight while they continued their cards game. Their voices carried through the hallway as they joked and debated with one another. I liked seeing John and William so at ease. I hoped returning to London would be better for William; I would hate for him to suffer through more nightmares. Beth followed me out and retreated to her own bedroom.

The next day, Beth had once again manipulated me into getting a gown made. I swear, I didn't know how she managed it. A short man with an unfortunately large mustache was measuring my body in a small dress shop on Bond Street. William and John, surely aware of Beth's intentions to get everyone a new wardrobe, had said their goodbyes as fast as they could after arriving. John said they had some business elsewhere, and they would meet with us later for tea. I highly doubted his vague excuse; they were probably going to a pub to sit, chat, and people watch. Beth had grown on me though. Heck, she felt like a sister, a sometimes-annoying younger sister that you couldn't help but love. There was a twinge of guilt about spending John's money, but I should stop feeling bad especially after the deal I made with Mrs. Ashbrook. I would do my best to repay them both anyway I could, but I had to look the part of the fashionable society girl now, and nothing would make Beth happier than dressing me up like a doll.

"What accessories do I need," I said to Beth, as the man wrote down my measurements and added the pretty green fabrics Beth had picked for me, so they could be sewn and delivered to Hawthorne at a later date.

"I know just where to go," she said, linking her arm with mine. We picked up gloves in a lighter shade of green and a matching reticule at another shop. Beth stroked her hands across a fur hat displayed outside at one of the small stands. I thought she muttered, "He would love this," while the salesperson distracted me with a spread of colorful ribbons.

"Who would love this?" I asked Beth after I told the salesperson no thank you.

"Oh, nothing," she said, a little too fast. "Let's go find us some shoes," she continued with added enthusiasm.

I actually got lucky and managed to find a sturdy pair of boots that would be perfect for hiking around the estate. I did have to relent and purchase more slippers and stockings than

I was comfortable with in exchange, but Beth was difficult to say no to after she insisted ever so seriously.

"You have to get a pair of boots as well if you want to go hiking with me," I said jokingly.

"Fine, I will if you promise me you'll dance with my brother at Mrs. Ashbrook's ball," Beth said with a mischievous grin.

"I'm sure he has another partner in mind," I spluttered, my cheeks growing red.

"If you mean Anne, then I am sure you are mistaken. Besides, I'd much rather he'd dance with you."

"Fine, but only if he asks me," I said, to hopefully end this topic of conversation. Besides, I was quite sure that John wasn't interested in dancing with me. Beth just liked having me around as a friend and confidant and if John was interested in Anne, that might spoil me staying. From what Beth knew, I had the option to stay with Mrs. Ashbrook since I was now the heir apparent and could choose to do so on any whim. She didn't know I might leave out of the blue anyway and completely disappear. I would do my best to say goodbye, of course, but I wasn't sure how I got here, and I definitely didn't know how I'd leave, if I'd leave. My grandmother had been able to though; therefore, so must I, right?

Appeased by my answer, Beth accepted our bags from the shop lady and followed me out the door.

"I am feeling peckish," she said, sticking her nose up in the air. I agreed with her sentiment once the sweet smell of freshly baked pastries from a nearby shop reached my nostrils. My stomach rumbled loudly, which made Beth giggle. "Let's go find a bite to eat. It's nowhere near teatime, so we can still join William and John later." Our arms were laden with bags from all the purchases and I had even managed to find a gift for Mrs. Ashbrook.

I giggled as Beth took a big bite of a honeyed bun covered in powdered sugar, which puffed up and coated her face.

"You should see your face," she said, snorting with laughter. "You are just as covered in powdered sugar as I am." We brushed each other's cheeks clean and stifled our laughter so we wouldn't draw attention to ourselves any longer. Of course, William and John chose that moment to find us. Beth started hiccupping at the sight of them, her face flushed.

"What happened?" John asked, confused, which only made Beth laugh more.

"A shopping and sugar high I'm afraid," I said with a smile, nudging Beth in the ribs.

"It sounds like you two ladies had a grand time without us," William said. "I hope you managed to find what you were looking for and are ready to go home and join us for tea at my apartments. John and I have a fun surprise for later tonight." The notion of a surprise sobered Beth up.

"William, tell us, what is the surprise," she said.

"I think I will let your brother tell it," he said.

John smiled at his sister and me. "We've got tickets to go to the theater tonight," he said with excitement.

"Oh, how wonderful. Now we definitely have to go back to our rooms immediately. Rose and I will need time to get ready," Beth blurted out.

"As you wish, my lady. We shall leave straight away," William said.

"We'll get to wear our new hair ribbons and, oh John, you

should have seen the beautiful fabric I picked out for Rose's new gown, and all the new slippers and gloves. She will look so beautiful," Beth gushed on our way back to William's residence. I blushed and stared straight ahead without making eye contact.

"I am sure you both will look lovely in your new outfits," John told his sister.

21

Champagne and Velvet Drapes

Anticipation ran through me like a live wire just as it did with John, Beth, and William. Beth and I were dressed to the nines in empire waist gowns with light beading and heavier velvet overcoats with colors that complimented the gowns beneath them. One of William's servants helped us put our hair up in small ringlets. Beth had lent me one of her necklaces to wear, the silver one with the jade stone she had been debating on bringing.

A valet opened the door to the carriage and John and William held out their arms for us to hold on to. Beth took William's arm, and I rested my hand on John's. I swallowed to get rid of my dry mouth. John smiled down at me and I couldn't help but admire how handsome he looked in his tailored jacket.

"Are you ready for the show?" he whispered in my ear, his lips gently grazed my earlobe.

"I can't wait," I said, stepping sideways to create more space between us. My heart was pounding. He hadn't said anything scandalous but somehow the tone of his voice brought all kinds of naughty imagery to mind. Imagery that wasn't appropriate out in public. I swear John could read my mind because he gave me a knowing nod of his head. He bowed slightly and invited me to take a hold of his arm. I rested my hand lightly in the crook of his arm as we ascended the steps leading up to the large theater; Beth and William following behind us.

Sconces along the outer wall lit up the building, a bright beacon in the midst of a city full of shadows. Entering the grand entrance hall, I had to crane my head to take in all the sights. There were golden details on the wall and ceiling with enormous chandeliers illuminating the room with the soft glow of candlelight. It must have taken some poor servant ages to light every candle in this place. John let go of my hand and made his way to a server circulating the room with glasses filled with a sparkly beverage, presumably champagne. He returned with one for each of us. Beth and William accepted theirs and I gladly took a glass as well. The fizzy, slightly tart liquid hit my tongue and I knew my assumption was correct.

"Mmm," I let out a small moan. "This is delicious."

"I can fetch you another if you'd like," John said with a crooked smile.

"Maybe later, after the play has started. There will be an interlude, I assume?"

"There will be," William nodded.

Guests in beautiful dresses and costumes flocked together and started filing in lines in order to get to their seats. My foot skidded on the marble floor as I took a step in the direction of the grand staircase. I would have to take small steps, so I wouldn't accidentally slip and fall. John steadied my arm and led me up the staircase all the way to the top floor, leading to the balcony seats. William showed our tickets to theater personnel at the top of the stairs, one of the valets pointed us in the right direction. John held open the heavy curtains separating our intimate viewing area from the hallway, and I slipped through together with Beth and William.

"These are amazing spots," I told William.

"This was such a great idea." Beth nodded, "I love Westbridge, but London has much more to offer. I might have to convince John to take up residence in London," she said, with a sly glance at John.

"Westbridge has a theater," he said.

"Yes, with performances from the Braggs and extended family." Beth shuddered.

"I don't seem to recall you complaining about going to one of their recitals whenever you were sent an invitation by the elder Lady Bragg."

"That is because you don't let me go anywhere else," Beth pointed out.

William guffawed, earning a glare from John. "She is right, if the abysmal performances of the younger members of the Bragg family are the only things she can look forward to, then perhaps you might need to be more lenient with her outings."

"I don't remember asking for your input," John said.

"Are their performances really that bad?" I asked Beth.

"Horrifyingly," she said.

"Terrifyingly," John added.

"Terrible," William finished.

"The Bragg children are sweet, but unfortunately, sweetness isn't an indicator of talent. There is a half-decent singer, actor, or instrument player every once in a while; however, most of them wouldn't recognize talent if it bopped them on the nose and danced a jig on their stage," Beth explained.

"Very accurate description," John said, grinning.

"I guess I should be grateful there hasn't been an invitation from the Braggs then," I said.

"Yet," Beth warned.

I took the chair on the right and John sat down next to me, William and Beth took the other two chairs. From my seat, in one of the brocade chairs, I had a clear vision of the entire stage, which for now, still had its curtains drawn. I bent over the balcony so I could check all the other people filling the seats downstairs. I loved going to the theater; although, back home, it wasn't nearly this impressive. Every summer, I would check the theater schedule and pick my favorites of the visiting Broadway musicals. The last one I had been to was Anastasia; I had loved the music and costuming. Dressing up and going to the theater held a certain charm even if it wasn't done often; most other events were casual to the point that people would show up in jeans and a hoodie. There wasn't anything wrong with loungewear or jeans, but I did like to put in some effort when I'd go to a party or if I went out for dinner, and I appreciated it if the people around me dressed up as well. It made the occasion a bit more special in my opinion. John tapped my shoulder so I could sink back into my seat as the curtains slid open. I moved around and got comfortable so I could focus on the actors portraying a story on stage.

It made me happy that Beth was enjoying herself as well. She deserved to be away from Hawthorne more often, even though her overprotective brother didn't agree. Her eyes lit up, and she laughed loudly when the characters on stage made clumsy mistakes. Beth sparkled in a crowd and she was entertaining to talk to. During a more intimate scene, where two lovers were discovered and subsequently drawn apart from each other, she used her pinky to brush away a tear. She wasn't the only one showing emotion; the scene had made me well up too, and John and William were both looking overly composed. John noticed my sniffles and held out his napkin to me. I used it to dab away the moisture underneath my eyes. I held it out for him to take back, but he waved my hand away, so instead, I folded it up and put it in my purse. Sooner than I expected, we had reached the halftime break. We all stood, shuffled out of the viewing box, and followed the large rounded stairs down to the lobby where servants were waiting with more champagne.

"Would you like another glass of champagne?" John asked me.

"Wait, I'll grab our drinks," William cut in, heading for the nearest servant carrying a tray of drinks.

"Did you pay attention to the lead actor?" Beth asked, leaning towards me. "He's so handsome. And isn't it romantic the way they plan to elope, so they can be together? I hope they manage to outsmart that evil king," Beth gushed.

"It is a good story," I agreed. John smiled at me and I gave him a quick wink.

"Here you are," William said, handing us all a glass and taking a big swig of his own.

"If you are all ready, let's return to our seats before the other guests start moving," John said.

Today had been an amazing day so far, in my opinion. I would've never experienced anything like it back home. And even though it wasn't like I was somewhere dangerous, I still felt proud of myself with how I managed to go along with everything and not be terribly out of place. This was still a foreign place and time, and I had no answers towards what might happen.

The play was about to start again, and we all sat comfortably in our chairs. With my hand dangling at my side, I had the sudden urge to reach out and touch John's, to entwine our fingers. The way I used to as a teen watching a movie with a boy I liked, the hesitation and nervousness heightened by the darkness of the movie theater.

There was a rustling behind us and a gaunt looking man with gray hair clawed his way through the heavy curtain. Both John and I turned our heads and watched as the man tapped William on the shoulder and then whispered something forcefully in his ear. William looked at first shocked and then haunted. He stood fast and turned to leave but John grabbed him by his wrist.

"What is going on?" John demanded.

"Just some business I need to take care of. I won't be gone long. I'll meet you back at my apartment," William said.

"Should I be worried?" John asked. "If you need assistance," he trailed off.

"No, I appreciate your concern, but nothing is going on.

Please enjoy the play and I'll find you later. Perhaps we can talk then. I'll be fine; there is nothing to worry about." William dove through the velvet drapes, following the strange gray-haired man.

"What do you think that was about?" I whispered.

"I have no clue. We should probably do as William said and enjoy the play; otherwise, it would be a waste of tickets," John said, glancing furtively behind him. "I'm sure if anything was wrong, William would have said."

Beth wasn't too perturbed by the disturbance, and was soon completely engrossed in the play again, forgetting the odd way William had left. John on the other hand didn't forget. He pretended to pay attention to the play but the gears in his head were turning, including a certain twitch of his jaw, which I had noticed before. Only when he seemed to intently think about something, and, of course, there was that time when he was arguing with me about Beth.

"He'll be okay," I said, splaying my fingers on top of his hand.

"I hope so," he said softly, looking up at me, then firmer he continued, "He said he would be, and he'll be back tonight. I'm certain I am worrying about nothing." I squeezed his hand and looked back at the stage. Beth was grinning; the lovers had prevailed and all was good in the fictional world on stage. There was still a bit of champagne left in my glass; I picked it up by the stem and drank the last dregs, savoring the flavor. Then, the three of us stood and clapped for the actors now taking their bows up on the stage.

"Can we attend another play while we are here?" Beth asked John.

"I doubt we'll find the time," John said. "But there is always another time at a future visit." He raised his brow. "Why, I thought you only wanted stay a few days. Have you reconsidered?"

"I was just wondering," Beth said.

22

A Gentleman's Club

It was an easy carriage ride back to William's apartments. Beth was yawning the entire ride as exhaustion from all the excitement of the day coursed through her. As soon as we got back, she said goodnight and retired to her room. I thought about retiring as well but John was evidently still on edge by the way he kept tapping his fingers against his leg. He was restless because William hadn't returned yet, so I vetoed going to sleep even if the covers were calling my name and chose to keep John company.

"Could you make us a cup of tea?" I asked one of the staff, a young girl with wide hips and a freckled face.

"Yes, ma'am," she bobbed and hurried to the kitchen. John took off his coat and hung it by the door.

"Let's sit in the parlor for now until William gets back," I said. John nodded and followed me down the wainscoted hall and into the room that had a couch and chairs and two side tables to get comfortable at. I liked William's apartments, but the color palette was overwhelmingly beige and brown. It reminded me for some reason of second hand stores and old folks' homes. William should get it redecorated, put some life and color in to the place so it would fit his own style better. But then again, I wasn't from this time and my taste was a bit eclectic. In my own apartment— if I still had it, that is— I decorated my living room with a gorgeous green velvet couch I found second hand, a rattan chair, side tables made from reclaimed wood, and in every corner and also hanging from the walls I had plants— bamboo, pathos, yucca, and spider plants. I was also fond of decorative pillows, the brighter the better. The outdoor wasn't very green, so I made sure to bring it inside. I think my love of plants and bright colors is what drew me to John's hothouse; it's the only spot in this world that feels remotely familiar.

The servant girl returned with our tea and set the pot and cups down between us. "Thank you," I said to her. "You can retire for the night if you'd like. We'll handle it from here." The girl looked at John for confirmation, but he simply nodded.

"Do you take any sugar or milk?" I said to John while I poured us both a cup of tea.

"Splash of milk and a small teaspoon of sugar," he said.

"So, you like things sweet," I jibed, as I fixed his cup and kept mine plain. I preferred hot tea to be unsweetened, unlike the thick sweet almost syrup like consistency of iced tea back home.

"Not always," John said with a quirk of his brow. He took a sip of his tea and leaned back into the chair. "You know it is quite daring to not be chaperoned with a gentleman present. What might the servants think?"

"I don't see a gentleman, do you?"

John flashed a grin and took another swallow of tea. "You are quite different, Miss Hart. Has anyone ever told you? I can't put my finger on it exactly."

"My family did repeatedly," I retorted, then drank some tea.

"I never suspected that things were so different in America," John said, thoughtfully. "A bit less constricting perhaps, especially with the social classes; however, that still doesn't explain someone like you."

"Like me?" I said, feigning innocence.

"Don't play coy," John laughed. "You know perfectly well how you behave as if you were raised as a man of station sometimes. Beth can be demanding, but she is my sister and still follows society rules. You on the other hand, flaunt the rules at all times."

"What can I say, my parents were progressives." John chuckled. "Would you rather I simper and fawn over you and stick to needle work?"

"Sometimes," John said, staring at me pointedly. "But, no, I suppose not. You have been somewhat of a breath of fresh air, even if a vexing one at times. Beth clearly loves you as a sister and Mrs. Avery also likes having you around despite slowing her down in the kitchen. Your stay with us has been interesting to say the least."

"I am grateful that you and Beth have taken me in. I love spending time with Beth."

"And me?"

"And you," I nodded. "Although I wasn't sure at first."

"The feeling was mutual," John said. "At first." He finished, leaving behind a loaded silence.

I savored the rest of the tea and after finishing it, I spent the time pacing around the room looking at the artwork. The walls were decorated with some random landscapes elevated with mills and quaint round-faced peasants. I also talked to John, but he had other things on his mind, so his answers were monosyllabic.

We had gotten home from the theater at 10 o'clock, but by now it was almost midnight and William still hadn't returned. The clock in the corner struck twelve times and John's jaw hardened. He jumped up and stared at the clock before turning to me.

"It is getting late; you should go to bed," he said.

"What about William?"

"I think I'm going to head out to find him. Who knows, perhaps he's already on his way and I'll merely intercept him." The expression on John's face told me he didn't believe this.

"I'll come with—"

"You can't go out at this hour; besides, it may be a bit rough where I am headed."

"William is my friend now as well and two are better than one."

"Rose, this is no time for games. It might be dangerous," John said, scowling. "You should go to your room."

"If it might be dangerous, there's even more reason for me to come," I said, hands pressed against my waist." We stared at each other with narrowed eyes.

Then, finally, John broke and said, "Fine, but let's hurry. I have a bad feeling." We grabbed our coats and headed out the door.

"Where should we go first?" I asked while John hailed a carriage.

"I figure we try the gentleman's club William is associated with first. Hopefully, we find him there. If not, we'll have to go to some seedier places." The carriage dropped us off in Pall Mall at a tan brick corner building that stood about three stories high with tall windows outlined by cast iron railings and decorative stonework, similar to a lot of the buildings I had seen around here. There were a few men loitering outside on the sidewalk. They were laughing, smoking, and clapping each other on the back.

"You won't be able to come inside, which means you will have to be careful and wait for my return," John said. Then, pointing at the wall, he continued. "Just stay close to here and stay out of sight. I won't be long."

"Fine, but what are they doing in there?" I said, glancing again at the men outside, one of which was now flashing a gaudy pocket watch to his comrades.

"A gentlemen's club is an excuse for wealthy men to get together and drink and gamble," John said, with distaste.

"Not fond of making bets?"

"It isn't one of my vices, no," John said. "Just give me a minute, I should be right back. And please do stay out of trouble." I leaned against the wall while John strode to the front door and knocked on the hard wood. He had said to stay out of sight, but I couldn't resist taking a peek through the window closest to me. Through the glass and past the blue velvet and sheer white curtains, I could make out a large room filled with small tables and chairs, people scattered all around in various poses pointing at the cards and each other. Bright

chandeliers illuminated the many men gathered there, playing cards, or dice, or simply just drinking. The room was almost hazy with the amount of cigar smoke that circulated the
air. It was such a strange sight, seeing these men in their tight
pantaloons red-faced and heated over a game of cards, their
voices loud enough to be heard outside through the panes of
glass.

Smoke filled my nostrils, and I waved my hand to disperse
the foul odor.

"What are you doing there, luv," the man that been showing off a watch to his friends said. He had crept up behind me
without me noticing.

"Perhaps she's looking to sell her wares," his companion, a
beefy man with a less than intelligent expression, snickered as
his eyes raked over my appearance.

"I'm waiting on a friend," I said, trying to be direct and
firm, so I wouldn't give them any ideas.

"Yeah, what's your friend paying then, luv. Sure we can top
'im," the first man said, taking out the timepiece again from
his coat pocket and dangling it in front of me.

"Like I said. I am waiting on my friend. I am not for sale!"
I said, glaring at them.

"Come on, luv, don't be like that," the man said, with play-
ful interest.

"Yeah, come on. We can make it worth your while," the
beefy guy repeated.

"Leave me alone," I said, angry this time but also a bit worried. What was taking John so long?

"We juz wanna 'ave some fun. Come with us to our place
fer some entertainin'." The man with the watch looked side to

side to see if anyone else was around and grabbed my wrist. I had to brace myself against the cobble stones, so he wouldn't drag me away from my spot.

"Let go of her hand," John boomed as he ran towards me.

"I didn't mean nuffin," the man with the watch said, dropping my arm like a hot coal.

I rubbed my wrist as the beefy friend piped up, "We didn't know she was taken."

"Leave now," John said, anger evident in his voice. "Or do I need to notify a constable. I believe we have a captain inside playing whist?" Both men looked stricken as their eyes moved between the entrance of the gentlemen's club and us.

"No need to trouble the cap'n. We's be off now," the man with the watch said, while nudging his friend. "Ave a good night."

Together, they scrambled away into an alleyway, probably to find some other seedier place to hang out, or to find some other poor woman to harass. John sighed and turned towards me.

"See, this is what I was afraid of. Are you certain I can't drop you off back at the apartment before heading to the next place." Then he took my hand and brushed up my sleeve so he could examine my wrist. The skin was chafed a bit raw but wasn't damaged otherwise.

"Are you alright? Does it hurt?" John asked, his full attention on my face while his thumb brushed the tender skin at the base of my hand."

"No, I'm fine," I said, taking back my hand. It crossed my lips feeling a bit like a lie, but my wrist was fine, which meant I was fine, even if the two men had scared me. "Did you get any info on William?" I asked, ignoring the first part of what he said.

John grimaced and shook his head. "I spoke to a few gentlemen; they recalled seeing William about a week or so past which means the last time he's been here was before he came to Hawthorne. One of them, a Mr. Sutcliffe, did say he'd seen William visiting certain gambling hells; in particular, one called 'The Tempest'."

"Did he say where you can find this place?"

"I have an idea, but the more difficult trick will be to get inside. Usually you need to be introduced by someone already a member. It will be a more challenging task with you by my side," John said, looking thoughtful.

"I will not be left behind," I said, poking at his chest. "We go together."

"We'll go together," John nodded, glancing at my wrist again.

23

The Tempest

Finding William had turned into a sight-seeing tour of the darkest places of London, and in some parts, also the smelliest, I noted as the stench of human waste and stagnant puddles of water in this particular alley reached my nose. The brick walls exuded moist breaths that probably contained every pathogen known to man. I kept my arms tight against my sides as I followed John through the narrow passage; a rat scurried past his feet and out of our way. This place was a far cry from the charming shopping street I had visited with Beth or the glittering opulence if the theater. Period dramas never showed this side of history on TV. Instead, it was all balls in fancy gowns, drinks from crystal glasses, games on beautiful groomed lawns, and a lot of lounging on velvet fainting couches. I'd rather be at the Netherfield Ball, or safe at Hawthorne with John and Beth, instead of on a scavenger hunt in the dirtiest places. But William might be in trouble, and we had to find him.

"I believe we've found The Tempest," John said, as we left

the bowels of the alleyway behind and entered a regular, if somewhat dilapidated, street.

"Where?" I said, looking around. I was expecting something similar to the gentleman's club, if a bit smaller and, well, less nice. I didn't see anything resembling a gambling den. The street we now stood on was flanked on both sides with worn down row houses in a brownish color that reminded me mostly of drab days and disintegrating leaves. Aside from a thin man smoking on the stairs leading up to the second story on the corner house, there was no one around. He eyed us suspiciously as John took my hand, and we walked further down the street.

"Gambling hells look like regular houses," John whispered. "They'll leave a door open so regulars can enter, and they usually have someone on lookout."

"That man over there," I said, nudging my head towards the man on the stairs.

"Yes, I assume he is assessing us this moment and if he thinks we might be trouble, he'd run off and notify the person running The Tempest."

"Do you really think William would visit a place like this?"

John huffed and brushed his fingers through his hair. "He didn't use to, but war seems to have changed him. I haven't had much of a chance to talk with him since he got back from Belgium but word spreads fast in our circles and I received information he got in deep with a loan shark. William hasn't said anything to me even though I gave him the chance, but he's different, more withdrawn, although, he manages to hide it well. Something must have happened when he was abroad that changed him."

"He's been having nightmares," I said, biting my lip. "Did you know that?"

"I didn't," John said, shaking his head. Then he looked up at an open door at one of the middle row houses. "Let's go in and hope for the best," he said, taking hold of my hand. We stepped over the threshold and into a short hallway with peeling wallpaper and scuffed wooden floorboards. At the end of it was another door, this time closed. John rapped his knuckles against the wood and the door cracked open to reveal a broad red cheeked face with a large bulbous nose framed by a salt and pepper mustache.

"Who are you?" the man said, his eyes narrowing as he scrutinized our appearance.

"A friend told us about this place, said it was a good spot to play cards," John said. "I'm Mr. Easton and this is my companion, Miss Hart. The man nodded at John's answer and must have thought he looked rich enough to be worth letting in. But then his gaze returned to me and I could see his gears turning again.

"We don't let ladies in," the man said.

"She's my lucky charm," John lied. "I always take her with when I play games.

"I won't be in the way," I added, trying for innocent.

"What's this then?" I heard coming from behind the doorman. The door cracked open wider and I could see the space behind them filled with men drinking and gambling. A second person, tall and wiry with graying hair and dark glinting eyes, now stood next to the doorman. The man wore an outfit with flashy colors that fit slightly wrong as if he had taken mismatched pieces from other people and thought this was what a gentleman should look like. He was dressed like a caricature of what John and even William, regardless of his vices, actually were.

"This 'ere's a Mr. Easton and 'is companion, Miss Hart; they wanted to gamble," the man with the massive mustache and nose said. The wiry man opened his arms wide and flashed a toothy grin.

"Well, how can we not let this gentleman and lady enter our beautiful establishment. I hope you will enjoy your visit," he said loudly. I could tell the men inside were paying keen attention to our little exchange, besides a few young men who were better dressed and must have been there to gamble away their futures, the way they were focused on their cards. "Let's start with the introductions, my name is Stevens and I'm the proprietor of this place." He held out his arm towards me. "How about I show you around inside while your friend here chooses a game he likes," Stevens said.

I reluctantly connected my arm with his and forced myself to smile. John gave me a little nod and found a table to join. "Wonderful place I've got here," Stevens said, leading me around the tables. "But I must say that a lady such as you does brighten the place up a bit."

"You are too kind," I responded. The dusky cramped space could hardly be considered wonderful, but it made the man money, so I guess that was all that mattered. The same peeling wallpaper with drab flowers that was plastered in the hallway was also decorating this room. Sparse furnishings, besides the card tables, and wall sconces were covered in grime and years of filth and dust. It was probably a good thing that the room let in so little light; it made the room appear more hospitable than bright sunlight would have done. My arm was still linked with Mr. Stevens, and we almost came full circle from the walk around the room. John was leaning towards a man playing cards on his right, probably asking if he'd seen William or someone fitting his description.

"I must thank the friend that recommended my humble little place to you and your companion. Who did you say it was," Stevens said. I stammered as I wondered if I should even say William's name but then again, we were here to find him and maybe the owner of this place might know.

"My companion is old friends with Mr. Chambers; he's told us about your place," I said, making sure to pay attention to his body language. "Matter of fact, we had hoped we'd run in to him here," I continued.

Stevens did stiffen a bit but then smiled even wider. "Ah, my dear Mr. Chambers. How wonderful. It is a pity I haven't seen him in a while, so I can't help you there," he said, sounding apologetic. The tone of it however sounded false and his behavior too slick. He reminded me of those car salesmen that helped me when I bought my car. It kept me on edge wondering what else the man had up his sleeves. "It seems your friend is enjoying his game. You must be a good luck charm," Stevens said, pointing at John. He was pulling part of the pot of winnings in the middle toward himself.

"Yes, I should probably join him," I said so I could excuse myself from this Mr. Stevens. "Thank you for showing me around."

"It was my pleasure," he said with a small bow and a flourish of his hand. "Do inform your friend Mr. Chambers that I am also looking for him." That last bit had some bite to it.

I shuffled away and went to stand behind John who was still gambling. Bending over, I whispered in his ear.

"Did you find something out?"

John shook his head then introduced me to the other players. "This is my lucky charm," he said jovially, pulling me against him. "Play along," he hissed in my ear so no one else could hear.

"Ya wanna be my lucky charm then, love? That one doesn't need it," one of the men shouted while pointing at John, earning hearty laughs from the others.

"Have you been lucky," I gushed at John, and he showed off the winnings in front of him.

"This one should go to my lady," he said, taking a locket from the random trinkets and coins and placing it around my neck. It was a pretty silver necklace with fine filigree work; I knew if I opened it there would be space for a small portrait. "With you by my side, I shall use the rest to win more," he said, pushing the rest of the jewelry and coins back to the middle of the table. The men nodded in agreement and joined in for another round. This time, I could tell John was losing and if I wasn't mistaken, he was losing on purpose. I wondered why. A couple of men stood near the drinks at the back of the room, the same men that caught my attention when we entered, playing cards dressed in more expensive clothing. I excused myself from John's side and walked over to the men.

"Such a fun diversion," I said to no one in particular, while making myself look busy choosing a drink, not that there was much to choose from besides mugs of foamy beer.

"What is a lady doing in a place like this?" one of the men, dressed in snug tan pants and a sharp pinstriped flyaway coat, said, swaying a bit. They both had quite a bit to drink.

"My companion wanted to try his hand at cards," I said, pointing at John who was still busy losing. "Our mutual friend recommended this place. In fact, I thought we'd see him here tonight but alas I can't find him," I said, feigning sorrow and moving my head as if I was looking for him. Instead, I used the opportunity to make sure the proprietor Mr. Stevens wasn't around.

"We come here often," the man said, eager to talk to me and be useful. "Who is your friend?"

"Mr. William Chambers."

"He hasn't been here tonight," the other man with a cravat tied tightly underneath his bulging chin said.

"Yes, but I think I saw a man that could have been him on my way over. I believe it was around King Street in the direction of St. James Park," the first man continued.

"You've been very helpful," I said, giving them both a smile. I left them behind, quickly walked to John, and tapped him on the shoulder.

He folded his cards and, in a voice tinged with faux sorrow, said, "My companion is in need of me, so I must adjourn." He gave the other players a nod. "Goodnight, gentlemen." Mr. Stevens must have retired because he wasn't lurking anywhere, but I was sure his henchmen were around keeping an eye on things inside and out.

"Those men I spoke to said they'd seen someone that looked like William around King Street heading towards St. James Park," I whispered in John's ear. "Do you know where that is?"

"I do. Let's go," he said, with determination.

24

Bad Vantage Points

I hoped the man at the gambling den was right, that he had given us the correct directions to William, and even more so that William was alright. John clasped my hand as we hurried out the doors and back into the London night. My shoes made loud noises as we picked up the pace, running down the cobbled street, following the row of buildings until we reached the edge of St. James Park.

The adrenaline in my veins had petered down and exhaustion set in which was not helped by the late hour. I'd need a long nap after this. But no matter how late it was, the park was bustling with life. Torches lit pathways around the park where revelers were singing and dancing. Salesman were hocking wares, mostly liquor and food, and men and women that worked the oldest profession were plying their trade. John and I ignored calls from the people trying to sell their things. The men and women that were scantily clad and signaling at anyone passing them by made me uncomfortable, not because of their lack of clothing— people back home in my time often wore even more revealing outfits— it was the desperation in their eyes. The idea that they were forced to sell their bodies or starve. I averted my eyes and held on tight to John.

"We should comb the park; he might still be here. If not, I suggest we head back home, perhaps he has returned or at the least we can start fresh in the morning or alert the authorities," John said.

"I think that's a good plan," I said. I didn't want to leave without William but if he wasn't here, we didn't have another lead and London was a big place. It would be like finding a needle in a haystack. However, as luck would have it, when we walked past a group of heavily inebriated men, two of them already asleep perched against a tree, I spotted a man leaving the park and crossing the street. He was following another.

I nudged John and pointed. "Is that him? It looks like him, but he's too far away."

John stared at the man disappearing into a side street. "I think you might be right," he said. "We should hurry and follow them." John grabbed my hand and together we rushed to cross the street. The side street we saw the two men disappear into was empty, but we kept moving forward, slowly to listen for sounds. There were voices coming from the right and I saw the corner leading into another alleyway covered with small awnings and clothing lines with some poor persons' laundry.

John pressed his finger to his lips and signaled me before we slowly crept around, moving forward into the shadows. There, William stood with his back towards us pressing another man against the wall. Were they fighting, I wondered briefly before the scene changed and William crushed his lips against the other man's, his hand grazing his hair. I stumbled and grabbed John's shoulder; the sound must have been loud enough to warn them because the man kissing William opened his eyes. He looked scared, pushed William away, and took off running. William looked confused but then he spotted us and froze.

"Will," John edged.

"How much have you seen. How long have you been here," William said, he looked mortified.

"We were worried about you. We didn't know where you were, and we heard rumors about gambling debts."

"Well, now you know." William seemed to steel himself for whatever John was going to say next.

"Are you alright? No one has hurt you?" John said softly. William clearly hadn't been expecting that question. He seemed to deflate and sank to the ground. I was shocked too, not by William kissing a man, but by John's calmness. From everything I had learned, even the most recent past had been less than forgiving to anyone loving differently. I hated how bigots had treated my cousin after he came out. Another thought did pop up. My mind went back to that night at Hawthorne when William was having a nightmare, when he told me he had lost his friend in Belgium during the war.

The ground was dirty and moist from who knows what, but that didn't matter at the moment. I knelt down next to William and grabbed his hand. "Do you remember when you told me about your friend you lost? He wasn't just your friend, was he?" I said.

William looked up at me and tears snaked down his cheeks. "I loved him."

"Why didn't you tell me?" John asked.

"How could I?" William said, his voice breaking. "I couldn't tell anyone and still keep my place in society. Surely you can understand that my feelings would be seen as amoral. Society would disown me; I'd be shunned."

"You could've told me. You can tell me now. You are my best friend; we have known each other since we were children. I hope you know you can trust me with your secrets," John said, with frustration, then softer he continued, "What happened to your friend?"

"James," William said, with a watery smile. "We bonded during training. We only got closer once we were shipped out to Belgium. Every night, we talked about our lives and families, discussed our fears. Then, without realizing it, we started talking about our futures. It became clear that I couldn't imagine a future that he wasn't a part of. We were going to rent apartments in London as bachelors together. That was the plan. He was perfect," William continued, his voice trembling. "The war was supposed to be almost over; we thought we were both going to make it through. But then our higher ups left for a party at an allied house. We had been camped for days with the Prussian army with no word on enemy troops. Our own reinforcements were still on their way and not due to arrive until the next day. I guess we should have stayed on high alert because we were ambushed. Even our vantage point at the windmill hadn't helped our troops spot the French militia coming our way, until it was too late. Our officer wasn't able to get word from the commander and ordered us to join the Prussians in the battlefield. A French soldier shot Jacob as he was loading his weapon right beside me.

I'm lucky I managed to get away with my life, but I can never forget how it felt to see the life leave his body, and our hopes and dreams with it. A piece of me died that day."

"Is that why you've been gambling and drinking so often?"

"When I'm alone, I think of him. I'm trying everything I can to drown out the feelings and thoughts racing through my mind."

"Here, let us take you home," John said, as he reached out his hand and lifted William up off the damp ground. I stood as well and brushed some random debris off my skirt. He swayed a little and smelled like alcohol as he walked in between John and me. "You aren't going to tell anyone?" he said, as John led him towards our carriage.

"We will talk more later but I would never tell anyone," John said. William turned his face towards me.

"You are my friend as well. Your secret is safe with me," I said to comfort him. John nodded and smiled at me as he helped William into a seat. We kept silent while John ordered the driver to take us to William's apartment. We couldn't discuss things when they could be overheard. Back at the apartment, I made sure to pour William a glass of water. He would need it with the amount of alcohol he had probably imbibed. John left William on the chair in the drawing room and pulled me aside in the hallway.

"You will not breathe a word of this to anyone," John whispered. I understood that he was trying to protect his friend and had to make sure I wasn't going to spread rumors. It hurt a little, but I couldn't hold it against him. After all, he hadn't known me for that long. All he knew of me was that I had turned up at his estate out of the blue and had needed rescuing.

"I meant what I said earlier. William is my friend now too, and I would never talk about him behind his back. Furthermore, I believe that every person has the right to love whomever they choose. It isn't anybody else's business who William loves or doesn't love."

The worry lines marring John's forehead smoothed; he let out a sigh, then grabbed my face and kissed me. "Thank you," he said, his breath hot against my cheeks. "He's my best friend, and I was so worried a debt collector had gotten to him or something worse. Thank you for coming with me and helping me find him." Then he stepped back realizing he had overstepped, even though I wasn't complaining. "I apologize. I shouldn't have kissed you. My emotions were heightened. We should return to William; you should probably get some sleep."

"Don't worry about my sleep," I said as I touched my fingers to my lips. They still tingled with the pressure of John's kiss. "I'll sit with you both until William is ready to retire." I followed John back into the room where William was downing the glass of water.

"What happened?" he asked. "You both seem flustered."

"We were just worried about you," John said.

"I'm going to be alright as long as I get Stevens off my back about my debts. I feel relieved that you know about me. However, I don't want you to think differently of me."

"You are the same person that stole apples from Mr. Danvers' orchard and blamed it on me. I think we'll be fine," John quipped, on a more serious note he added, "Is Stevens the proprietor of The Tempest? Let me take care of your debt. Just promise me you'll stop drinking and gambling so much and I urge you to be careful and discreet. Not everyone is as open-minded as of course you are well aware."

"I couldn't possibly expect you to clean up after me," William choked out.

"You are family which means that you can and will take my help when it is offered," John said.

William let out a sigh and nodded. "Would you be so kind as to fetch me a pen and some paper?" he asked me. I found some at the secretary in his office and brought it to him. He scrawled down an address for John. "Stevens' office, it's in downtown London. If he's not at his gambling hell, then he's there." John took the paper from William.

"I shall pay him a visit in the morning; I don't doubt we'll be able to get to some kind of arrangement and you will never have to deal with him again." John frowned before he continued speaking, "On a more delicate subject, the man you were with, do you know him? Do you think he might talk?"

"He was a stranger; I doubt he knew who I was. There's a lot at stake for being like us; I would be surprised indeed if he chose to tell anyone."

"I hope so; I just worry for your safety. Come on, let's get you up to bed." Together, John and I helped William to his room. I sat with him and brushed his hair with my hand until he fell asleep while John stared at us from a wicker chair standing near the window.

"Come, you should get some rest now too," John said. He put his arm around me and led me out to my room. "Thank you. For everything," he whispered as he closed the door behind me.

25

A Reveal

"Are you certain you don't want to come with us and stay at Hawthorne for a bit longer?" John said to William. They had been talking for most of the morning after John had returned from his meeting with Mr. Stevens.

William waved away John's concern. "No, I'll be fine. I promise. With my debt paid..." William looked a bit embarrassed. "My words alone can't sufficiently cover my gratitude and you must let me repay you, but for now, I won't have to worry about Mr. Stevens or his goons, and I will stay away from gambling and alcohol. I still have to get settled in to this place," William said, motioning at the walls surrounding us. "And this might be the right time. A clean slate so to speak."

"Gratitude isn't necessary, and you can always come to Hawthorne," John impressed. "We love your company, but if you have any other problems, please send a letter to me." Then stepping closer to William, he said, "Oh, and before I forget, do you remember what I asked you?"

"If I find out anything, I will let you know," William said, embracing his friend and patting Beth, who looked a bit confused, on the top of her head. Beth had been sound asleep beneath her covers the entire time John, William, and I had been out only to return near dawn. I didn't know how John was still standing upright with so little sleep; he had left only a couple of hours later to deal with Mr. Stevens and had already returned by the time I rolled out of bed and joined them for breakfast. Beth had reprimanded me for my tardiness and poked fun at my appearance. I wasn't the most pleasant person to be around in the morning with barely any sleep, so I bit my lip and said nothing. It wasn't her fault, and I would have joined John again if I had to. She was eager to pack and return to Westbridge. I wondered why since I would think she'd want to explore more of London, but maybe she missed her own home and her own bed. I could certainly relate to that.

"Stay safe," I told William and hugged him as well, his arms tightened around me.

"You and John can always come back and visit me as well," he said. His valet loaded up the carriage with our trunks and new purchases. The clothing we ordered would be delivered to John's home in a week or so. With William waving us off, we took our places on the cushioned seats and left London behind. The sight of the large hedges and columns framing the entrance to Hawthorne brought me joy. Finally, I would be able to sleep without the noises of the road, jostling of the carriage, or the attention of John and Beth. My eyes stung like they were being poked by a million tiny needles, and I was sure that if I looked at myself in a mirror, they'd be bloodshot. I needed to sleep ASAP. Together, we grabbed our belongings and lifted them into the entrance way. Then I yawned loudly while John and Beth set down her trunk in the middle of the floor.

"Rose, you look exhausted. Go retire for the day. Your things will still be here tomorrow," John said.

"But I wanted to give Mrs. Ashbrook her gift."

"Beth can join you tomorrow," John said. "Go on up to bed," he said as if he was talking to a child.

"Okay, I will," I said. There was no need to argue, I could barely stand straight and knew he was right. The bed was soft like heaven when I let myself fall into its fluffy depths, my limbs finally letting go of their tension. My feet were tender from all the walking John and I had done; the rest of my body didn't fare much better, especially with the uncomfortable sitting position during the carriage ride. I napped on and off from the time we got home which was in the mid to late afternoon until the early evening. Then I stretched my legs, used the chamber pot, and took a moment to bend and stare out the window.

The view was lovely. It was still light out, but I could tell by the softening glow encasing the green fields, trees, and garden topiary and glistening off the pond that I had fallen into when I appeared in this place, that the sun would set in an hour or so. There was a figure walking along the path leading past the pond and towards the edge of the estate. I squinted my eyes to see if I could make out who it was. The person was too slight to be John. Beth, I thought, once I recognized the particular sway of her hips. She walked as if she'd rather dance, almost bouncing everywhere she went. I liked that about Beth; she had so much excitement for life that even her body couldn't contain it; there would be no shy shrinking away for her. It was something I could learn from her; I often felt uncomfortable in the spotlight— insecure, worried about the opinions of other people. I watched her dark figure bound further away. She had been interested in hiking, maybe she wanted to go for a walk after such a long time sitting still. Well, it was her home. I shrugged and went back to bed. The pillow and I had an appointment.

* * *

Downstairs the next morning, the gift I had bought in London was beautifully wrapped in a small navy box with a baby blue ribbon tied around it.

"Mrs. Ashbrook is going to love it," Beth said, looking at the package. "Should I have bought something as well?" she said, frowning.

"I don't think Mrs. Ashbrook is going to mind," I said. "Besides, if you are that worried, I can always say that it was from the both of us."

"Oh, could you? I would greatly appreciate that. I wouldn't want your great aunt to think less of me."

"Of course," I said with a smile.

"Oh, that reminds me. John said to ask Mrs. Ashbrook about the dance in your honor and when she might like to hold it and if there is anything he might be able to assist with."

"That is very kind of your brother," I said. The whole idea of faking a family connection with Mrs. Ashbrook still made me a bit uncomfortable.

I thanked Hugh, our driver and handyman, once he

dropped us off at Granhope Manor. "We should only be an hour," I told him.

"Yes miss, I'll be back here waiting for you and miss Beth," the slim middle-aged man said while bobbing his head. Beth linked her arm with mine while I held the small box meant for our host and walked down the gravel path and up the walkway where we were let in by Mrs. Ashbrook's valet. Indoors, the space looked just like I remembered, a Roman revival. It was as if I was walking through a museum with a giant exhibition on statues and marble. The valet led us to the drawing room where Mrs. Ashbrook sat in an ornate chair flanked by two smaller ones, her legs crossed, clearly awaiting our arrival.

"How wonderful to see you both, my dears," the woman said, with the confidence of someone who grew up wealthy and respected. Authority had always been a part of her; once Mrs. Ashbrook told you to do something, declining wasn't an option. "I was told that you two and Mr. Easton traveled to London to visit his friend, what was it, Mr. Chambers."

"We did, ma'am," I said. "And," I continued, holding out the navy-blue gift box to her. "Beth and I brought you a small gift we thought you might like."

"How thoughtful," the woman mused as she took the box and undid the baby blue ribbon. She let the ribbon fall into her lap and opened the lid to reveal a soft, light gray patterned scarf. "It is lovely," she said, running the fabric through her fingers. "Thank you very much. But, please sit down," she said, pointing at the chairs. Beth and I obliged. "Did you have a good time in London?"

"Oh, yes. My brother and Mr. Chambers took us to a play," Beth said. "And Rose and I had a grand time shopping."

"That does sound like a lovely trip," Mrs. Ashbrook agreed.

I figured it'd be better to get John's questions out-of-the-way, so I turned to Mrs. Ashbrook, "Mr. Easton was wondering if you had settled on a date for the ball, and if so, if there is anything he could do to assist."

Mrs. Ashbrook looked thoughtful. "No, my staff has everything well in hand. I was planning on Saturday in a fortnight. Invitations shall be sent out soon. My dear, are you still alright with being announced my heir during the ball?"

"Yes," I nodded. With Beth there, I couldn't discuss our deal in depth.

"I do wonder," Mrs. Ashbrook continued. "Why Mr. Easton would offer to assist me when he has his own party to plan?"

"His party?" Beth said, looking puzzled. I was confused as well.

"What do you mean?" I asked.

"Surely he has told his sister and his ward," Mrs. Ashbrook said, twirling her hand. "I heard from Mrs. Blakeley that he and Anne are to be married. I wondered why you all left for London and thought it might be to put in orders; although, it made no sense why Anne and her mother wouldn't come along." Beth looked shell shocked.

"He hasn't said anything," she stammered.

"Oh dear, I hope it wasn't a surprise," the woman said. "Anne's mother told me that her daughter said that John had pledged himself the day of the picnic. I figured you all would know. My apologies, I shouldn't have rambled on." Beth was quiet but thankfully Mrs. Ashbrook did continue talking because I didn't know what to say either. While my fake great aunt draped the scarf around her broad neck and went on and on about its quality and how the proper choice of gift reflected well on the gift giver, I couldn't help but think back to the day of the picnic. The way Anne had hung on John's every word, kept by his side, the way they had looked together. She wanted John, and now, according to Mrs. Ashbrook and Anne's mom, she had him. But if he was engaged to her, why would he kiss me. His kiss in the hallway after we had brought William back surprised me, but it also had awakened something. No matter how much I wanted to deny it, I was incredibly attracted to John. The more I got to know him and Beth, the more my opinion of his character started to change. His rude initial behavior revealed a man burdened by a lot of responsibilities, including his sister's well-being but also a man who was kind, funny, and generous. I couldn't be sure, but I thought he had warmed up to me as well. This news, if it was true, felt wrong. The idea of John and Anne together made my stomach turn. But what right did I have to be upset? This wasn't my time or place; didn't I want to leave?

"Perhaps John is planning to surprise us with his news, together with Anne" Beth said, contemplative.

"My, that is probably right," Mrs. Ashbrook said.

"Wonderful news," I said, faking a smile. Mrs. Ashbrook gave me a weird look. The woman was perceptive and probably already realized I had warmed up to John. If it was true though, I would keep my distance. I would not be some random dalliance before his wedding. If that was what he wanted, then my esteem of him would sink. Better to keep my distance, even if I had no idea how to get home yet.

26

Isolation and Misunderstanding

"We should probably keep quiet for now," Beth said, biting her lip. We sat together in the carriage with Hugh taking us back to Hawthorne, an uncomfortable tension hung between us. "If John did mean to surprise us, I would hate to spoil it."

I nodded. "I won't say anything." Beth shifted around a bit on the padded seat.

"It isn't what I expected. I kind of thought that," she trailed off. "Well, anyway. His happiness is important to me and if Anne will give that to him then that is all I can ask for."

"Yes," I said, sullen. "Perhaps I should move in with Mrs. Ashbrook."

"Oh no," Beth said, shocked. "I'm sure you can stay; I'd like you to stay. Besides, we still have to wait and see what happens."

"We will wait and see, I suppose. But," I said with a wry

smile. "We both know that Anne isn't my biggest fan and once she is the lady of the house, she might not want me around."

"We will wait and see," Beth repeated a bit sadly. We had promised to keep quiet and not ask John any questions, but it hurt to see him when we got home. Would he tell us the news tonight? He didn't act any different during dinner; he was upbeat and asking us questions like regular.

"Did Mrs. Ashbrook like the gift?" he asked me. I was still caught a bit off guard.

"She loved it," Beth said, sounding almost like her usual self. "Rose was kind enough to say it was from the both of us. Mrs. Ashbrook wore it straight away and regaled us with compliments on our gift giving."

"Did she say when she planned on hosting the ball?" John asked, looking at me.

"Saturday, two weeks from now," I said in a clipped voice. I couldn't help it, faking my demeanor had never been my strong suit.

Beth swooped in once again, "She said she will send out the invitations soon and wanted to thank you for your offer but that her staff has everything sorted." If John noticed anything out of the ordinary, he didn't show it. He simply drank a sip of wine and speared some meat while nodding at Beth.

"Are you looking forward to the ball and your big reveal?" he asked, once again directing his conversation to me after he finished his bite of chicken.

"I'm not sure," I said honestly. "I don't really like to be the center of attention." I looked down at the plate of food I was poking my fork around in. The gossip of John's secret engagement had put me in a foul mood, and I hated pretending to not know while he acted like everything was normal. It felt disingenuous. "I'm sorry, I'm not feeling so well," I said. "Do you mind if I retire for the evening."

"Naturally, I do hope you feel better," John said, he looked a bit taken aback. I wasn't sure if it was worry about my health or if it was about my brusque manner.

"Good night," I said, leaving the table.

"Good night," Beth muttered. Once I left them behind, and I sat in my room, alone and in the dark, I felt silly for being angry with John. It wasn't his fault. Of course, he'd marry Anne; she'd be the top pick for anyone, and it would have happened regardless, whether I did or didn't show up here. I didn't plan on staying, so why be upset with him. I could acknowledge that, but it still didn't mean that I wanted to see or talk to John any time soon. I needed a bit of time and space. Ugh, I thought with vehemence. I just wish it had been anyone but Anne. Avoidance was my plan the next day.

I got up early and ate breakfast in the kitchen with Mrs. Avery busy cooking and cleaning around me. I just nipped at a piece of leftover bread.

"Are you sure you don't want to wait for breakfast with the others? I can make you some porridge; it might be gentler on your stomach," Mrs. Avery said.

"No, thank you, some bread is more than enough for now. But I am going to retreat myself today, so I could use something for lunch that I can take with me," I said.

The stodgy cook and housekeeper fluttered through the kitchen stirring this pan, checking on that pot, and picked up a few odds and ends around the room that she wrapped in a cloth and lowered into a bag for me. I thanked her profusely and slunk out of the kitchen, took a detour to pick up a few books from the library, then left the large home through the back door.

With the gray cloudy sky overhead that promised rain, I figured the safest place to be left alone would be the hothouse. I doubted anyone would want or need to go there during a rainstorm, but I used to love listening to the sound of rain-drops hitting the glass windows in the sunroom of my child-hood home. It rained so rarely that when it did, it was almost magical when those first drops hit the glass with dull pings. I'd curl up on the love seat with a book. My parents deco-rated their house in a kind of western themed farmhouse chic, so the room was embellished with cutesy signs of boots and horses, mason jars filled with easy to keep alive plants, and faux distressed whitewashed furniture.

I leaned back into a bench in the corner of the hothouse in between two large potted plants with green fronds, pulled up my knees, and opened up a book. The clouds had opened up and the rain started, it's soothing pitter-patter on the roof. It was comfortable in there, surrounded by plants with just myself and my own thoughts. Maybe tomorrow I'd be able to fake enthusiasm, but today, I wanted to just be by myself.

A while later, I had to stretch my legs to get some blood flow back into them. I had been engrossed in one of the books I picked up from the library and the drops of water sliding down the glass had lulled me into a faraway world. My fingers slid along the different pots while I walked a circle around the room and did a few awkward lunges. The door creaked and opened behind me.

"There you are," John's voice said. I swirled around and

watched him walk inside. "I wondered where you were. Beth said you weren't in your room and Mrs. Avery told me you were planning to be alone. Is anything wrong; are you still feeling unwell?"

"No, I am fine. I just didn't feel up to company today, that is all," I said, turning around and walking back to the bench. He followed me and sat down next to me.

"I know we haven't had a chance to talk since leaving London, but I thought we should, or at least I wanted to explain a few things," John started.

"It's fine," I said, cutting him off. John frowned.

"I feel like I have done something to offend you. If there is something that is bothering you, I hope you would share it with me. I know that the situation with William must have been jarring for you and I admire your bravery and ingenuity during the whole ordeal. I would also like to apologize for overstepping. My emotions were heightened, and I shouldn't have kissed you."

"I'm not offended," I said. I hoped John would leave me alone again. I knew I shouldn't care about him, but now he was telling me that his kiss was a mistake when it hadn't felt like that to me, even if it couldn't happen again what with Anne and his secret engagement.

"I hope that is true," he said, taking a hold of my hand and squeezing it for a moment. "Something unexpected happened these past few weeks, something I didn't plan, but I have come to care for you. You challenge me when I need it," John said, then hesitated for a moment. He was so charming, sitting next to me in the hothouse surrounded by the flowers he tended to. "I hope you might be amenable to my attentions. I would very much like to kiss you again," he finished with a roguish smile.

"You what?" I stammered, growing red in the face. Then his words dropped, and I got angry. How did he dare to tell me he wanted to kiss me when he was engaged to Anne?!

"What is wrong with you?" I spat, lurching away from his grasp.

"What do you mean," he said, confused.

"What do you think I mean? How can you tell me you want to kiss me when you are engaged to someone else? It's not fair to play with my emotions like that."

"Now, wait a moment," he said, as he stood. "This is the first I heard of that." He reached out for my wrist, but I pulled my arm away and backed up more, bumping into the wisteria.

"Mrs. Ashbrook told Beth and I all about your upcoming wedding to Anne Blakeley," I said. My face ashened, tears started running down my cheeks. This was one of my character flaws that I hated the most; whenever I got angry, I would cry. How could anyone take me and my anger serious if I stood sniffing and crying in front of them.

"Why didn't Beth say anything?" John said, way too calm for my liking.

"She didn't want to spoil the surprise reveal she thought you were planning."

"Oh," he said. "Rose, I'm not engaged," he added, his eyes boring into mine.

"You are not?"

"No, I am not."

"Oh." I shuffled on my feet and swiped at the wetness beneath my eyes.

"Is this why you were ill and why you wanted to be alone after you got back from Granhope Manor?" John asked, his face softening. I nodded. My nose runny.

"It was a bit of a shock," I added lamely.

"I want you to know that I would never do that to you," John said. "I meant what I said, I like you. I don't have any kind of understanding with Anne Blakeley.

"She told Mrs. Ashbrook that you proposed the day we all played croquet."

"I don't know why she's telling people that story, but I've only ever talked pleasantries with her. Anne has always been interested in me, or more likely my name and estate; it's easy to know that, but she's never been my type." He reached out for me again and this time I let him. He pulled me towards him and enveloped me with his arms. "Rose, my sweet Rose. Please don't think the worst of me. I want to pursue you, but only if you are willing. We can take our courtship as slow as you'd like, as long as you let me have the first dance at your ball."

I giggled; I couldn't help myself, then gasped from the tears. My face was smashed against his chest and my weepy cheeks left splotches on his shirt. John took my face in his hands and laid a soft, chaste kiss on my lips. He still managed to have a roguish twinkle in his eyes when he added.

"I promise I won't soil your reputation." I gave him a friendly little shove and wiped my face with the back of my hand.

Then more seriously, I said, "I feel dumb for being so upset. I should have just asked instead of believing what I heard from Mrs. Ashbrook."

"If I was in your position, I would have thought the same thing," John said magnanimously.

"Well, I promise I won't get fake engaged then," I retorted.

"Will you come back inside with me? I'm sure Beth would enjoy your company, and we could tell her together that Anne Blakeley will not be a part of the family."

"Thank god," I said, with a deep sigh. John let out a rumbling laugh. I picked up the bag with food and the small stack of books while John led me outside with his hand resting at the small of my back.

27

The Heir Apparent

The dresses Beth and I ordered in London had arrived a few days before the ball hosted by Mrs. Ashbrook was to take place. Everyone who was someone in town had been sent an invitation on an elegant piece of paper. It had no mention of me except that there would be a surprise to be announced by the hostess herself. The town gossips had been buzzing all week, even dropping by our doorsteps to pump Beth for information. More often than not, I had to disappoint the ladies because Beth was nowhere to be found. I wondered what she was up to, but it wasn't my business to investigate if she wanted to be alone.

Estelle was styling my hair and helping me dress for the event. It was odd that Beth wasn't there yet. Normally, she wouldn't shut up about fashion and going to social engagements. I was about to go find her when she walked in to the room.

"Rose, I hope you'll forgive me if I don't join you tonight," she said.

"Are you not feeling well?" I said with concern. She didn't look sick, but she did look a bit flustered; her cheeks were red, and she was fidgety.

"Yes, I think I just need to stay in bed today," she said, avoiding eye contact and looking down at the ground.

"That's too bad; I know you like balls and dancing. I can tell you all about it when I get back," I said. "Are you sure?" Something felt a bit off about her. "Do you need me to stay with you?"

"No, you enjoy the ball. I am fine. I'm just going to go to bed," Beth hurried to say. She seemed eager to leave.

"If you are sure," I trailed off.

"I am. You enjoy your evening." Beth nodded and sidled back out of the room. Her behavior was odd but I chose to set it aside so Estelle could finish the updo she was creating in my hair. I was both nervous and excited all at the same time, but the gorgeous dress I was now wearing helped to put me in the right head space. Dressing the part always made everything better. As a teen and as an adult, whenever I got sad, I would cheer myself up by doing my make-up and picking out a cute outfit even if I had nowhere to go. Clothes were there to be worn in my opinion, unlike my mother who only took out her "good" dresses for special occasions and expressed that it was wasteful to wear nice clothes at home. I missed her and my father though; they would have marveled at the way I looked tonight. My grandmother would have agreed as well; she believed in dressing up for yourself just as I did. She wouldn't go anywhere without a strand of pearls around her neck and hanging from her ears. When she was younger, she wore pretty dresses, but from the time I could remember, she had changed those in for tailored pants, classy shirts, matching cardigans, and a petite leather watch on her left wrist. I ignored the sadness that squeezed my chest; her loss was still so immediate. I still couldn't wrap my head around the fact that she had been here in Westbridge just as I was now. Thankfully, Estelle had finished my hair, so I gushed and thanked her for her help. Now wasn't the time to go down memory lane; I had a party to go to and, I thought quirking my lip, a man to dance with.

Mrs. Ashbrook had outdone herself. The entire driveway to her large home was illuminated by candles that combined with the Roman statues and neatly trimmed hedges forming pathways in her garden with small seating areas in hidden alcoves, creating a romantic setting with the sense of wonder that anything might happen. John and I weren't the first guests to arrive; the front door stood perched open and there were clusters of people all throughout Granhope Manor, leading from the foyer to the ballroom, up on the first floor and also outside through the French doors, admiring her backyard. Everywhere you looked, her staff had placed candles and lit sconces, bathing the entire estate in a golden glow that made the furnishings richer and the guests more attractive. A couple in the hallway were taking in the splendor of a statue of a nude man posing thoughtfully, yet another was staring at a painting of maidens dancing in flimsy dresses.

John linked arms with me, and we both followed the guests until we reached the ballroom which had a busy floral wallpaper and gold trimmed wainscoting. Little seating areas were created around the room. A group of musicians was getting ready to play in a corner. On the opposite side, a table with refreshments was set up which is where I spotted Mrs. Ashbrook talking to her valet.

"I'll go talk to her," I said to John.

"I'll wait for you," he said. "As long as you remember our deal."

"I do," I said and walked towards Mrs. Ashbrook. Halfway there, I turned around and flashed him a smile; John winked back.

"Ah, there you are, my dear," Mrs. Ashbrook said as soon as she saw me heading towards her. "Alphonse, will you hand Rose a glass of champagne?" she directed her valet. "One for me as well." I accepted the bubbly drink with a smile. Mrs. Ashbrook took a sip of hers and stared at my dress. "The gown suits you," she said.

"Thank you," I said, a bit nervous now that the announcement would be soon and then the full attention of everyone in attendance would be on me.

"I see most guests have arrived, so it will be time to officially start the ball. I hope you are ready, my dear. Just remember to smile," she said, giving one of her own rare warm smiles. "Let's begin," she said, striding to the center of the ballroom. I looked around again for John. Quite a crowd had shown up by now, but I spotted him standing by an elderly couple, he gave me a quick nod. I strengthened myself and went to stand beside Mrs. Ashbrook.

The clear ringing sound of the small spoon hitting the side of her crystal champagne glass drew the attention of all the guests gathered in the ballroom and even the ones outside were now filing in to see what was happening.

"Thank you all for coming this evening," Mrs. Ashbrook

started, and I had to tell myself not to fidget with my fingers or dress while I stood next to her. Already, I could hear people whispering, wondering what I was doing there. "In my invitation, I promised a surprise," her deep authoritarian voice said, with a flair of the drama. "This evening, it is my pleasure to introduce you all to my grandniece and heir to my estate, Rose Hart. Now, without further ado, Rose will open this ball with the first dance."

The stout woman ended her speech and without aplomb, strode away leaving everyone in the room to come to terms with her revelations. I could see the shocked faces staring at me. The musicians were starting the first notes of a waltz and John thankfully rescued me from standing awkwardly by myself in the middle of the room. More couples joined us, and I heard snippets of their gossip.

"Heard she just appeared out of nowhere," a tall woman with a pointy chin said.

"Took advantage of Mr. Easton," a girl with glasses and mousy hair said.

"-swindling the old bat," a rotund man in a black suit said to his wife who was equally wide. Not everyone was as negative, but almost everyone was curious about me and about the news.

"Just ignore them for now," John whispered, while leading me through the steps. I nodded. Focused on John twirling me around the room, everyone else vanished. I might have fallen into a strange situation but at that moment, dancing with John, was meant to be. There were other handsome men in the room, something about the formal attire did it for me, but no one looked as dashing as John.

My heart fluttered as his lips turned into one of his dimpled smiles and his eyes sparkled with mirth. "I hope you've made a decision," he whispered into my ear. John smelled like something manly and woodsy, like he'd been chopping fir trees near a campfire. I couldn't help but picture what he would smell like on top of me.

"Why are you blushing?" he said, as he pulled back.

"It's just a bit warm in here," I said. "And as for your question, I might be amenable," I added, a little shyly.

"How amenable? Only a little or—," John goaded. His hand trailing down my back.

"Let's wait and see when we are back at Hawthorne," I said with a grin. John and I followed the music, moving across the floor where we reached the side of the ballroom once the waltz ended and the musicians moved to the next.

"Mr. Easton, what an extraordinary story, taking in a young woman on her own and then finding out that she's Mrs. Ashbrook's grandniece. How marvelous," a middle-aged man in a severe suit with his brown hair stiffly plastered down said. His companion, a pretty young blonde, turned towards me.

"Miss Hart, you must be so excited to have found your family. How has living with Mr. Easton been? My name is Jane Rigsby; my husband imports silks. I do hope we will see you at one of our parties."

"Mr. Easton has been incredibly kind and generous and Beth has become one of my best friends," I gushed.

"Is she somewhere around here?" the blonde asked.

"She unfortunately felt ill so chose to stay home," I said. "I do hope you excuse me; I see someone I know," I added to get away from the young woman. John led the silk merchant to the refreshment table. His wife followed them, so I could sneak away from the crowd for a moment.

The Blakeley's were also in attendance. Mrs. Blakeley looked shell shocked; the poor woman probably still had to reconcile the fact that her daughter would never inherit this place like she hoped. Anne, for her part, was glowering at me from afar. Only Mary and her brother, Rudolph, appeared to be enjoying themselves. Mary was dancing with a young man in a military uniform, grinning from ear to ear and Rudolph was being attentive to the refreshments laid out on the table, his plate piled high with sugary treats. I squeezed past the guests blocking the doorway and walked down the hallway, nodding and smiling at people that were congratulating me.

The attention was a bit overwhelming and I just needed a breather before I returned to the ballroom; although, I wouldn't mind another dance with John, thinking back to the way his fingers skimmed my dress. Just one wasn't enough. I should've gone and thanked Mrs. Ashbrook, but I didn't know where she had wandered off to. There were a lot of people in the foyer as well, but I didn't spot my supposed great aunt. I did see what I thought was her silver haired head up on the landing. I climbed the grand staircase leading to the first floor.

Looking down at the foyer, I could have sworn I saw William's wavy hair cut through the crowd. However, that was impossible; William was in London. I did look around the crowd gathered near the entrance but didn't see the man I thought I saw. My nervousness must be making me see things. I was never one for crowds and now this was my second ball, and I was being accosted by strangers. Perhaps Mrs. Ashbrook wasn't a fan of crowds either, and she went upstairs for some space. That didn't fully fit with my impression of the woman though. She took charge and said and did as she pleased. I highly doubted something as insignificant as a crowd would fluster or bother her.

28

Conversations of a Con Artist

At the top of the grand staircase, I found Mrs. Ashbrook solitary and admiring the view of guests mingling on the marble floors below. "How did you find the attention?" she asked, a champagne glass clutched in her bejeweled fingers. The woman in front of me was such an enigma. On the one hand she enjoyed gossip, hosting a party, and to judge by the amount of jewelry dripping from her, she also liked being the cause of envy. But then she separated herself from the crowd willingly to be by herself and appointed me her grandniece so the ladies in town would stop bothering her. I wondered what her story was; she must have an interesting one, living the way she did.

"I needed a breather from the crowd, and I wanted to thank you," I said.

"You were perfect, my dear," Mrs. Ashbrook said. "You looked lovely on Mr. Easton's arm, opening the ball. He is interested in you for more than a companion for his sister; I can tell." I blushed. " I thought so," Mrs. Ashbrook said with a knowing smirk. "I see it is reciprocal. Pretending to be my grandniece has been beneficial for you. Without my accolades, you probably wouldn't be able to make that match."

The woman perhaps thought I agreed to her scheme to marry well but I had only gone along with her plan so I wouldn't be kicked out of John's house. He was so suspicious when we met, and where would I have gone if that happened? "I think I chose well," she said, with an air of superiority. "None of the girls in town seemed gentle and deserving enough. With you, I won't have to worry about interference in my estate any longer. Will you come live at Granhope Manor? I could always use a companion for when it suits me."

Shaking my head, I answered, "If it is alright with you, Mrs. Ashbrook, I would like to stay with John and Beth."

"Yes, I assumed you would want to stay and snare that handsome young man. His sister already adores you. If I was a betting woman, I'd say we could expect a wedding soon."

"Oh, I don't know about that," I said, slowing her train of thought down. She motioned at me with her hand, her lips puckered a bit.

"Be a dear and help me to the chair over by the side table." I held on to her arm and walked her to the small chair standing next to the side table which was overlooked by a large, gilded painting of what appeared to be Mrs. Ashbrook in her younger years, the proud aristocratic chin and piercing eyes gave it away. I wouldn't have considered the woman in the painting conventionally beautiful, but she was striking. Back in those days, she would have had her pick of suitors, another reason it was odd she now lived completely alone, besides her staff members. "My gout acts up in the evenings. You should leave an old woman alone; Alphonse will see to me soon. You should go and enjoy the ball, dance with your man; the party is in your honor, after all."

"Thank you again, and I will go and do just that," I said, with a genuine smile. I should find John because one dance with him wasn't enough.

I left the elderly woman behind and started my descent down the staircase. There, a few steps down, so he was just out of sight, stood John.

"I was just coming to find you," I said, but he didn't appear happy to see me. His expression was odd. Downstairs near the entrance, I saw William looking up at us. I gave him an excited wave which he returned. "I thought I recognized William earlier but thought I had imagined it," I told John. "What is he doing here?"

John frowned and ignored my question. "Rose, I need you to come with me now," he hissed.

"What's going on? Is something wrong?" I said. What could have happened to change his mood so suddenly?

"Just come with me," he urged as he grabbed my hand. I followed him down the stairs, through the crowd of people. I flashed a quick smile at William as we passed him by, then John took me down another hallway. There were fewer people there, but he still wasn't satisfied.

"John, talk to me. What is going on?" I asked.

"In here," he responded as he opened a door, looked around for witnesses, and shuffled us into a small room.

"Was it your plan to get me alone," I said, with a quirked brow. The glower on his face made me quickly lower it.

"How long have you been planning to con Beth and I?" he asked, his hands curled into fists at his sides.

"What do you mean?" I said, backing away and bumping into the wall. John turned the lock on the door.

"I overheard you and Mrs. Ashbrook talking."

"Why were you spying on me?" I demanded.

"Dammit, Rose, answer the question," he said, slamming his palm against the wall.

"I'm not conning anyone. I would never," I said, stricken.

"You've been lying about your family, and for whatever reason, Mrs. Ashbrook has been helping you. Was the inheritance of one estate not enough so you had to go for me and my sister as well?"

"No, I swear it's nothing like that."

"Then what is it, Rose? Tell me the truth." John looked disillusioned and disappointed, but how could he ever believe what happened to me?

"I can't," I said, resigned.

His disappointment turned to anger, and he yelled, "William came to find me today because I had asked him for a favor. I asked him to find information on Mr. Danby. He was new in town and Beth clearly liked him, so I wanted to make sure he wasn't hiding something. William found out that Mr. Danby is actually a con artist that travels around, visits towns like ours, and promptly marries young women with large dowries. The man has left a trail of broken-hearted and ruined girls everywhere he's been. Now, imagine my surprise when I wanted to find you so you could greet William, and I

could tell you the news, just to overhear you and Mrs. Ashbrook talk about how you lied about your identity and how
you planned to snare me into a marriage."

"I didn't mean it that way. You misunderstand; you heard
all wrong," I said. I reached for him, but he shrugged my hand
away.

"Then I started to put things together," John continued.
"How could two strangers just show up nearly simultaneous
in our little town, both liars no less. I have to give it to you,
the fake family story and the way you seemed to care about
Beth almost had me believe you. To imagine," he said, trailing
off. "I thought we were real." John sounded anguished.

"You should tell Beth about Mr. Danby," I said.

"You have no right to mention my sister any longer or fake
concern. Against my better judgment, I trusted you. I thought
there was something between us worth exploring. You played
me like a fool."

"John, please—"

"What could you possibly say," he said, his face pale.

"Let me explain."

"No, this has gone on long enough," John said, pacing
around the small room which, upon second thought, might
just be a storage closet. "I want you gone. You are going to go
to Hawthorne to pack your bags and then you are going to
leave and not come back."

"Don't do this; I haven't done anything wrong," I pleaded.
I grabbed John's bicep and stopped him in his tracks. John
looked me straight in the eyes.

"I forbid you to talk to my sister. If she does see you, you
will say nothing and fake an excuse. I'm sure you can lie one

more time; it must come natural to you by now," he said, with a bite.

"Where am I supposed to go?" I bit back. A mixture of sadness and anger was coursing through me; the heartbreaking way John looked at me caused guilt to flare through me for ever lying to him, even if it was to protect myself. It made my heart ache that the man I wanted nothing but to kiss was treating me like an enemy. Despite the sadness, his hotheadedness and quick to judge attitude set my teeth on edge. Hadn't he known me long enough to know that I would never con him or Beth? He wouldn't even hear me out.

"Where are you supposed to go?" John said in a strangled voice. "How about your co-conspirator, Mr. Danby, or what about Mrs. Ashbrook? What did you promise her that made her name you her heir, or does she not know the full picture? Should I inform her?" he said, crossing his arms.

"Don't bother," I said, dropping my hand off his bicep. I didn't know what to do or where to go, but it became clear John would not listen to me. "I will go," I said, biting my lip to hold back the tears now forming in my eyes. The last thing I wanted was to draw attention to myself in the midst of this party and all the guests.

I wiped my cheeks with the back of my hand and scraped my throat, then I unlocked the door and quickly stepped out. I knew my face would still look red, but I hoped the people at the party would take the bright cheeks as a sign of a healthy flush.

William still stood in the foyer, mingling with a few other guests— a lady with thin lips and highly coiffed hair wearing a burnt orange gown with frills, and a man whom I assumed was her husband with a large mustache and a cravat tied underneath his double chin, matching her dress. I shook my head at him which made him look confused and concerned.

"What's going on?" he mouthed. But I couldn't talk to him. John would soon probably fill him in about my supposed misdeeds and I hated the idea of everyone I liked in this time and place thinking of me as some kind of criminal. He tried to stop me, but I sped past him, avoiding his gaze. I wanted to leave the foyer before John would reach me. Seeing him again was the last thing I wanted. I had to use the anger that was driving me at this moment because I was afraid that soon that feeling would leave and all that would be left was sadness and fear. To think that last night, when I was lying in bed, I had actually contemplated staying. What if I could go home, would I want to? Yesterday evening, snuggled up in the large poster bed, with John's soft kiss fresh in my mind, I wasn't sure what my answer would have been.

"Excuse me," I said to an elderly man I had nearly bumped into as I hurried out the front doors. He huffed a bit, muttering about youths and their disrespect of their elders. Out in the front garden, the dark sky stretching above me, and surrounded by candles, I stopped and breathed in deeply. I just had one question for myself. What should I do now?

29

An Old Acquaintance

I would still need clothes. However, did I really want to return to Hawthorne at the moment? Would I be able to stay with Mrs. Ashbrook? What if John told her his theory about my teaming up with Mr. Danby and she also kicked me out? My mind was racing with questions and trying to think of solutions. Oh, why couldn't I figure out how to get home, I thought angrily.

John and I had arrived here by carriage, but I didn't see Hugh parked anywhere. Would he have gone to wait at the stables or was he back at Hawthorne waiting until a later time to pick us up? I figured the least I could do was check.

Following the illuminated pathway through the gardens, I walked around the perimeter of Granhope Manor, past the west wing, and into the backyard. I was heading north to sneak off towards the stables at the back of the estate, when I heard a voice calling my name. Oh, no, I thought as I turned around and recognized the woman calling for me. On a bench between two statues of women in gauzy dresses, sat Mrs. Blakeley and her eldest daughter.

"Mrs. Blakeley, how lovely to see you." I feigned a smile.

"Is everything alright? You look a bit out of sorts," she said.

"No not at all, I merely went outside for a breath of fresh air."

"One can get overheated from all that dancing," Mrs. Blakeley agreed. "Anne and I were just talking about the wonderful news this evening." Judging by Anne's face, she didn't think it was wonderful. "To think when you first arrived at Mr. Easton's doorstep, we all thought you were someone of low birth, only to find out you were Mrs. Ashbrook's long-lost grandniece. You must be thrilled."

"I am very grateful."

"Since you have found your station, it would perhaps be useful to find more ladies of your standing to surround yourself with. My Anne perhaps," Mrs. Blakeley said, nudging her daughter who reluctantly grimaced at me.

"Maybe," I said, looking around. I wanted to leave. "I should go though."

"It would be beneficial, especially since Granhope Manor borders the Hawthorne estate, and as I'm sure you've heard from Mrs. Ashbrook, my Anne has an understanding with Mr. Easton," Mrs. Blakeley conveyed as if she was telling me an important secret. Anne smirked. I couldn't believe they were trying to sell me the same lie they did Mrs. Ashbrook. What was their end game? With everything going on, I didn't care anymore about fitting in or playing it safe.

"What understanding is that?" I said darkly.

"We will soon be engaged to marry," Anne sniped.

"Ah, from my understanding, Mr. Easton isn't aware of this plan at all," I said, wiping the smiles of both the elder and younger Blakeley's face. "Should I fetch John and tell him the good news?" I asked, motioning towards the ball room. The two women looked stone faced. "No?" I said. "Well, then I shall be going. Enjoy the party."

The small victory over Anne didn't make me feel any better. Who was I kidding, with me out of the way, she would probably still manage to finagle her way into marriage with John. She for sure would be gloating when she found out about my current predicament.

The music being played could be heard through the open French doors, which enabled guests to roam the gardens and ballroom freely in case they wanted a breath of fresh air. At the moment, the musicians were playing an upbeat tune, probably some kind of folk dance. I gazed back at the billowing sheer white curtains framing the doorway and the smooth dance floor that lay behind. I had been looking forward to another dance. Standing in the middle of the doorway, staring straight at me, was a familiar woman. She wore different clothing than when I last saw her— a navy-blue empire gown with sky blue gloves that fit in with the surrounding crowd. But I recognized the glasses that were too modern and which, when I would get closer, would have vivid green eyes behind them, and her bushy hair even if she had it restrained into a regency up do at the moment. As soon as our gazes crossed, she turned and disappeared into the crowd. I forgot about my plan to check the stables for Hugh; I had to find her. It took me a moment to remember her name, Melinda. A lot of time had passed since I saw her, and I only met her once in that bookstore, which is where I was before I turned up here.

I raced across the grass, balancing on the balls of my feet so my heels wouldn't sink into the dirt, slid through the doorway and into the ballroom, then craned my head to see where she went. I caught a glimpse of dark blue fabric at the entrance to the main hallway.

"Ah, there you are; I hoped I would find you. Would you do me the honor of dancing with me," Randolph Blakeley said, stepping away from his conversation with an elderly couple.

"I'm sorry, I have to go," I quickly shot out as I pressed past him and another group of guests. The people gathered in the ballroom stared at the way I was hurrying, but I had no time to lose. I broke into a sprint down the hall as soon as the pathway opened up, my heels pounding the marble floor. A few guests ducked out of my way, pressing themselves against the walls, muttering curse words at the insane woman racing past them.

Maybe the stress of it all had finally done me in. I was going crazy and actively seeing things that weren't there.

"Excuse me," I yelled at a couple standing in the middle of the foyer. They skipped back, looking angry, and I continued out the front door, sliding a bit when my feet hit the gravel. My heart raced. It wasn't my imagination. Melinda the bookshop owner, she was really here. She stood outside calmly waiting for me as if nothing strange was going on.

She smiled gently and said, "How about we take a walk?" I nodded, wheezing and trying to catch my breath. I hadn't kept up with my cardio as much as I should have while living the regency lifestyle and Mrs. Avery's cooking was very good.

"Who are you?" I asked as soon as I could breathe without my lungs burning.

"Melinda, the bookshop owner," she said, without a hint of sarcasm.

"No, really? Who are you? How are you here? Why am I here?" I rattled off. We walked along the gravel driveway, away from Mrs. Ashbrook's house.

"Well," Melinda said, turning towards me. "Those are a lot of questions, so how about we take them one at a time. My name is Melinda; I am the owner of the bookshop. For your second question, I traveled to your story to check up on you."

"Check up on me?" I said, gob smacked.

"Yes, I wanted to know how it was going," she said, as if she was asking me about the weather.

"I have no idea what anything you said means. What do you mean when you say that you traveled to my story? Why do you need to check up on me?"

"My bookshop is special," Melinda said. "It recognizes when someone is in need of a story of their own. Your mind called out to my store and it appeared for you so you could find the place you were meant to be."

"The bookshop is sentient?" I said, worried.

"Not sentient exactly, but certainly intuitive. You," Melinda said, poking my chest, "were in need of it and now you are here. I dropped in to see how you were handling your new surroundings. Did you find what you were looking for? I remember you said you were looking for adventure and romance."

"I showed up here without knowing how or why. The person I was staying with yelled at me and kicked me out of the house, and now I have nowhere to go and the whole town will think I'm a criminal. Can you or the damn bookshop take me home?" I said, scowling at the woman.

"Oh my, you have been through a lot," Melinda said. "Yes, I am here so you can make a choice. Do you want to stay here, or do you want to go home?"

"That's it? And then I'll be back home? Will time have passed? Wait, the book—"

"Which book is that?"

"My grandmother's, the book that led me to your shop. I met a man here that knew her when he was younger. She was here just like I was.

"Yes, but she decided it would be best to go home. She didn't want to leave her parents. You will have to make your own decision; stay or go, it will be up to you. Whatever you decide, you will find yourself back with no time passed."

"I need a moment," I said.

"You can, but don't take too long; I don't have forever."

I left Melinda standing near the end of the driveway while I paced around in circles. Home, I could go home. I still had no idea how this worked, but she said I could be back home without anyone knowing I was gone. But... John and Beth. Could I really leave without saying goodbye to Beth? John had yelled at me and kicked me out of his house, but I couldn't help that my heart clenched at the thought of never seeing him again. But if this was all some kind of story in a book, then what should I care, I tried to tell myself. It didn't work, this world felt real, not at all like a story. However, there was no future for me here. I had a life, family and friends, and a job back home. Here, John was never going to speak to me again and with his interference, I might not even be able to live with Mrs. Ashbrook. What was I going to do? Be a beggar on the streets? John hated me and I didn't belong here.

"I want to go home," I said, returning to Melinda. I flinched when I said it.

"Are you absolutely certain?" she said.

"Yes," I said, even as doubt was coursing through my mind, making my eyes water. I glanced back at the grand house, hoping against all odds to catch another glimpse of John. Of course, he wasn't there; he was probably off in a room some-where, talking to William. Melinda took out a book from a fold in her dress— a slightly worn pale green hardcover with my name etched on the spine.

"This is your story. Once you open it, you'll return home." She quietly watched me as I took the book from her hands. I grazed the soft fabric stretched over the hardcover, clenched my teeth, and flipped it open.

30

Pride and Prejudice

"If life were predictable, it would cease to be life and be without flavor," was one of my favorite quotes by Eleanor Roosevelt, even if it had absolutely nothing to do with my life. I had always chosen the easy, predictable path. I listened to my parents, went to school for teaching because it seemed like the safest bet, and I stayed with Michael. He was good-looking, from a good family, and had a good career. So what if he didn't make my heart flutter? Heck, if he had asked me to marry him, I would have agreed without a second thought. My life was following a checklist. And then he cheated, and my grandmother died, and I ended up back in time, relying on myself in a situation I couldn't have imagined in my wildest dreams.

I was still holding the book with my name on it but now, instead of standing next to the gravel driveway leading up to Mrs. Ashbrook's estate in the dark of night, my eyes were adjusting to the bright dessert sky, the sun glinting off the storefront windows I was standing in front of. A homeless person holding a sign stating he was a veteran in need of a job was boldly staring at me, open-mouthed. I looked down at myself. No wonder he was staring; I was still dressed for a ball. A couple of shoppers exiting the store pointed and giggled at me. My equilibrium was returning, and I recognized where I was. It was where the bookstore had been. But while the dollar store was clearly thriving, the space the bookshop had occupied was boarded up and a for sale sign was tacked on the door. I didn't know how to feel about that. Something inside myself was telling me that I had made a huge mistake. I had lamented to Nicole about how I needed an adventure and as soon as I got one, I did nothing but think about how to get out of it. That conversation with Nicole felt like it was ages ago. In fact, it was. I had been gone for weeks. Living at Hawthorne with John and Beth. For my friend that same conversation would only have been a couple of days ago.

I walked the few blocks to my grandmother's house, drawing attention from anyone I came across, used a spare key hidden in a fake rock in her flower bed, and entered the empty home. The purse holding my phone, wallet, keys, and other odds and ends was at the bottom of John's pond, so instead of taking out my mobile phone, I used the landline to call Nicole. I needed someone to talk to.

She found me a couple of hours later, sitting on the couch, staring at the wall, still wearing the gown. "Are you okay? I came as soon as I could," she said, as she walked into the room and went to my side. "What are you wearing?" She grabbed a fistful of the slick fabric.

"I think I made a horrible mistake," I said, burying my face in my hands. Nicole hugged me tight.

"What is going on? You can tell me. Is it about your grandmother or Michael?" I shook my head.

"This may sound strange, but please hear me out."

"Hear you out about what?" I fidgeted with my nails then jumped up.

"I need some coffee."

"Okay, and then you'll tell me? I have to say that you are kind of worrying me."

The coffee pods were where my grandmother had left them in the kitchen cupboard. I popped one into the machine and waited for the water to heat. Nicole pulled out a stool and sat down at the kitchen island. Strange how much time had passed for me since my grandmother's funeral, but now that I was back home, it really wasn't that long. Her home still looked the same, as if she could walk in at any moment. The banana cream pie my aunt made for the funeral was still in the fridge; I cut Nicole and I a large slice. I pulled a stool around and went to sit across from her at the marble topped kitchen island. After a sip of hot bitter black caffeine to fortify myself, I continued.

"Something strange happened to me. Do you remember that book I found? The one with my grandmother's name on it?"

"Yeah." Nicole nodded. "Did you find out where it's from?"

"Well, kind of—"

"Kind of?" She took a large bite of pie.

"Well, it led me to this bookshop and then I kind of went back in time."

"Wait, hold on," she said, dropping the spoonful of pie

she was shoveling towards her face. "Back in time? Like some Outlander shit?"

"Like some Outlander shit," I agreed.

"Are you pulling my leg," she said, raising her right eyebrow. She had the warmest dark brown eyes that reminded me of hot chocolate, which were now looking at me like I was being an idiot. Nicole had one of these faces where everything she thought would be plain to see for everyone. If she didn't like something, you would know even if she was being polite about it.

"I am not," I said. "Look at my dress," I added, grabbing the full skirt and lifting it above the marble top.

"I agree that your dress does not look like something you can buy at Ross. You said you went back in time, to when? And why haven't we missed you?"

"The Regency era, right after the war with Napoleon. I was in England."

"In England?" she said incredulously. "Did you meet Mr. Darcy?"

"I'm serious, Nicole. Do you remember the book with my grandmother's name?"

Nicole scrunched her eyes. "I remember you mentioning it. You said you found it when you were cleaning out her bedroom."

"Yes! That book, it zapped me. Then, when I went for a run, I couldn't help myself. I ran multiple blocks until I reached a bookstore. The owner spoke to me. Then, when I browsed the books, I remember disappearing. It was strange. One minute I was inside the bookstore, the next I was outside in the grass. I spent weeks there. Until the owner of the bookshop reappeared, The owner of the bookshop, she found me there and gave me the choice to return or to stay." I ran to the living room and retrieved the hard-covered book with my name on it. "Look," I said, handing it to her. "She gave me this to return home." Nicole was weighing the book in her hand and checked out the first few pages.

"Have you read this?"

"No."

"You should. I would read mine if I could. I am wondering though, if you were in the past, why didn't we miss you? It doesn't seem like any time has passed."

"The book shop owner said that time worked differently. I was there for several weeks."

"Who is John?" Nicole asked, pointing at the first page. "Is he why you said you made a mistake?"

"I don't want to read it," I said, shaking my head.

"Are you sure? I would, if I had the chance." Her finger brushed my name embossed on the cover.

"No," I said fervently.

Nicole closed the pages and put it aside.

"John," I said. "We had a fight. I was living with him and his sister at his enormous house and I had to lie about where I was from so I could stay. He found out, thought I was a scam artist, and kicked me out." My hand was shaking as I took another sip of coffee.

"You liked him," Nicole stated.

"I really, really did. Not at first though. At first, I thought he was a pompous asshole," I said with a wry smile. Nicole laughed.

"And then?"

I glanced at my book and back at Nicole. "Then I got to know him, saw how much he cared for his sister, how he shouldered the responsibilities of running a household, the lengths he would go to help a friend in need. He was arrogant and funny, infuriating and kind."

"And hot," Nicole added slyly.

"Yeah," I giggled. "Definitely hot. You should have seen him in his tight pants and tailored jackets; they really showed of his butt. There were a lot of things I wanted to do to him behind closed doors." Then I sighed. "But he hates me, and I chose to return home."

"Are you sure that's what you wanted?"

"I don't know if I have that option. Besides, even if I could return, what would I do there when I couldn't even go back to him? You are here, and so is my family, my job. No, what happened to me was an adventure. I told you I wanted one and now I can go back to living my life." I steeled myself for what I was about to say. "John and Beth and my life in Westbridge will just have to be an interesting memory." Suddenly, the gown constricted me. I pulled at the sturdy fabric. "I need it off," I said urgently. Nicole stood and pulled at the laces, then helped me slip the dress over my head, so I was left standing in the air-conditioned kitchen wearing just a shift dress. I dumped the dress over the back of a kitchen chair and found a tee and a pair of leggings in the bedroom I was staying in while I was supposed to be packing up my grandmother's home.

"Do you feel a bit better now that you are comfortable?" Nicole asked, settling in downstairs on the couch. "I think we need pizza for dinner, and I am going to stay here tonight."

"You don't have to; I'm okay."

"Yeah, nah. You went through something insane. I am here if you need to talk some more. Or we can watch a movie. How about Pride and Prejudice?" she said with a wink.

"With Colin Firth?" I laughed.

"As if there is another choice."

While Nicole ordered in dinner, I put away the cups and plates we had used earlier. I didn't really know what to think or feel about being back, but I was grateful for Nicole's presence. My day had been strange, emotional, and exhausting and after a few slices of pizza I fell asleep halfway through the movie, cuddled up on my grandmother's old couch with Nicole. In my dreams, I saw John's face and Beth's.

"Why didn't you say goodbye?" Beth was saying, anguish evident on her face.

"I didn't mean it," John was shouting at me. I turned away from his looming figure and ran, tripping over my own feet. Then I was on the stairs, but I couldn't move. Estelle, Hugh, and Mrs. Avery were all staring up at me.

"How could you?" they said in tandem, as they raised their arms and pointed at the balustrade. My eyes followed the direction of their fingers and I screamed as Beth toppled over and fell down in a flurry of fabrics. I squeezed my eyes shut so all I could sense was the sound of her body hitting the floor. My heel slipped and instead of on the stairs, I was now outside at the Sunny Acres Cemetery, standing beside an open grave. My grandmother and John, dressed in all black, were throwing flowers in the dirt hole.

"You weren't there," John said accusingly.

"I wanted to be," I shouted.

"But you weren't," John said, shaking his head. "You weren't here."

31

Home Is Where The Heart Is

I woke up drenched in sweat, my shirt clinging to my back. The dream still spooked around in my head, the distorted versions of Beth, John, and my grandmother. Shrugging off the clothes I slept in, I headed towards the bathroom and turned on the shower, then dropped the shirt and pajama pants in the laundry basket.

The warm water beating down on my head and back helped soothe the ache in my body and mind. There definitely wasn't anything quite like modern plumbing; a shower made you feel much cleaner than just washing yourself with a cloth and the occasional soak in a tub would do. I lathered up with soap and added plenty of hair conditioner to my strands. An hour later, I walked out of the bathroom with my hair wrapped in a towel, finally ready to face the day. Nicole had also woken up and was pouring a cup of coffee.

"Black, right?" she said, sticking out her tongue at me.

"Yeah, thanks," I said. I preferred my coffee dark and bitter, but Nicole liked hers to hardly resemble coffee at all with the amount of creamer, sugar, and other flavorings she would add. During winter, she'd spice it up with a packet of hot cocoa in a concoction she called "café cocoa" to sound fancy. I've tried it and it actually tasted pretty good, even if it didn't taste like coffee, but I would never tell Nicole that.

"Did you find any creamer for yours?" I asked, picking up the mug of hot liquid and taking a big sip.

"Yeah, there were some powdered packets in the cupboard and I just added a bunch of sugar. Do you wanna pick up breakfast on the road? You needed to stop by your mom's and your own place, right?"

"Sounds like a plan. Mom has a spare key to my place, so I'll be able to get into my apartment and get the rest of my stuff that I need, like my other set of car keys."

"Let's swing by your mom's first then."

Nicole and I sipped our coffees then headed over to my parents' house which was only a fifteen-minute drive. Mom was asking us to stay for breakfast, but I waved away her invitation, even though Nicole gave me the side eye. She loved the pancakes my mom made; they were a frequent occurrence whenever Nicole and I had sleepovers when we were teenagers.

"Did you have to make us miss your mom's pancakes?" she whined when we were back in her car with the key to my place in my jeans pocket.

"I know, I just didn't feel like talking. I'd want to say something but what good would it do? You know how crazy my story sound."

"Hmm, I guess so," Nicole said. She tapped her phone and pulled up a list of breakfast places near us. "I don't have long; I'll have to go in to work soon but how about we grab something to eat here before I drop you off," she said, showing me the page.

"Sure," I nodded. "Sounds good to me."

We ate at a breakfast and brunch place that specialized in egg dishes; Nicole stuffed herself with pancakes drizzled with blueberry syrup and a side of bacon and scrambled eggs. I ordered a southwest omelet with tomato, Cotija cheese, and avocado. After that filling meal, we stopped by my apartment so I could grab my keys, then she took me back to the place where our morning started. I waved goodbye to her from the driveway and climbed into my own car.

Next stop, the bank. I spent my entire morning and most of my afternoon getting a new bank card, then got a new phone and synced it to the cloud so it had all my data again. My final errand was picking up some groceries: yogurt, bread, tortilla's, ground beef, and some random fruits and snacks. Once everything was stored either in the fridge or pantry, and I sat down again on the couch, the mundane nature of the day sinking in. If I had never ended up in Westbridge, then I might not have even realized how boring my life really was. Work, cook, eat, clean, sleep, repeat. Nothing more than the same things repeated ad infinitum. Sure, life there could be monotonous as well, but mostly, there was so much to learn and explore— social engagements and balls, learning how to cook and bake from Mrs. Avery, hiking and horseback riding, and that was just the tip of the iceberg. It was also the first time people were interested in me as a person where what I said and did mattered. Here, I had Nicole, and I was grateful for her, but on the whole, people here lived their lives never fully connecting with one another, only drifting past each other on their way to various obligations, sometimes forgetting to see each other in person at all. Just a "like" on a shared picture as a reminder that they are still there.

Checking the messages on my phone, a notification that said I had a new voice-mail popped up. I pressed play and held the slim metal case against my ear, a familiar voice started speaking.

"Hey Ro, I know it's been a while since we talked, and I just hate how we left thi-" I had to pause the recording. What the hell did Michael want, calling me after the way we broke up? I continued the message again. "-ngs that day. We both said some things we didn't mean, and you know I always cared about you. I just, I've been thinking that we should give it another go. Whaddaya say?"

My jaw about hit the floor. He wanted to get back together after he cheated on me and called me boring? The thing was, if he'd asked before I went to Hawthorne, I probably would have said yes, would have justified his cheating as somehow being a symptom of me not being everything I should be in our relationship. However, that Rose was gone. I learned I could be resilient and strong and that I didn't need a man like Michael to feel like I'm fulfilling some path to adulthood. I tasted something rich and sweet in Hawthorne and it's my fault I am missing out on that; John was upset for good reasons and I should have fought to stay, to explain to him. Instead, I took the cowards way out. I accepted Melinda's offer and was whisked back to a safe time and place that offered me only stagnation.

Shit, I really did lose it all. I looked at the green book Nicole put on the dark wood coffee table draped in a large doily, picked it up, and weighed it in my hands. I wondered if I should read it. Perhaps it would give me some closure. Or, it would ram home how much I gave up. The idea of all the people in Westbridge being reduced to words on paper bothered me. They were real people with hopes and dreams, and I couldn't imagine a world where I couldn't see and hear Beth's loud laughs or Johns cocky struts, and winks that he seemed to reserve only for me.

I decided that even if it hurt, at the very least, reading my story would be like reliving some of it. The parts with John definitely came across the same on paper, his thawing towards me and the glimpses of vulnerability. Then I reached the part of our fight at the ball. He felt so betrayed and disillusioned, it was hard to read with my regret still so fresh. I expected that to be the end of the book but there were still some pages left.

John, together with William, left for Hawthorne. London was too far to go back to that night. John went to check on Beth but found her room empty. I read on with shock and dawning horror; she had left a note.

Dear brother and Rose,

I apologize for the deception, but I do have some great news. When I return, I shall be Mrs. Danby. We have been meeting in secret and due to some unfortunate family trouble, my Ambrose

*wanted to keep our impending marriage between us secret. I do hope
you will be happy for us and welcome us both with open arms.*
    Yours faithfully,
    Soon-to-be Mrs. Beth Danby

John had accused me of being in league with him but after
the revelation of his character, I never thought he managed to
get to Beth. I knew she liked him, but they'd hardly seen each
other and then only in public. She'd been heading out hiking
a lot, I thought. Maybe that's when she'd meet with him. The
rest of the pages weren't much better news; John and William
set out to find them but had no idea where to start. In the
end, Beth returned to Hawthorne alone with her dowry and
virginity gone and her husband off to scam new unsuspecting
women.

That couldn't happen to Beth. John had to find her before
it was too late. She had such a bright light, and that man
should not be the reason it was snuffed out. I stuffed the book
into a bag, snatched my car keys, and drove to the dollar store
I had reappeared at. The same homeless man with his veteran's
sign was sitting out front, leaning against a sign.

I got out of my car and started shouting "Melinda" and "I
need to go back". My hands raised and I pleaded at the skies,
subsequently worrying every person in my vicinity about my
sanity. I couldn't give up even if I looked like a crazy person.
Somehow, I had to get back, and if her and her store had
found me once, they could do it again. I stared at the empty
storefront then angrily walked around the buildings, but
nothing happened. Upset with myself, I plopped down on the
sidewalk not too far away from the homeless person.

He was looking at something behind him then yelled, "That's it. I've had enough, I'm out of here."

I got up. The empty storefront was gone. I walked into the building and in the middle of it stood Melinda.

"You didn't have to shout, you know," she said.

"Can you take me back?" I said urgently.

"If that is your wish, then I can make it happen. But I hope you understand that I don't run a taxi service."

"I do. And it is; I just need a moment," I said, pulling out my phone. I was going to leave home, more than likely forever, and I wanted Nicole and my family to know where I was going and that I'd be alright. I texted Nicole and asked her to explain it to my parents.

"I love you Rose and I want you to be happy. Go live your adventure," she texted back. Her support felt good even if it might mean that I'd never see her again. I pulled the book out of my bag after I put the phone back in my pocket.

"Are you ready?" Melinda said, as she stepped towards me and tapped the book with her fingers. She handed it to me. The cover exuded heat in my hands.

"I am," I said and opened the page.

32

Wild Goose Chase

I stood in the middle of the gravel driveway. Mrs. Ashbrook's brick home, with large symmetrical windows framed by shutters, and an entrance way embellished with ivory columns, loomed in front of me. The party was still happening, no time had passed. I didn't care that I now looked out of place, my feet pounded down the gravel. It was imperative that I found John.

"Excuse me, have you seen Mr. Easton?" I said to an elderly man moseying around in the foyer.

"Err, I'm not sure," he said, bewildered by my appearance.

"Okay, thanks," I said, moving on down the hall. Anne was walking down the hallway talking to her mother. I tapped her shoulder. "Hey, have you seen John?"

"What," she murmured as she turned around and took in the sight of me.

"What in God's name are you wearing?" her mother uttered with shock.

"That's not important right now," I said, waving away her question. "Do either of you know where Mr. Easton is?"

"Why do you need to know?" Anne said suspiciously.

"Do you or do you not know?" I said. I didn't have time for her attitude.

"Did you have a falling out?" She quirked her brow.

"Anne, can you answer the question?" I said scowling.

"Fine, I believe I saw him out in the back garden talking to his friend."

"Thanks," I said and ran off. The look of surprise on her face was almost comical, if I had had the time to laugh.

Her mother shook her head and muttered to Anne, "I can't believe she is the heir to this place."

At the doorway, I hesitated for a moment. The ballroom was still packed with guests so there was no way I could sneak by unnoticed. Screw it, I thought, and I walked in, head held high. A hush fell over the room; even the musicians stopped playing their instruments, notes ending falsely. The gathered guests who were socializing in small groups here and there were now all gawking at me. Mrs. Ashbrook had returned to the dance floor and stood arm in arm with an older gentleman in curtails wearing his hair greased back; she looked displeased with what she probably thought was a dramatic social faux pas on my end.

"Where is her dress?" a lady with blonde curls piled high upon her head gasped. I pretended I couldn't hear the low murmuring gossipers as I strode deliberately through the crowd, cutting across the dance floor and out the double doors. The band picked up a new tune, but their music was now overshadowed by the loud discussions the guests were having about my appearance and what it would mean for my social standing.

"Now, now. There must be a good reason. It might be a new fashion choice for ladies in America," I heard Mrs. Ashbrook say as she tried to do damage control.

John was talking while William waved around a cigarette that he was busy smoking. I strode briskly towards them.

"What are you still doing here?" John said, at the same time that William said,

"What in heavens name are you wearing?"

"I'm sorry, William, I need to speak with John," I said.

"I have nothing more to say to you," John said, pointing in the direction of the driveway. "You should leave."

"John, perhaps you should hear her out?" William said, dropping the cigarette bud to the ground and extinguishing it with a twist of his shoe.

"How can you defend her after what I told you?" John snapped at him.

"You didn't give me a chance to talk," I said. John shook off William's hand.

"No, I didn't need to. I heard enough."

"No, you presumed to know," I said pointedly.

"You said it yourself. You lied to me. And Mrs. Ashbrook confirmed that you were trying to seduce me into marriage."

"She doesn't know the full story."

"So, there is more?" John said, uttering a laugh utterly devoid of humor

"What is the full story?" William frowned.

"I just, I, dammit." I tried to think of how to explain it to William, but I didn't know how, and I thought it was easier if

I just got John alone. "John, this is about Beth. I need to talk to you alone."

"What about Beth?"

"Come with me," I said, grabbing John's hand. "I'm sorry, I'll explain to you later," I told William. He looked a bit perplexed.

"Fine," John said with venom as I pulled him away from his friend. Once we were far enough away that we couldn't be overheard, I stopped. "So, what is so urgent that you had to accost me while I was with William, dressed in whatever clothes those are," John said, crossing his arms. "You were wearing a dress only a short while ago, why change?"

"Okay," I said, swaying a bit from the nervous energy that had been building up inside of me. "This may sound strange, but you have to promise you'll hear me out."

"Why?"

"Please, just promise," I urged. John nodded with suspicion.

"I promise."

"The story I told you and Beth was a lie, that is true, and I deeply regret that I had to do that. However, at the time, I didn't have another option. You see, I'm from the future, almost two-hundred years."

"What are you getting at?" John said, shaking his head in disbelief.

"Let me finish. You promised you'd hear me out." John nodded again for me to continue. "When you jumped into the pond and helped me out, I had just been dumped into this year and place; I had no idea what was going on. I lied for my survival when I had no clue how long I'd be here or who you all were."

"That makes no sense," John said.

"Just look at my clothes," I said, gesturing at my denim jeans and teal peplum shirt. "When you left me after your angry accusations, the person that sent me here showed up. She gave me a choice; stay here or go home. I went home."

"If you went home, then how are you here now?"

"I was getting to that. For me, it's been two days since that conversation. I touched a book which led me here and when that person showed up with the same book. I touched it again, and I was back in America, in my own time. But this time, the book had writing in it, everything that happened while I was her and even after I left."

"Rose, that sounds like a fairy tale. How do you expect me to believe that? Your clothes do look different and I don't understand how you could have changed out of your dress and styled your hair differently so fast, but you are asking me to believe in the unbelievable."

"Look," I said, pulling the cell phone out of my back pocket. "This is proof. This is my phone." Johns' eyes were flitting between my clothes, phone, and the place William was standing in the distance, probably because with this unreal bombshell being dropped on him, his only urge was to run. He did the opposite; instead, he stiffened even more. "Here." I handed him the phone. I had unlocked it and opened the photo gallery. "We use it to talk to people that are faraway, just like we are having a conversation now, and to take photos, portraits, of ourselves or our friends or things we like.

"How does this work?" he said in awe. He swiped through the pictures and observed my phone from every angle.

"Well, I'm afraid I don't really know. We just buy it."

"So, you really are from the future?" he said tentatively, staring at me.

"Yes." John held out the phone toward me again although he hesitated, his fingers tight on the metal as if he didn't want to let it go. "John, there is more," I said, taking the phone and putting it back in my pocket.

"What is it?"

"The reason I came back. It's Beth. I read the book and found out about Mr. Danby. John, he took her." My voice filled with urgency. "He seduced Beth into eloping; they could be on their way to London as we speak. We need to go after them right away."

"Eloping? Are you sure?" John said. "They've never been alone together."

"That's not true. Reading the book, I found out that she's been sneaking off to meet him in secret. I did see Beth walking outside a lot but at the time, I thought she was just taking up hiking. I never imagined she was meeting him."

"We'll have to hurry. I'll need to tell William," John said, his eyes wide. John and I ran towards William who was standing around waiting for us to be done with our talk.

"What is going on?" He noticed the worried look on John's face.

"Beth's in trouble; she's eloped with Mr. Danby. They are on their way to London as we speak. William, can you find a driver to take you to the constable? Rose and I will go after them, but we could use the backup."

"Of course. I will go right away," he said, looking at the both of us. "But does this mean that John was right," he said, his question directed at me.

"No, I was wrong; Rose is helping us." John squeezed Williams upper arm. "Now, go and alert the police. We will go after them. Rose and I will explain everything to you after."

William nodded and took off towards the side of the house. John grasped my hand and together we ran towards the stables. Hopefully, Hugh was there with the carriage ready to leave.

We found the gentle groundskeeper and driver resting his eyes, sprawled out across the seat. John tapped the glass and Hugh shot up.

"What's that," he muttered, looking around, then he spotted us through the glass. "Mr. Easton, Miss Rose, how can I help?"

"Hugh, I need you to take us to Hawthorne, post-haste. We have no time to waste. And when we get there, I will need you to saddle the two fastest horses; I think Damian and Brutus will do."

"Yes sir, right away sir," Hugh said. He reconnected the horses in front of the carriage as fast as he could and had us on the road to Hawthorne in record time. John and I were bouncing in our seats with the speed we were moving across the uneven terrain and a myriad of potholes in the road. Hugh drove up the main entrance and stopped so we could jump out, then led the horses around towards the stables.

"I just want to check her room," John said.

Mrs. Avery greeted us pleasantly at the front door. "How was the ball?" she said.

"I'm sorry, but do you know if Beth is still here?" John said.

"What do you mean?" the stout, motherly woman asked, with her hands on her hips. "Beth went to her room early tonight; she wasn't feeling well."

"Let's hope we are wrong, and we find her sound asleep, but we'll have to check," John said to me as he ran up the steps.

"What is going on?" Mrs. Avery asked me.

"We think she might have eloped with Mr. Danby. We found out that he is a con artist and has seduced other wealthy women before."

"No!" Mrs. Avery exclaimed. "Not my Beth, she wouldn't run away with a stranger."

"I hope you are right," I said. "But Hugh is saddling horses for us in case we have to go after them." John emerged from the upstairs hallway and headed down the stairs with a crumpled paper clutched in his hand.

"Is she?" I said, but he shook his head.

"No! John, you have to find her, bring her back," Mrs. Avery said, frantically clutching her apron." I grasped her shoulders.

"We are going after her immediately. We will find her." John hurried down the stairs, and we left Mrs. Avery behind in the doorway, her hand lifting as if to wave us off but then she wavered and pressed her fingers against her mouth. Hugh handed John the reins to Brutus then proceeded to give me a boost to Damian's back.

"Are you sure you'll be able to keep up?" John asked. I nodded steely. "Alright, let's set off then."

"Good luck!" Hugh shouted after us. We rode in tandem down the path leading to the main road which was lined with a green ditch on one side and a row of knotted willows on the other.

"Which way do we go?" I asked, looking at John's profile.

"You said they were headed to London. They could take the main road, the same one we took when we visited William, or the back roads. However, I doubt he would take the back roads; they might go unnoticed that way and be harder to follow but the point of leaving while we were detained at a ball was to gain distance fast. I hardly think that crook would worry about us following them any time soon."

"I agree," I nodded. John sped up and I spurred on Damian to keep up. "What was on the paper?" I shouted over hooves hitting the dirt. It was fortunate I returned wearing my jeans; the idea of horseback riding in a ball gown didn't sound appealing and changing in that case would have taken too long with the many layers that left me trussed up like a goose.

33

A Great Big Whack

We followed the main road from Hawthorn to the cross-road where we could either turn left for the center of West-bridge or right to follow the country road until we connected with the larger main road that led through the bigger towns and cities to guide travelers on their way to London. Our clothes were already getting dusty from the road and it was a chore to keep an eye on every bend and twist when it was black out except for the moon and stars which offered little light to guide us.

"Are you still alright?" John said, looking back at me. He was keeping up the gallop but both horses were winded, Brutus had spittle flying from his bit.

"You don't have to worry about me. I'm fine. We just have to keep this up until we find Beth," I said, brushing flyaway hairs out of my face with one hand and holding on to the reins with the other.

"Ho, boy," John said, gentling his horse down to a trot and patting him on his flank. I pulled up beside him. We couldn't keep up the gallop the entire time, but neither could Mr. Danby and he'd be driving a coach with Beth and whatever things she brought. The extra weight meant they were traveling slower than us; it just depended on how much of a head start they had gotten.

"On the main road, a coach can reach up to eight miles an hour," John was explaining. "But that is in perfect conditions, depending on the horses and the state of the roads. Especially in evening conditions, it might be half that, whereas we are riding light on two of my best horses. If they aren't too far ahead or have taken a different route, there should be no reason why we couldn't find them before they reach London.

"London was about a four-hour ride, wasn't it?"

"Yes, it's about thirty miles away. However, we do need to get to them before they reach the city. Once they disappear into its depths, we'd be hard-pressed to find them. I wouldn't know where to start. Danby could be taking my sister anywhere; London is a large place to get lost in."

"We'll find her," I said, hoping my conviction would reassure John. He contemplated the situation while we rode on in the dark, a bristle from Damian here, a neigh from Brutus there, and the constant rhythm of hooves hitting the dirt.

Coming up on our right was a tollbooth, its guardian already stepped outside to welcome us. John leaped off Damian and led him to the round-faced man. I followed suit.

"Have you seen a carriage come by not too long ago?" John said.

"Perhaps," the man said, noncommittal. "This is the main road to London; we get a lot of traffic."

"Even this late at night?" John asked, looking around. We

hadn't seen anyone on the road after we left behind the smaller ones that led back to Westbridge. "We are trying to find my sister. A man took her; he would've been driving a carriage with a young blonde woman; he'd be dressed like a dandy."

"Now that you mention it," the man said. "Might've seen them no more than a hour past, could be less. Tall fella, had an ornate cane just for show. He was in an awful hurry and tried to stiff me on the tolls. But as I always say, tolls gotta be paid, else we get no maintained roads, and no one wants to be riding o'er naught but potholes."

I gasped excitedly. "John, that has to be him."

"You are quite right," John told the toll booth man, and paid him his dues. "Is there some water for the horses?"

"Behind the booth, there's a trough," the man said, pointing in its direction.

"Thank you," I said, at which the man nodded, then John and I led our horses around to let them drink.

"If we hurry, we'll be able to catch up with them soon," John said to me when the horses were watered, and we were back in our saddles.

"I just hope William manages to get the police to us."

"We can hope for the best but assume that they may take a while. We probably will have to confront and stop Danby on our own." John let out a wry smile. "I might have to keep Beth locked up in her bedroom after this is all said and done."

"I know what you mean," I said, shaking my head. Then, more serious, I continued, "Mr. Danby is an asshole, taking advantage of Beth when she's seen so little of what happens beyond the walls of Hawthorne."

"I didn't know," John said, downcast. "I was just trying to keep her safe but by trying to protect her, I made her vulnerable, naive."

"It's not your fault. You did what you thought was best, as any parent would have done. You had to raise Beth after your parents died and I think you have done a marvelous job. Not every man would have taken up those responsibilities and been so caring with his kid sister."

"I didn't have a choice," John said plainly.

"That's not true. Everyone has a choice and your reaction right there tells me everything I need to know about who you are as a person. Beth is lucky to have you as a big brother, and I am lucky that I've gotten to know you."

"You say that as if we won't have more time to get to know each other," John said, staring at me, his gaze a bit uncomfortable.

"I don't know. I mean, when I left the first time, it was because of our fight."

"Do you want to go back after we find Beth? Did you only come back because you felt obligated to tell me about her well-being?" John asked.

"No, God no!" I exclaimed.

"Because I'd understand, if you wanted to return to your own time, that is. You must miss your family and the conveniences you have like that phone thing you showed me."

"I mean, I would miss them," I said. "And yes, I'd miss some modern inventions."

"You must tell me about some of them before you go," John interjected with a painful look.

"But I don't want to go. I'd like to stay here with you and Beth, if you'd have me."

"Are you completely sure?" John said, straightening his back. I nodded. "Just to make sure there are no misunderstandings then, I intend to court you after this, if you let me."

"I would like that a lot," I said. John grinned widely.

"That is settled then." I smiled a toothy smile as well and immediately guilt hit me that I was so happy when we were still racing to find Beth.

Our chase wasn't done yet. We had been riding for many miles and there were still more to go. My butt and calves were aching from being in the saddle for so long; my muscles would need a long hot shower to relax, something I couldn't do anymore.

"I think I can hear them," John hissed. I pricked up my ears and tried to listen past the sound of our own horses beating down the road. He was right; it was faint, but I could hear something heavy creaking and hooves hit the ground in the distance. We urged Brutus and Damian on and soon saw the dust kick up in front of us from a wagon riding fast ahead. I had to shield my eyes from the sand and grit being flung our way.

"Are you sure it's them?" I shouted towards John.

"No, but it has to be them. Who else would be out here at this time. A normal person would have found an inn to stay at." John sped up Damian even more.

"Beth," he shouted hoping for an answer from his sister. John caught up with the carriage and rode alongside it.

"For God's sake man, stop the coach," he shouted at the man sitting in front. Danby looked back at John and me with anger and determination written in the lines of his face. He slapped the reigns, so the two horses spanned in front of the carriage picked up their speed. "Danby, don't be a fool. Your coach won't be able to outrun my horses," John urged.

"Let us go," Danby shouted.

"I will not let you go but, if you stop so I can return with my sister, I promise I won't follow you." Danby shook his head and kept driving the horses on. John slowed down a bit and reached out and tapped the wooden shutters as hard as he could.

"John, what are you doing here?" Beth said, as she opened the shutters and saw her brother riding to keep up with the carriage.

"Beth, Danby isn't what he seems," John shouted out of breath.

"What do you mean?" Beth said, then she directed her voice at Mr. Danby. "Percy, please stop."

"Return to Westbridge," Mr. Danby slung at John.

"Beth he's trying to marry you to get to your money. He's done it to other girls." Beth looked horrified.

"He can explain," she yelled. "Percy, stop the carriage. Let us talk." She looked even more horrified when the man showed no intention of stopping, and he was instead urging the horses on, jostling the carriage erratically, shaking her around inside.

John hurried beside the two horses and made a grab for the reins. My heart skipped a beat seeing Brutus so close to the wheels of the carriage and John bent away from his horse, his right arm stretched out towards the leather leads. One false step could make him fall and get caught between hooves and heavy turning wheels; they'd turn him into pulp. Beth stuck her face out of the window.

"John, be careful!" His fingers tapped at the leather and slipped. I held my breath. He reached even more.

"Danby, stop this madness," he shouted. John lifted almost completely out of his seat and with a big heave, he grabbed a hold of the lead and leaned back into his saddle. Pulling the leather towards him, he managed to get the two horses to slow down. Danby was seething.

"How dare you," he said, but control of the coach was now fully in John's hands. A few hundred meters further, the horses and carriage made it to a full stop. John jumped out of the saddle and ran to the coach door. I jumped off Damian as John held the door open for Beth.

"John, look out," I screamed. Danby emerged from the driver's seat at the front of the carriage with a gun pointed at us.

"I told you to let us go," he said. "Beth go back inside," he motioned with the gun.

"Beth, get behind me," John ordered. Beth's eyes flitted between the two men and the inside of the carriage, then backed up slowly to stand behind John.

"Percy, what are you doing?" she said, a tremble running through her every word.

"He was going to take you to London to get a hand on your dowry and then leave you with nothing, weren't you Danby?" John said.

"Is that true," Beth said, cowering behind John.

"You might've been the last one, with the size of your dowry," Danby sneered while he gestured with his gun.

"I trusted you," Beth said as if she couldn't believe the turn of events.

"I have to thank your brother for your naivety," Danby said, then straightened his aim and he returned his focus to John.

"How did you know where to find me?"

"Simple deduction," I yelled from the side of the road. Danby turned his head towards me, and John rushed forward to snatch the gun from him. Danby, however, noticed and reacted too fast; he pulled back his dominant arm and with the other, hit John square in the chest. John stumbled.

"Beth," I hissed at my friend and John's sister, while wildly waving my hands. She ran to me just as Danby fired his gun and narrowly missed John. Beth ducked down next to me in the weeds at the side of the road. John had leaped behind the carriage for coverage, but Danby was still holding the gun. It wasn't a fair fight.

"You should've let us go," Danby said again, his attitude bolstered by the metal in his hand. "Perhaps I should settle down with your sister after all. Once you are gone, she would inherit the entire place, isn't that right? That's easy enough to take care of," he pointed the barrel towards the sky.

"Danby, man, see reason. The constable is coming for you. Your scheme is up," John said from his hiding place. There wasn't anywhere else for him to go and Danby was inching closer.

"Stay quiet," I whispered to Beth. Then I crept along the side of the road, hoping that Danby wouldn't notice me. I was glad it was nighttime, which helped hide us. It seemed I was in luck as he was too focused on his own ego at the back of the carriage, regaling John with what he would do with the money. I tiptoed my way to the front of the carriage on the left side. John noticed me from the other side and shook his head, but I held my pointer finger against my lips and continued to look for anything I might be able to use. My hand felt around on the floor by the driver's seat and my knuckled bashed against something hard and smooth rolling around. I pulled it out as quietly as I could and recognized it once I had it in my hands. Danby's cane, he had used it for show when Beth and I met him when we went to Norah's.

My fingers curled around the stick and I stalked close to the side of the carriage. I wasn't sure what I should do but then I heard Danby's slick voice again.

"There you are," he said, together with a cocking noise. I could hear John trying to shuffle away.

"No," roared out of me and I leaped around the back and whacked the cane as hard as I could, aiming at Danby's skull. It connected with his head with a hard thud. A deep grunt left him, and he sagged to the ground like a sack of potatoes. With my eyes closed, I gave him another whack for good measure; the man deserved it. John ran towards me.

"Are you alright?" he asked, then snatched the gun out of Danby's hand and checked the man's breathing. "He's alive, but you hit him hard. He will most likely be asleep for a while." John took the cane from my hands. "Rose, you just saved me. Your bravery astounds me; I don't know how to thank you." I squeezed my arms around him. No reason to keep up propriety any longer, I thought. I needed a hug, and I needed his body against me. At first, he stiffened at my sudden attack, but then he relaxed and rested his cheek against the top of my head and squeezed me back.

"Are you both safe, what happened?" Beth said, as she tentatively walked towards us.

"Rose here gave Mr. Danby a great big whack with his cane and saved my life," John said as he let me go. Beth gasped.

"Good. I wish I would have." John looked back at the man passed out at our feet.

"Can you help find some rope? We should tie him up before the constable and William arrive and before he wakes up." Beth nodded.

She found some inside the padded coach benches which John used to tie Danby's hands and feet together. With a quick pat down, to make sure the man didn't have any knives or other sharp objects on his body, John carried him inside the carriage, dropped him on the seat. He fastened the end of the rope around a beam. Strung up like a chicken, Danby was unable to even hop away from us.

34

An Indecent Proposal

"I have to ask again," John said. "Are you certain you want to stay here, with me, and not return to your own time and your own family?" I nodded and opened my mouth to answer but he pressed his index finger against my lips. "Because, if you aren't, I will let you go even if it would pain me to do so. However, if you say you are, I will never let you go and you will not get the chance to change your mind. I don't think I could bear to say goodbye after I let you into my heart."

He grabbed a loose lock of my hair and tucked it behind my ear. We were standing in his study, dusty from riding, and a bit sore, but safe despite everything that happened. John and I explained everything to Beth, to her growing wonder and horror. Shock finally took its toll on her and she was now sound asleep in her own bed. The same couldn't be said for Mr. Danby; he was now in custody of the law and wouldn't be sleeping in his own bed for a long time, if not forever.

"I instructed my friend to explain my situation to my parents. They will know where I am and why I have chosen to go. I can't pretend that it wasn't a difficult decision, but I've grown fond of Hawthorne, of Beth, and Estelle, and Mrs. Avery, and Hugh."

"And me?"

"And you."

"Just fond?" John said, coming closer. "Or..."

"Well, let me think."

"Seems you need to do a lot of thinking," he grabbed me by my waist and pulled me towards him. "I think we might have to change that." His body pressed solid against me.

"Oh, fine, I give up." I said, as John nuzzled my neck. "I love you; I wouldn't have returned for anything else."

"You," he said, as he placed a kiss right below my ear. "Love," he murmured, kissing the tender skin on my neck. "Me," he finished with a kiss at my collar bone. John looked back at me with such hunger that a shiver ran through my body. "I think we need total privacy for what I'm about to do." He turned the key and locked the door to his study.

"What are you about to do?"

"I think I need to thank you," John said, lifting me onto his desk. "For saving Beth, for saving me, for being so brave, and so damn stubborn."

His lips crushed mine and I wrapped my legs around him to pull his body even closer. John's hand raked across my body and pulled down the fabric covering my breasts. "You are so beautiful," he groaned as he looked at me. "I love you, too." I kissed him again, tasting him.

John caressed my cheek and stared into my eyes. "Say you'll marry me." The words tumbled out of his mouth in an urgent plea.

"Yes," I said softly. "I will marry you." Then another thought hit me. "Beth will be so excited for us," I said.

"Let's not talk about my sister in this moment; I have different things on my mind, things that are definitely not suited for conversation," John growled, as he caught my lips. With a big sweep, he lifted me off the floor and carried me to the sofa in the corner of the room.

Once he was done thoroughly kissing me into a stupor, he came up for air and said with a mischievous sparkle in his eyes. "Daresay, I am looking forward to our wedding night, future Mrs. Easton.

"I might have to agree," I said and kissed him some more. "He was a traditional man but, judging by his kisses, I had something to look forward to. "I think I liked not talking," I said, lazily tracing patterns on his broad chest. He rested his hand on the small of my back, kissed my temple, and grinned.

"We might have to not talk more often."

I looked up at him. "Do you think Beth will be okay?"

"Once she's processed everything that has happened, I suspect she will be fine."

"I hope so. She really thought she loved Mr. Danby."

"She was fortunate that nothing but her pride was hurt," John said. "It could have been much worse. We caught them in time and, except for the constable and William, no one else needs to ever know what happened. I don't want her reputation and prospects to be ruined over a man like that. Mr. Danby will be locked up in London, and thanks to Beth's secret elopement scheme, no one will ever know they were leaving together."

"All is well that ends well," I muttered.

"Indeed," John said. "Now, future Mrs. Easton, what do you say we leave my study and find something to eat?"

* * *

John announced our engagement the next morning over breakfast. Beth, who was just about to take a bit of a bread roll, quickly dropped it to her plate.

"Married? Oh John, I am so happy for you and Rose." Beth reached for my hand and squeezed it. "I couldn't wish for a better sister, and I can't think of anyone better suited for my brother. I do have one request."

"Which is?" John said amused.

"That I can plan the wedding and help pick the outfits, of course."

"You'll be my maid of honor; I would love it if you helped me choose a dress."

"John, you might have to send word to William. I think we might need to stay with him while we visit London."

"Why would we need to go to London, pray tell sister?"

"Rose will have to get married in the latest fashion, of course. When are you planning to have the wedding?" John and I glanced at each other and smiled.

"We haven't decided yet," I hedged.

"Soon," John cut in with determination. I blushed. Beth's eyes crinkled and she laughed.

"Congratulations, sir," Mrs. Avery and the rest of the staff said. Mrs. Avery especially appeared pleased as punch. She had taken a liking to me during the times she taught me how to bake and I helped her with odd jobs around the kitchen.

It would be strange to become the mistress of the house,

to really claim Hawthorne and the Eastons as my home and family. I'd miss my family and friends and I was sad that they wouldn't be able to see me get married, but I had faith that Mom and Dad were proud of me for going after what I wanted, even if what I wanted was two-hundred years back in time.

"Rose, can I see the pictures on the metal box again? You showed me last night, but I was too exhausted to focus," Beth said when it was just the three of us in the dining room again.

"Yeah, I'll get it real quick." I ran up the stairs to my bedroom and fetched my cellphone from the drawer in the desk. It only had thirty-two percent battery left. Once that was gone, all that was left was a useless piece of junk. Preserving the battery and turning it off until a later time crossed my mind, but the things on my phone didn't matter. My life was here now, and at least I got to share a glimpse of my life with John and Beth.

"I don't know how much longer we'll be able to see the things on my phone," I said when I returned.

"Why?" Beth said as she grabbed a hold of it and examined a picture of me and my mom in front of my childhood home.

"Do you see those numbers in the top right?" Beth nodded. "It tells me how much battery is left." I frowned as I thought about how to explain so Beth might understand. "The phone uses energy; once that energy is depleted it stops working— the same way a fire burns until all the wood has been consumed. I just don't have more wood to keep it burning."

"Then we will have to make the most of it." Beth swiped to a new photo, one of Nicole and I. John scooted in closer and offered commentary on every picture. He had already seen them all; we'd gone through them together. That didn't matter because he still looked just as amazed at the small glimpse into my life before I met them. I couldn't help but giggle at the absurdity of these two people that I adored, that lived in a vastly different time, and were completely fixated on the small screen of my phone. John looked up from the phone at the sound of my giggle.

"It's just miraculous. You've given up so much to be here with us. I just hope we live up to your expectations."

"You have already far exceeded them," I said. "Now, I have something else to show you that you might like." I scrolled through my music folder and started "Claire de lune", probably best to start with something they'd recognize instead of more modern songs.

"How," John started, as the notes poured out of the tiny phone. "It really is like magic. Perhaps, I am the luckiest man alive to be engaged to a woman who is not only beautiful but also miraculous."

"And smart?" I quipped with a smile.

"And very talkative." John grinned.

"That's a hazard you were aware of."

"And I wouldn't want it any other way."

Beth pushed herself up from the table. "I think I am going to go outside for a bit by myself so you two can have some space." She caught my eye and shook her head with a grin.

John barely noticed his sister get up, nor did he react as she inched out of the dining room. My phone and everything else was forgotten as he fixed his eyes on me.

"I think I might like to see what I would need to do to stop you from talking," he said, winking.

"It would take quite a lot."

"Is that so? Then I will have to give it my best try," he said, as he snatched me by my waist and tickled me.

"Oh, stop," I gasped in between bouts of laughter. Finally, he stopped his attack, and I could catch my breath. His eyes darkened and he held out his hand.

"Will you join me?"

Afterword

If you made it this far, I would like to thank you for reading this book and taking a chance on me as an author. It truly means the world to me. I hope reading 'Rose Through Time' brought you as much joy as it did for me when I wrote it.

If you feel so inclined, I would love it if you left a book review. Or for updates on my future work and sneak peeks into what I am writing, you can subscribe to my newsletter on;
www.harmkebuursma.com

Hopefully I'll see you return to the world of Westbridge, or see you visit one of my other worlds.

Acknowledgments

I want to thank my amazing husband; without his support I wouldn't have the freedom to write. Despite not being the biggest reader, he cheers me on every step of the way and will listen to me drone on about every plot-point and character I create. I'd also like to acknowledge my family and friends who have offered all their support along the way and have been some of my very first readers. Without their support whenever I doubted myself this novel would have never made its way into your hands or onto the devices you are using. Much appreciation also goes to the coffee that kept me going, my two dogs that provided some adorable distractions, and all of you who are reading 'Rose Through Time' right now.

About The Author

Harmke Buursma is a writer, and author of the novel Rose Through Time. She uses her background in Journalism to help bring her fictional characters and worlds to life. When she isn't writing, she likes to read as many books as she can get her hands on. Originally born and raised in The Netherlands, Harmke now lives in Las Vegas with her husband Matthew and two dogs.

Harmke Buursma
Photo by Patterson Photography

For more information about Harmke and her books, visit www.harmkebuursma.com.

Books By This Author

ROSE THROUGH TIME

WILLIAM THROUGH TIME

William Through Time

#2 in the A Magical Bookshop Novel series

Still wrestling with the loss of the man he loved, William receives a letter from his friend John. Spurred by its contents William leaves his apartments in London behind to travel to Hawthorne. There he meets Austin, a man who just like his friend's wife Rose has traveled from the future. William wrestles with feelings of guilt, nightmares about his military service, and strict Regency Era society rules as he becomes more and more intrigued by the strange and modern young man. Will love slip through his hands once more or can he hold on to it?